NO DEADLY MEDICINE

TRUDEY MARTIN

This book is a work of fiction. Names, characters, businesses, organisations, places, and events are either the product of the author's imagination or used fictitiously. Any resemblance to actual persons, living or dead, events, or locales is entirely coincidental.

ISBN: 9781838396510

Excerpt from The Hippocratic oath:

"I will prescribe regimens for the good of my patients according to my ability and judgement and never do harm to anyone.
I will give no deadly medicine to anyone if asked, nor suggest any such counsel."

Your free book is waiting

Claim your free book!

EVEN MONEY A Verity Spencer short story

After uncovering a web of corruption in No Deadly Medicine, Verity has to decide what she wants to do with her life now. Still mourning her husband, she's started to fill her time by chasing errant husbands and wives for money. Susanna Means approaches Verity believing that her partner, too, is being unfaithful...but as Verity looks into his life, she realises he may be holding a much darker secret...

Visit the website to download:
https://trudeymartin.co.uk

MONDAY

Chapter One

Looking back, I probably shouldn't have picked it up. I should have left the notebook lying on the ground where the elderly gentleman had dropped it and walked on to my rendezvous with Collette.

I was already ten minutes late, and I knew she'd be anxious. She was one of my oldest friends; I mean oldest as in 'known the longest time' rather than in terms of her age. She was a good five years younger than me. She had been an absolute rock since John, my husband, had died about twelve weeks before, in a car crash. He'd been on his way to a meeting in Hull, driving the Volkswagen Golf that we'd shared. He hadn't been far from Hull, a few miles away, when he'd been hit head-on by a lorry that had just disembarked from a ferry. The driver was from Norway, or Denmark, or somewhere Scandinavian and had been tired, had lost concentration and had been driving on the wrong side of the road. Sometimes I hated this man I had never met for being so careless. Sometimes

I felt sorry for him, having to live with the consequences of what he had done.

John, I was assured by the police, had died instantly. Not that that was much of a consolation; he had only been forty-five years old, way too young to die, and I had been struggling to find my balance ever since then.

John had, thankfully, paid into a company pension, which meant that I'd received a sizeable lump sum and a would get a reasonable portion of it for the foreseeable future. It meant that I had a choice; I could give up work. I wouldn't have as much money at my disposal, but at least I had time to think about it. I could use my time off to see whether I wanted to return to my job at the local college, teaching the drivel dished out by the government to uninterested students who had little motivation to learn. I seriously doubted that I did.

My life with John had come to a shattering, shuddering halt with his death and although it had been a few weeks now since I'd had a day where all I wanted to do was lay in bed and cry, I knew Collette would be worried that I was late.

I was rushing from our home, my home, on a little road called Steeple Lane just beyond the top of Steep Hill in Lincoln. It was a bright and crisp autumn morning, and the city looked beautiful tumbling down the hill ahead of me. I didn't always look to my left as I passed the cathedral, having passed it almost every day for over twenty years, but I did that day. The autumn sun bathed the stone towers in a rosy hue. No doubt about it, it was an impressive building inside and out.

I had just reached the bottom of the hill, where the

street widens out and the shops become more mainstream than the quirky individual ones that line the hill. I had arranged to meet Collette in our favourite little independent coffee shop and was striding towards it when I saw the man drop the notebook as he walked in the opposite direction towards the start of Steep Hill. He was a tall, slim, elderly gentleman with a full head of grey hair and a matching grey moustache. He was wearing a heavy camel-coloured wool coat and he carried a walking stick, although he didn't look as if he needed it. The notebook he'd dropped was a small pocket size beige-coloured Moleskin. Without really thinking, I picked it up and shouted after him.

"Excuse me." I took a few steps back up the hill towards him and tried again. "Excuse me! Sir!" But he didn't hear me, the wind carrying my voice away towards the High Street. He carried on striding up the start of the hill. I flipped the notebook open and on the first page glimpsed an address. I'd pass it on my way home. For a second, I considered running after him, but then I thought of Collette waiting for me and decided that it wasn't that important. I'd drop it in later.

I pushed open the door to the coffee shop and immediately spotted Collette sitting at our favourite table near the back, the one with the comfortable chairs. She'd grabbed a newspaper and was reading that whilst she waited, with a half-drunk cup of coffee in front of her. I was almost next to her when she looked up and saw me.

"Vee," she said. "How are you doing? Are you okay? I was a bit worried when you were late."

"I'm fine," I answered. "Just got a bit delayed. I did think about texting but then thought I'd be even later, so I just ran out of the door. Do you want more coffee?"

"No thanks. I'll finish this one. I'll have a scone though." She grinned. Having a scone, or a cake, with our coffee was our weekly treat.

I went up to the counter, ordered a coffee and two scones, and then went and joined Collette on the comfy chairs. She looked at the notebook and raised an eyebrow in query.

"An old man dropped it. Almost outside here, actually, just up the road." I gestured vaguely in the direction the man had been walking. "I picked it up and shouted after him but he didn't hear me. It's got an address though; it's on my way home so I'll pop it through his door on my way back."

A young waitress came over with my coffee and the two scones, which we ate whilst we chatted. Collette picked up the notebook. It was slim, with an elastic band incorporated in the back cover, wrapped around to mark a page. Collette flicked through it. There wasn't a lot in it. She put it back down on the table.

"I'd be tempted to just throw it in the bin. It doesn't look as if there's anything important in it."

"Well, it's right on my route home. It isn't any trouble. I'll just poke it through the letterbox. I'm sure the old guy will be pleased someone took the time to return it."

"Softie."

We spent almost an hour catching up on what was happening with Collette's two children, Charlotte and Sophie—seven and five, respectively.

"I'm so frustrated with the school," Collette vented as we started on our second cups of coffee. Charlotte was having a few problems at school with bullying. She was a bright girl, but was a little awkward and something of a bookworm. Her bottle-bottom glasses didn't help, and the other children exploited it a bit. Collette got exasperated with the school for not handling things as well as they could. She was a very protective mother. Charlotte would be ok; she'd grow up to be some kind of intellectual, a scientist maybe, or a novelist, and everyone would marvel at her uniqueness. Sophie was the polar opposite, outgoing, lively, and cute as a button with long, curly blonde hair and eyelashes that made me very jealous. She had settled into school without a problem, and although she was nowhere near as clever as Charlotte, she enjoyed school a lot more.

"I've organised another meeting with the head teacher," Collette announced. "I need to keep an eye on the time. Don't want to be late." She paused. "They have to do something, I'm seriously considering moving the children to another school."

I told her I thought it was a bad idea; Sophie had settled really well and had loads of friends, and Charlotte, well, I thought she would still have problems in another school, but I didn't voice that opinion out loud. Collette rolled up her sleeve and looked at her watch.

"Look at the time!" she exclaimed as she stood up and put on her coat. "I'd better be heading off. I'm in town on Thursday again if you fancy meeting up?"

"Great. I'll be here. Same time?"

"Yeah, see you then," she said before rushing off out of the door for another meeting with the long-suffering head teacher.

Chapter Two

I left the coffee shop feeling brighter than I had done in quite a while. It was good to talk about someone else's problems and really take an interest, rather than feeling that I didn't care about what was happening to other people. Getting over John's death was a hard and slow process, but I was gradually becoming less self-absorbed. I adored Collette's children; I was godmother to them both. They were so different, and each had a vibrant and interesting personality. I loved watching them grow and develop and become their own little people. Thinking about them, and the difficulties they were encountering as they grew, had taken my mind in a different direction, and I smiled at that as I drew in the crisp autumn air, setting off back towards home.

I double checked the address in the notebook. It was written in an immaculate script that could only belong to an elderly gentleman and had been written with a fountain pen.

Dr Michael Neasden
3, Prosper Lane
Lincoln

I knew the road well; it was just off Steep Hill to the right, about halfway up. I sauntered up the hill—it is not called Steep Hill for no reason—and looked in a couple of shop windows on my way up. There were lots of people going both up and down the hill, brought out by the sunny Monday morning perhaps, or being extremely well prepared and starting Christmas preparations early. My heart lurched. I hadn't even thought of having a Christmas without John. Memories of the last few flooded into my head; choosing a hotel, packing the car, cosying up together by log fires. We had no children so staying at home on our own would have been too like every other day of the year. I had loved going away; I hadn't a clue what I would do this year. The thought filled me with dread.

I slammed back into the present when I was almost knocked over by what I assumed to be someone out for a run. Dressed in a scruffy tracksuit, he pushed past me, tutted, and ran off down the hill. *Easier going down than up*, I thought to myself as I realised I'd almost missed the road, and I turned into Prosper Lane.

Dr Neasden's house was the third one along the lane, the numbers going up in sequence as there were only houses on one side of the street. A tiny but well-kept garden, with a few shrubs and flowers, prettied up the red brick frontage. To one side a passageway led around the back of the house, where I assumed the door had to be. The windows could have done with a lick of paint, but the outside of the house seemed in reasonably good condition. I followed the path down the side of the house and saw the dark red door towards the rear. The path opened out onto a paved yard, a beautiful sun trap. A few planters lined the space with the last remains of summer flowers in them. Dr Neasden seemed to be preparing for winter colour, as a couple of packs of baby pansies and chrysanthemums stood near the far wall. In the corner, just beyond the door, there was a small table with a couple of chairs. An empty mug stood on top of a daily newspaper, its pages rustling in the breeze. The door was ajar, so I gave it a light knock but got no answer. I knocked a little louder, thinking perhaps Dr Neasden had left the table to go to the bathroom and was upstairs, but there was still no response.

I pushed at the door. It opened into the kitchen. I was going to shout out Dr Neasden's name, but the state of the kitchen took me aback. Drawers were open, cupboard doors were gaping and all of the contents pulled out. Cutlery and crockery littered the floor, saucepans and frying pans piled on top of them. A toaster lay on its side on the worktop. The bin spewed its contents onto the floor with the rubbish spread across the vinyl. Letters and papers covered the kitchen table. I walked into the kitchen and called out, "Dr Neasden." There was no reply. My heart pumped faster with each image I took in; dread wound its way round my stomach and chest. I tried again.

"Dr Neasden! My name is Verity Spencer. I picked up your notebook earlier. I was just calling round to return it."

I heard something. I stopped and held my breath, listening intently. I heard it again. A muffled *hmmmph*.

I took a step into the kitchen. A window over the sink looked out over the courtyard, and a door on the other side of the kitchen led through to the hall.

Placing my feet with care, I trod through the debris and made my way across the room. I pushed the door open and crept into the hall; this presented a similar picture. Coats and hats lay under an empty coat rack. An old-fashioned telephone sat on the floor next to a little table, its handle and curly cable off to one side. Water from a smashed vase seeped into the carpet, the flowers drawing me forward like a romantic trail of rose petals.

Between the kitchen and the stairs there were two doors on the left of the hall. The first was a small dining room furnished with old, dark wood furniture. The room was a vision of chaos. I ignored it, holding onto the wall as I crept further along, and I called out again. The same faint *hmmmph* came back in return.

Moving faster, I darted towards the front of the house. My mind raced, trying to take it all in. On the floor by the far door was Dr Neasden's walking stick, discarded and lying across the doorway. *This is not right. This is not right.* I ran the few feet down the hall, past the upturned vase, to the front room and stopped in my tracks. The room had a plain but old-fashioned three-piece suite, which had all the cushions pulled off and piled into the middle of the floor. Broken ornaments littering the carpet surrounded an overturned coffee table. A smashed mirror hung at an angle above the fireplace. Instinctively, I put my hand over my mouth. I could not understand what had gone on here. Then I saw a leg sticking out from behind the sofa. The soft moaning was louder, closer. My heart turned cartwheels as a hundred thoughts of what I might find clambered for space in my brain.

I hurried around the back of the sofa, clambering over the pulled-off cushions, and saw him lying there. Dr Neasden was covered in blood and had clearly been beaten up. Red blotching and bruising covered his face. Blood trickled from a gash on his forehead. The sleeve of his tweed jacket hung adrift, severed from the body. His left arm lay across his body at an angle that I couldn't quite figure out. A neat hole in his midriff, surrounded by an expanding pool of blood, left me in no doubt that somebody had shot him in the stomach.

Chapter Three

I had no time to think. I gathered up one of the net curtains that had been pulled off its wire and made it into a ball, pressing it into the wound in Dr Neasden's stomach. Blood was coming out of his back and soaking into the carpet.

"Don't worry," I said, trying to hide my mounting anxiety. "I'll call an ambulance and the police, they'll patch you up in no time." Looking at the gathering pool of blood beneath him, I hoped it wasn't as bad as it looked. I yanked my iPhone out of my pocket to call the emergency services, the notebook falling to the floor as I did so. Dr Neasden clutched at the air with his good arm, raising his eyebrows and struggling to drag words from the back of his throat.

"No, no," he whispered, pointing at the book.

I pressed onto the wound with my left hand and concentrated on getting my call through to the emergency services and giving clear instructions to the woman on the other end of the phone. I turned my gaze from the doctor, still trying to get my attention and pointing at the notebook.

"You have to go to the top of the hill," I continued. "And then turn left to come back down to this point. There's no way in or out at the far end of the road." I disconnected, thinking that it was going to be at least ten or fifteen minutes before the ambulance arrived, and hoping that I could keep the doctor hanging on that long. I put my phone and the notebook back in my pocket before returning my full attention to the man lying on the floor in front of me.

"The book," he whispered, struggling to speak. "Hide it."

I stared blankly.

"Hide it," he forced the words out. Then, with the arm that wasn't all twisted, he fumbled for something in his pocket. His wallet. He was giving me his wallet. What on earth? I didn't understand.

"Give…give…that," he said, trying to lift his head off the ground.

I didn't want him exerting any energy or using his strength on anything other than staying alive, so I took the wallet and put it in my pocket. I found a cushion and put it under his head. He was struggling to breathe, and I was struggling to keep pressing the net curtain into his wound. It was soaked with blood, and he was becoming weaker. His eyelids were drooping, blood and mucous were bubbling at the corner of his mouth, and his complexion was taking on the grey tone of approaching death. My arms were beginning to ache, and I willed the ambulance to arrive. I was sure he couldn't last much longer—looking at the growing pool surrounding my knees, I didn't think he could have much blood left.

"Who did this?" I asked. "Was it a burglary?"

He didn't answer. His eyes started sliding upwards and his breath became more laboured.

"Dr Neasden," I shouted, trying to keep him awake. Trying to remember desperately anything at all from my first-aid course at the college, and then I had the sinking realisation that what Dr Neasden needed was way beyond first aid.

"Stfmmm," he mumbled.

"What? Sorry…what did you say?"

"Stfmm. Stefum."

I tried hard to decipher what he was saying but I really wished he would just concentrate on staying alive. "Stephen?"

He nodded. "Talk to Stephen," he whispered. "Prmiss. Tk t Stfmm."

"Talk to Stephen? What?" I had no idea what the doctor was talking about, but the thought kept circulating in my head that he ought to be conserving his energy and not trying to talk at all, so I left it at that. He tried lifting his head again; he was finding it harder to summon up the strength, but he wanted to tell me something.

"Nt buk."

"Notebook?"

He nodded again.

"You want me to talk to Stephen about the notebook? Stephen who? Where is Stephen?"

The doctor's eyes began to slide again and glaze over. "Prmiss."

At last the distant sound of sirens filtered into the room and I hoped that the ambulance was here first. I pressed the curtain tighter into the wound and prayed to anyone who cared to listen to get the paramedics in here quick.

And then I heard them screech to a halt outside. I heard the doors opening and closing and the footsteps of the ambulance men clattering down the passageway. Dr Neasden gripped my hand. He had shown no strength at all until that point but he clung on, pressing his hand hard over the hand I had pushing down on the bullet wound in his stomach. He breathed in sharply and tried to say something. Nothing. Each time he breathed in, it sounded like a whistle. He tried again. A whisper. And then, as the ambulance men came crashing through the back door and into the kitchen, and the wails of police sirens could be heard heading down the road, he pulled me to him.

"Trust no one."

Someone dragged me to one side, and I stepped back to let the paramedics take over. They put an oxygen mask over the doctor's face and checked his wound. They rushed around, calling to the doctor to stay awake, telling him he would be at the hospital in no time and that everything was going to be okay. They were lying. Everything was not going to be okay.

A young police constable had arrived and stood looking dangerously out of his depth in the middle of the chaos that was Dr Neasden's sitting room. I hadn't noticed him come in with all the activity going on by the window. He asked me what I was doing here. How had I come to find this—he struggled for the right word—situation.

"I came to return something that Dr Neasden had dropped," I said.

"What was that then?" said the police officer. I know it's a cliché, but he really did look young enough to be in school.

I glanced over at the doctor, and he caught my eye. Caught me looking at him. He tipped his head, a tiny little movement as if trying to nod. And then I understood. He turned away and closed his eyes.

"His wallet," I said, holding out the wallet that the doctor had given to me. "He dropped his wallet in town earlier."

"He's gone," the paramedic said, and stood up.

Chapter Four

An hour or so later I was sitting at the table in Dr Neasden's yard, talking to Detective Sergeant Mike Nash and drinking a take-away coffee that had appeared from somewhere. I didn't remember asking for it, but it was exactly how I liked it, so I guessed I must have told someone what I wanted at some point. I was cupping my hands around the takeaway cup to keep myself warm. Suddenly, I started to shake and shiver. It was shock, the police officer told me. He had listened to what I'd said, nodding and taking notes. He seemed okay, although he'd occasionally sounded a bit sceptical. Or maybe that was just my imagination. I had used the sink in Dr Neasden's kitchen to rinse the blood off my hands and arms. I couldn't believe how much of it there was. No matter how much I had washed, there had seemed to be more. There was a mirror near the sink, to the side, on the wall, and I had looked in that and removed the blood that had splashed onto my face. Then I had gone outside with Detective Sergeant Nash to answer his questions. A lady police constable hovered in the background. I assumed it was she who had fetched the coffee.

It turned out that Dr Neasden was a retired GP, and he'd lived here, in this house, for a long time; that was obvious from the décor, it felt like the home of an elderly couple. Well, what I could see of it under all the mess. I wondered if he had been married; I guessed that he had, the house was full of feminine touches. Then I wondered how long he had been a widower, on his own like me, adjusting to a different kind of life.

According to Nash, Dr Neasden was seventy-two years old, and spent some of his spare time doing voluntary work for an organisation that worked with people who had no recourse to public funds. He'd told me this because he had been trying to establish if I knew the doctor but I had never met him before, to my knowledge, and had never heard his name mentioned. When he had worked, it had been at a surgery just on the edge of the city; the opposite end of the city to my current GP's. I imagined that I could easily have walked past him at some point, but in a city of over eighty thousand people he would have gone unnoticed. I had a vivid memory of him striding up the hill with the stick he didn't seem to need, but if our paths had passed before then I couldn't remember.

"So run it past me again," said Detective Sergeant Mike Nash. "You are?"

"Verity Spencer, aged forty-two, live in Lincoln…"

I sighed. I'd been through it several times now. Every detail, every feeling, every impression. It was all one hundred percent as it had happened save for one element—I had told him I'd picked up Dr Neasden's wallet and not his notebook. I hoped I was convincing.

I was generally hopeless at lying. Perhaps it was the shock, but I was struggling to concentrate. My mind wandered to John; if I'd ever lied, he could always tell. Once, I had tried to organise a surprise long weekend away for John, but it had all gone horribly wrong as I had struggled not to reveal all. I'd ended up telling him what I was planning. I looked at the police officer, imagining he might possess the ability to read my thoughts, and I concentrated hard. It was perfectly believable that I could have picked up a wallet and wanted to return it. *Stick to the story, Verity.*

"So you went to have coffee with your friend, err…"

"Collette."

"Collette Smith."

"Yes."

"And you talked about her children?"

"Mostly, yes."

"You mentioned the wallet."

"I mentioned it, yes, I said I would post it through the doctor's door on my way home."

"How did you know the doctor's address?" The first time they had asked me that I had panicked. I hadn't looked in the wallet. I didn't even know if there was an address in there. Luckily, the young constable had been holding the wallet open at the time to assess the contents. I thought I'd seen a pink card in one of the credit card slots. I had taken a gamble.

"I looked in the wallet and his driver's licence was in there. It had his address on it."

"But when you got here you didn't just post it through the door. Why was that?"

I sighed again. "As I said earlier, I noticed that the door was open and the kitchen was in disarray. The newspaper and mug were still outside so it seemed odd. When I called out to see if there was anyone here, I heard a muffled sound. So I followed it."

"And you found the doctor lying in the front room?"

"Yes. I could see he'd been injured. He had a bullet wound in his stomach."

"You are familiar with bullet wounds?"

"No," I said, sighing with the weariness of the constant questions. "I am not familiar with bullet wounds. In fact, apart from on TV programmes, I have never seen anyone with a bullet wound."

"But you assessed it as such?" He sounded so like a stereotypical police officer.

"Well, the gaping hole in his abdomen and the blood pouring out his back led me to that conclusion. But I am willing to be proved wrong if the pathologist thinks otherwise." I didn't know why I was feeling like this. Probably trying to save someone's life took it out of you. Then having to answer the same endless questions over and over again didn't help. And there was no reason for him to be facetious in the first place.

"And you didn't see or hear anything suspicious?"

"No."

He paused and reviewed his notes. He looked up, and I thought he was going to ask me something else. I closed my eyes and sighed, feeling weary.

"Okay, thanks, Mrs Spencer. I think that should do it for now. Would you like someone to walk you home?"

"No, that's fine. I only live ten minutes' walk away. I'm fine, thanks." I paused. "What happens now?"

"If we need anything else, we'll be in touch. You may need to give evidence if we ever find out who did this." He gestured towards the house. He handed me a card. "If you think of anything else, let me know."

"What like? I've been over and over."

"You'd be surprised how often people come back later with details they remember that didn't seem significant at the time. Or that they'd forgotten until something prompted their memory."

"Okay, I'll bear that in mind." I put the card in my pocket. The same pocket that guarded the doctor's notebook. I looked up at the detective, thinking he would be able to tell what I'd felt in my pocket. I'd lied to the police officer. I had never done that before. Guilt was niggling at the back of my head. I had always been such a conformist; John used to laugh at me when I would run back into supermarkets to pay for items I had inadvertently hidden in the trolley. But this was nothing to feel guilty about, it was nothing major; it was only one small detail. Or that's what I was telling myself anyway. The doctor had been so sure. *"Promise me."* I brushed the thought away. My involvement had been adequately explained. The notebook was a sideline. It probably had nothing to do with this. This was most likely a burglary that Dr Neasden had disturbed. I smiled at Detective Sergeant Mike Nash.

He held out his hand. "Thanks for everything. Medics said you did a great job keeping the doc going until they arrived."

I smiled a weak smile. "Not good enough, clearly." I glanced towards the house, from where the doctor's body had been recently removed.

He shook his head. "I don't think the best doctor in town would have been able to save him. You did good, Mrs Spencer, you did very good."

I thanked him and, about four hours later than planned, headed up the hill to my house on Steeple Lane.

Chapter Five

I walked into the house that, for almost twenty years, I had shared with my husband. A photo of our wedding day greeted me as I entered. We looked so happy. I struggled to keep my emotions in check after all that I had just been through, and I glanced around at the house beyond attempting to delay the tears. But it just served to remind me that I was now alone here, just me and the wedding photo, with a version of me who had thought we had so much life ahead of us. We'd bought the house not long after our marriage. It was bigger than we needed for the two of us, but we'd always anticipated that we would have at least two, if not more, children. Despite our best efforts, that hadn't happened and, after a few years of trying, we'd become resigned to a childless marriage. We'd considered going for tests, thought about trying IVF, talked about adoption, but had decided that we would let fate take its hand. As it happened, we'd easily slipped into a childless exis-tence, doing whatever had suited us and not having to fit things in around a never-ending schedule of ballet and tennis and gym, which was what Collette's life seemed to consist of. I headed upstairs and got undressed; blood stains covered my skirt. As I took my black tights off, they left smears of dark, dried blood on my legs. There was blood on my bra and pants too; it must have soaked through my clothes. There was blood all over me; I didn't know why I hadn't noticed how much there had been before. I wondered what people must have thought as I'd walked through the streets. I put my clothes in a bag, deciding to throw them away despite the skirt being one of my favourite recent purchases. I got in the shower and stood there for what felt like ages, letting the hot water run off my head and shoulders and trying to wash all the memories away. I kept looking down, thinking I still had blood on my skin; I could smell it, that iron-like unmistakable smell. I scrubbed myself, like Lady Macbeth, trying to rid myself of the last vestiges of horror but I just couldn't get rid of it. Eventually I gave up. I got out of the shower and wrapped my hair in a towel, put on my dressing gown and slippers, then went back downstairs.

I made myself a cup of tea and sat at the counter in the kitchen, thinking about the events of the day. The shaking returned, my body convulsing with violent shudders. Goose bumps crept up my arms, causing all the hairs to stand to attention. Flashes of images played in front of me like a broken movie; the doctor squeezing my hand, the way he had looked at me just before he'd died, my lie to the police. Why had I lied to the police? What had I possibly gained from that? I had no answer to those questions. I could not fathom it, except that the doctor had been there, dying on his living room floor, and had implored me to make sure that I took his notebook to someone called

Stephen, or I talked to Stephen, I couldn't remember exactly. He had been struggling to speak, and I had been desperately trying to save his life. Despite having no clue what he'd meant, I had gone along with it. He had seemed so convincing. He had looked into my eyes and begged. He had turned to me as I'd taken up his lie, telling the police that it was his wallet I was returning. He'd died in the knowledge that I hadn't handed them his notebook. But I doubted myself.

I had to call Nash and confess. I'd tell him that I'd found the notebook in my pocket and forgotten that I'd picked it up with his wallet. That way I wouldn't need to tell him I was lying. That way I could fob it off as one of those 'details that people remember' after the event and had given no significance to. I could say that I'd found the notebook when I'd got home, and must have forgotten it in the heat of the moment. The shock I was suffering from, after finding the doctor shot and dying, would surely account for a temporary loss of memory, and if I rang straight away, as soon as I'd found it, that would sound convincing. Wouldn't it?

I reached over into my coat pocket and retrieved both my iPhone and the card that Nash had given me. As I pulled them from my coat, the notebook fell out and hit the floor. I picked it up and flicked through the pages. There was hardly anything there. I could not begin to think why it had been so important to the doctor. The first page had his name and address in his elderly, loopy handwriting. Then there were a few pages that had been torn out. The next few pages were blank. There was nothing on them at all.

One page had one word written on it. It simply said, in the doctor's distinctive handwriting:

Champion!

That was it, just the one word, 'Champion!', nothing else. Champion of what? *Had the doctor won something?* I wondered. I shook my head.

After a couple of pages, there was a short list of numbers.

43809760
63329916
72709588

A few pages further on, there was what appeared to be a list. It consisted solely of what I took to be acronyms.

RSDI
KTMD
ADDI

I had no idea what any of those stood for.

One page contained some more numbers. Nothing else, just numbers in blocks of three.

215
762
879

I flicked through the pages and there was only one more entry. But it made me stop in my tracks. At the top of the page was written:

Stephen Ibbetson

Beneath the name, on the bottom of the page and in the corner were three letters.

Stephen. This had to be the Stephen that I was supposed to contact. *Shit, shit, shit.* A name. A whole name, not just a faceless request. I reached for my laptop and Googled 'Stephen Ibbetson'. It delivered 654,000 results. Great. I didn't even know why I was bothering. I was a recently widowed, poorly paid further education teacher. Who had just lied to the police. That was probably one of the most daring and exciting things I had done in my adult life. What on earth did I think this had to do with me? Precisely nothing was my answer to that question. The imploring look in the doctor's eyes, as he lay dying in his living room, popped into my head temporarily preventing me from making the call to Nash.

I flicked back through the notebook; it was compelling. I wondered what it all meant. I tried the acronyms, perhaps there would be something there. On Google 'RSDI' netted 263,000 results, most commonly related to some US Admin fund called Retirement, Survivors and Disability Insurance. 'KTMD' returned 411,000 results. Nothing of interest. Highest up on the page was some Texan TV station. Both US based. Was there an American connection? I tried 'ADDI'. That brought in over 16 million results. Bizarrely, the majority related to knitting needles. *Knitting needles? Hmmm.* Not much to go on there. I put the notebook to one side and decided that I was clearly not cut out for this. I had no idea who Stephen was. I didn't even know if he was the Stephen Ibbetson from Dr Neasden's note book. There had to be plenty of other Stephens in the world. Although, it did seem too much of a coincidence that Dr Neasden had struggled to say the name in his dying breath if there was no connection with the person in the note-book. I was unsure why I should continue lying to the police and resolved once again to call Nash and hand the notebook over to him. After all, that was the police's job. If there was anything in there that related to the murder of Dr Neasden, surely it was the police who were best placed to trace them? And if the note-book held clues then they should have it. Shouldn't they?

Except Dr Neasden clearly hadn't thought so. He'd been very clear, having been the recipient of the bullet wound, that he did not want the police to have the notebook. Maybe it had nothing to do with his death. I remembered his firm grip on my hands.

"Trust no one."

I got out my sandwich toaster and made myself a quick cheese and ham toasted sandwich, poured a large glass of wine, and took it through to the living room. I ate my sandwich sitting on the sofa and leaning over the coffee table whilst watching some dreadful reality TV programme. A group of squealing young people were deposited in Ibiza or somewhere and given free rein in the local nightclubs and bars, and then the host not only ridiculed their drunken behaviour but secretly showed it to their horrified parents. What was the world coming to? After I'd finished eating, I pushed my plate to one side, turned off the television, replenished my wine glass, then picked up the phone and dialled.

Chapter Six

After three rings, Collette picked up. It was just after seven, and I knew they'd have finished eating, and it would be a good half an hour before the girls' bedtime.

"Vee, hi," she said on answering.

"Are you okay to talk?" I asked. "Are the kids occupied?"

"Sure," she replied, then instantly shouted through to answer one or other of them.

"Shall I ring back later?" I really needed to talk to someone about what had happened, and I wanted her full attention. My words caught in my throat as I spoke, and I struggled once again to fight back the tears. What I wanted was John's arms around me, pulling me in and telling me everything was okay, but Collette was the closest I had. She heard the snag in my voice and instantly became concerned.

"Are you okay? Vee? What is it? Do you want me to come round?"

"No, no." I genuinely didn't. "I'm okay. It's just... Oh, God, it's been a horrific afternoon."

I filled her in on the events of the day. I explained everything—the mayhem, the discovery of Dr Neasden, the call to the emergency services, the interview with the police, everything. She kept asking me to repeat things for her, and she was constantly interrupting with exclamations of amazement and disbelief at what I had gone through. She was suitably intrigued and horrified at the same time; asking questions, asking how I'd felt, what I'd done, what I'd said, and so on. Every now and again, I needed to take a breath. Remembering my fight to keep the doctor alive was hard. I didn't want to cry down the phone, and I needed a few seconds from time to time to gather my thoughts together.

"Whoa, what a day you've been through." She sounded genuinely concerned. "Are you okay? Are you sure you don't want me to come over?"

"No, don't worry, I'm okay, honestly, and it'll be the children's bedtime soon."

"That's not a problem, Marcus can put the girls to bed."

"No, it's fine. I'm fine. Thanks. It's just…"

"What? Just what? Anything. Just let me know."

"Well…." I hesitated. I didn't know how to tell her I'd lied to the police. It was completely out of character. I didn't know what she'd say.

"What? Verity, what is it?"

"Before he died, the doctor asked me to do something." I thought it might sound better if I got in there first with it being the doctor who'd asked. Almost like it wasn't my fault.

"He asked you to do something? Verity, are you okay? You're making no sense at all."

I swallowed. "He asked me to take his notebook to someone." I didn't mention that at this point I wasn't even sure who I was supposed to take it to, or if the doctor had said take it, or talk about it; I didn't think sounding vague would be useful at this juncture.

She calmed down. "Okay, that's not so bad then, is it?"

"Well, he also asked me not to tell the police about it. He asked me to tell them he'd dropped his wallet instead and that was what I'd brought back. So I didn't mention the notebook."

As predicted, this did not go down too well.

"Verity, are you mad?"

I said nothing.

"You're not thinking straight," she continued. "It's perfectly understandable with what you've been through recently. Losing someone close can do that. I mean, it can make you behave in strange ways. Then finding that poor man like that, it's not surprising that you weren't thinking straight. You have to tell them, Vee, you have to."

But I was not going to change my mind. In fact, the more she implored, the more determined I was that I had done the right thing. She veered between anger at my stupidity and worry at what would happen if anyone found out. She cried with frustration when I refused to hand over the notebook to the police.

"Collette, you didn't hold him whilst he died. You didn't see the look in his eyes. He implored me. What else was I going to do? He made me promise. He was so…convinced that I shouldn't tell them."

"Lying to the police is a serious offence; you might end up in court." But I could tell she had softened a bit.

"Look, I'll take the notebook to the friend and see what he has to say. If he wants me to go to the police,

I will. I'll tell them I found it in my pocket and forgot that I'd picked it up with the wallet. The Sergeant said people forget and then remember things after incidents like that. Ok? I promise, if the friend doesn't pan out for any reason, or if he thinks I should go to the police, I will."

Silence.

"Collette? Is that okay? I'll keep you informed all the way."

More silence.

"Collette, please."

"Okay. I suppose," she sighed, forcing the words out. "But it doesn't mean I agree with what you did, alright?" She lightened up a bit. "You're a very naughty girl," she said in her "cross Mummy" voice.

"I know. I don't know why I did it. But I've never sat with anyone who was dying before, let alone someone who's been shot and left in a ransacked house, with all their possessions thrown all over. I can't believe it all happened; it's like a nightmare or something. I don't understand what's gone on, and I guess it's for the police to investigate, but the doctor seemed genuine, and he seemed so desperate for me to hide the notebook and take it to his friend."

"Okay, well be careful. Make sure you deal with it tomorrow or very soon. If you leave it too long and then suddenly 'remember' that you found the notebook it won't ring true."

"I will. I promise. Oh, and, Collette?"

"Yes?"

"If the police contact you and ask what we spoke about, it was the wallet okay? Not the notebook."

"Jesus, Verity, what's got into you?"

But I knew I could rely on her.

TUESDAY

Chapter Seven

I slept the sleep of the dead that night. I thought I'd be awake all night but it was quite the opposite. I kept dreaming vivid dreams of chases and guns that dissipated the moment I reached full wakefulness, and then I would drift back off again. I woke early, just after seven, so I showered and dressed and headed to the city centre for a coffee. I put on my coat and took my laptop in its bag and headed for Caffe Nero as I knew it would be open. I walked down the hill, the sun just rising to the east and casting a soulful light across the city.

As I entered the cafe, I joined the short queue. Two other early birds stood ahead of me, studying their phones as they waited. I ordered a croissant and a large Americano with hot milk and asked for it in a takeaway cup, even though I was not going to take it away. I just preferred my coffee hot and it stayed warmer longer in a takeaway cup. Grabbing the cup off the counter, I resolved to buy a reusable one soon. I plonked myself down in a seat in the corner, took my laptop out and fired it up, connecting automatically to the Cloud. I searched for news about the doctor, but there was nothing, not even a mention in the local paper. That was a bit unusual, wasn't it? Maybe it was because he had been shot. Perhaps they weren't giving any details. I Googled his name to see if there was something I might have missed, but all I got was a newspaper article from a couple of years ago about his retirement and the send-off his patients had given him. It seemed that he was quite a popular guy.

I scanned a few of the dailies on my laptop. Not much going on really, the usual moans at the government for one thing or another, predictions of the weather turning bad in a few days' time, who was going out with who in celeb world. Pretty boring stuff.

I fished the notebook out of my pocket and flicked through it again. Nothing in it made any sense at all. I couldn't fathom the importance of it, but then I suppose all I had to do was deliver it to "Stephen." I didn't have to figure out what it all meant. I Googled Stephen Ibbetson again. Hundreds of Facebook and Twitter and LinkedIn accounts came up. I glanced at a couple, but they told me nothing, so I ignored the rest and moved away from social media. There were some firms, an accountant, a vicar. I spent ages ploughing through these, opening webpages and looking through to see if there was anything, anything at all that might connect these different Stephen Ibbetsons with Dr Neasden. I couldn't come up with anything. I looked at a couple of newspaper articles, but they were from ages ago and got me nowhere. Dejected, I took a swig of my now stone-cold coffee. I'd been sitting there for over two hours now, and still I was coming up with nothing. I ordered another coffee; perhaps the caffeine might help. When I sat back down, I flicked through the notebook again and sighed. I didn't know what to do, and would have gone home if I hadn't just bought myself another coffee.

The laptop had gone to sleep, so I opened it up again and tried Googling the name Stephen Ibbetson together with some of the acronyms in the notebook. That also got me nowhere; there didn't appear to be any connections there at all. Nothing of any use came up. I looked back at the page in the notebook where the doctor had written the name. It was written right at the top of the page. And right at the bottom of the page were the letters LBH. They looked unconnected but I thought I would give it one more try, and I Googled "Stephen Ibbetson LBH."

Bingo.

LBH, in this case at least, turned out to stand for the London Borough of Hillingdon. There was a Stephen Ibbetson who was an Assistant Director of Children's Services and worked for the London Borough of Hillingdon. There was only the one person. At the top of the Google results page, there were quite a few references to him, but beneath those were the results for "similar searches," so I knew there was only one Stephen Ibbetson that went with the initials LBH. The entries mostly consisted of some minutes from meetings he had attended, presentations he had given and so on, but they didn't tell me much about him. In fact, most of them just had his name listed as an attendee, or made a vague reference to "Stephen Ibbetson suggested that…" or something along those lines. There was one PowerPoint presentation which he had delivered, apparently, to a group of London Boroughs, and it was about changes to safeguarding procedures. It didn't look very interesting.

I looked on the website of the London Borough of Hillingdon. I wasn't even sure exactly which area of

London it covered, but it turned out to be the very west-most borough and the headquarters were in Uxbridge. On one page, I found a staff photo of Stephen Ibbetson, a smile beaming from his rugged, round face. Below the picture was a short biography.

Stephen Ibbetson has worked in children's social care for almost thirty years. He qualified at the North London Polytechnic and started out as a social worker in West Berkshire, working in both child protection and looked after children teams. Since then, Stephen has held various positions in several London Boroughs, including team manager, service manager, and head of service. Stephen has been at the London Borough of Hillingdon since June 2010, having joined us from his position as head of service for child protection in the London Borough of Ealing. He has responsibility for children's specialist services, including children in need, child protection and children with disabilities.

That was pretty bland and didn't tell me much. He looked early to mid fifties in his photo, which I guessed tied in with the information in the bio.

I double checked by looking at some of the other London Boroughs which also began with the initial H, of which there were quite a few, including Hammersmith, Hounslow, Haringey, and so on. None of these places had anyone called Stephen Ibbetson working for them. There was nothing else of any interest that came up when I just Googled LBH. This had to be Dr Neasden's Stephen.

On the website for the London Borough of Hillingdon, there were several contact details for certain members of staff, although not for Stephen Ibbetson. It was easy to figure out the formula for email addresses though. It went first initial, dot, surname and always had the ending lbhillingdon.gov-.uk. I opened up my Hotmail account and wrote him an email.

From:<Sugarandspice328@hotmail.com>
To: <s.ibbetson@lbhillingdon.gov.uk>
Dear Mr Ibbetson,
I am sorry for approaching you out of the blue, but I was asked to contact you by the late Dr Neasden of Lincoln. Would it be possible for us to arrange an appointment in the next day or two?
I look forward to a swift reply.
Kind regards,
Verity Spencer

I read it over. I thought about the doctor and his dying moments; his hand gripping mine. *"Trust no one."* I looked at my name again and decided that it might be prudent to use a different one. Perhaps I was being a bit paranoid, but what harm did it do to finish with a pseudonym, just in case? My Hotmail account didn't include my name, so that wouldn't give it away. I changed my sign off to Miriam Nathan, a combination of mine and John's mothers' names, then pressed send before I changed my mind. I figured that if it wasn't the right Stephen Ibbetson, he would dismiss it as a crank email, but if it was, then I could have just made contact. What did I have to lose? Unless he was on holiday, he'd make contact pretty quickly if he had any idea what this was about. As I didn't receive an out-of-office reply, I figured I'd hear from him soon if indeed he was the right Stephen Ibbetson. I felt elated as I marched back up the hill in the sun with a renewed sense of purpose. Hopefully, if I'd finally found the right Stephen, I was going to be able to fulfil my promise to talk to him on behalf of Dr Neasden about the notebook and its mysterious contents. Then I could tell Collette I'd done what I'd said I would and I could just get on with my life.

If only I'd known.

Chapter Eight

As I turned into Steeple Lane, my stomach dropped. Something was wrong. The front door was open, at least half-way. I felt sick; I knew I hadn't left it like that. My feet wouldn't move, they were heavy like lead and I stood there, stopped in my tracks, struggling to comprehend. Then I started to run. I ran along the road and up the front path, tumbling through the open door, throwing my handbag and laptop bag to one side as I went. For a while I just stayed there by the door, stunned, open-mouthed, gazing at my suddenly unrecognisable home.

My possessions were everywhere. I walked from room to room in a daze. In the kitchen, the front room, and all the bedrooms, the contents of drawers and cupboards lay scattered across the floor. I tiptoed over books and clothing, checking that the house was empty, but whoever had done this was no longer there. I retraced my steps. Nothing seemed to be missing. The contents of my jewellery box were strewn across the floor, but it appeared that it was all still there. As were the television, the stereo, and the expensive speakers John had insisted on buying because they "enhanced the listening experience." They weren't where I'd left them, but no one had stolen them. I paused in the middle of the chaos, adrift, unable to grasp onto a coherent thought. Thoughts of the doctor's ransacked house raced into my brain. Followed by images of him dying amongst the remains of his possessions. I looked at my floor, covered with smashed photographs, clearly just thrown on the floor with contempt. I picked my way through shards of broken glass, and ornaments; pictures of loved ones smiled up at me from broken frames as I walked. One of me with my mum had miraculously survived, and I picked it up and placed it on a shelf. I let out a heavy sigh; it seemed like a futile gesture in all this mayhem. I surveyed the chaos. Everything had been raked through, seemingly in a hurry, in a desperate search for something. *A desperate search*. Just like Dr Neasden's house.

I stopped. The notebook. *Oh shit. Oh shit.* Why hadn't it occurred to me when I'd first walked in? It had to be the notebook. It had to be connected with Dr Neasden; the way the house had been tipped upside down, with nothing stolen, was identical. This was no random burglary. There was no other explanation; it had to be the notebook. I'd had it with me; whoever had done this hadn't had a hope of finding it.

But who would know that I had anything to do with it? I'd never met Dr Neasden before yesterday. And who would know where to find me?

I pondered this last point for a while, going round and round, tying myself in knots, over and over it in my head. I hadn't told anyone about the notebook, apart from Collette, not even the police. Someone must have known about it and figured out that I might have it, or know something about where it was.

The notebook; it was the only connection between me and Dr Neasden and thank God I had been out when they'd arrived or I might well now have been lying on the floor with a bullet in my stomach. Whoever was searching clearly didn't care about leaving bodies in their wake. I was frozen to the spot. Frozen with fear and I didn't know what to do. Someone must have known that I'd been to Dr Neasden's house. But only the police knew about my visit, only they knew that there was any link between the two of us. And Collette, of course, but I wasn't even going to entertain the thought that she had anything to do with any of this. I hadn't told the police about the notebook, but if someone knew it existed and was searching for it and knew I had been round to Dr Neasden's house, they would assume that I knew something about it. Or indeed, think that I had it in my possession. *They were right on that one.* I sat down on the floor, my back against the wall.

"Trust no one."

No one knew about this except the police. Someone had to have found out that I had been at the house, and they could only have found out that information from one source; from the police themselves. I reached for my phone, instinctively wanting to call Nash and tell him what had happened, that someone had got information from them, somehow. But how could they have? Who would have access to that? Nobody could have accessed that so quickly unless it was actually someone on the force. Whoever had done this, whoever was looking for that notebook, had someone working for them inside the police. Either that, or they were the police. Perhaps that was why Dr

Neasden had been so keen to hide the notebook from them.

I put the phone down, sinking further into the floor, my shoulders slouched. I reached for one of the broken photo frames. It contained a picture of me and John on holiday in Spain a couple of years ago, smiling against the crystal blue sky, unaware at that point that he would be alive for only another eighteen months or so. I clutched the photo to my chest and sobbed.

I sat there, crying, wishing more than anything that I had not picked up the notebook, or that I'd chosen to run after the doctor and been a couple more minutes late for Collette. But I couldn't turn back time and, as I surveyed the surrounding damage, the realisation sunk in that I would have to do something. And fast. Whoever had done this would be back. They had killed Dr Neasden and I certainly did not want them to find me with a gun in their hand, whoever they were.

I left the house; I didn't know where I was going but I needed to think and to do that I needed to walk in the fresh air. I grabbed my coat and handbag and headed towards Steep Hill. There were a few people about and I was suspicious of everyone. Everyone seemed to be looking at me. Everyone looked shifty. I hurried along with my head down, but I felt uneasy. Something wasn't right. I tried to shake the feeling off, telling myself that I was just shaken by what had happened to the house. People milled about and turned away, into the cathedral or the castle, or into the shops. I was mentally kicking myself for leaving the house but I was there, out in the open, now. I wanted to hide; I didn't know what to do, so I slowed down and let several people walk past me. They chatted animatedly as they walked along. *You're being silly, paranoid*. But I couldn't get rid of the feeling of unease. I dipped into one of the little shops that line Steep Hill; it sold quirky shoes, and normally I would have loved to stay and admire the display. Today though, I lurked among the displays and peered out of the window from the back of the shop.

The street was quite busy outside with people going about their business. Some walked straight by, up or down the hill. Others took time to browse, looking through the window to admire the display of shoes. And then a man sauntered into view, looking for all the world like another tourist meandering down the hill. He peered through the window and into the depths of the shop, and although I turned my head away as fast I could, there was a brief moment when our eyes met. And I knew straight away that he wasn't shopping for shoes. He was looking for me.

I thought my heart had stopped. Everything stopped. Then suddenly it started pounding, loudly and quickly in my ears, the blood rushing through my head and making me feel nauseous. Sweat poured down my back. I was being followed, and I had no idea how to handle it. I was into something I didn't understand, and I was way out of my depth. *Get a grip, Verity, you can deal with this*. My mind was spinning, though, and I tried to slow down my breathing. Tried to clear my head. How was I supposed to lose someone who was following me? I struggled to even think of where to begin.

I glanced around the shop at the shoes, hoping that my unease wasn't evident for all to see, and tried to figure out if there was any way I could gain the upper hand. Well, for a start, he clearly wasn't very professional because I had spotted him almost straight away. I had to lose him. And I had seen enough movies to know that the best thing to do would be to find a crowd. It was much harder to spot someone in a crowd.

I came out of the shop and headed towards town. I tried to look as if nothing was amiss, sauntering slowly past the shops and glancing in the windows. All the time I could sense him behind me, but I didn't turn round; I didn't want him to know that I had spotted him. I wandered down the hill and past the High Street shops, stopping here and there for a look and checking reflections in windows to see whether he was still there. It was a Tuesday, so it was less crowded than it sometimes was at the weekend, but the High Street shops were always quite busy. I headed for Boots. That was a big store and there were lots of different isles, nooks, and crannies, places to get lost. And most importantly, it had a side exit towards the back. Just before I got to Boots, I upped my speed so that I would arrive a few paces ahead of my follower, hoping to catch him unawares with my sudden change in pace. I wasn't sure how close he was.

As soon as I got to the shop, I went in through the first door. I barged through the shoppers, brushing them out of my way and ignoring the impatient tuts. It was actually really busy and, luckily, being fairly average in height with shoulder-length brown hair, there was nothing too distinctive to make me stand out from all the other people. Forcing myself to slow down, I sauntered along, not doing anything that would draw attention to myself. I mingled in amongst everyone else on my way to the back of the shop; anyone looking across the top of the pool of heads would find it hard to pick me out. Then I dipped through the optician's at the back and out of the side entrance. Once out in the open, I sprinted across City Square and into the old, horrid seventies shopping centre building, now almost empty apart from the post office. I ran through the building, almost falling in my haste, and out towards the bus station, jumped into a taxi waiting in the rank, then went straight back home.

Chapter Nine

I knew I had to work fast, but I'd been planning. I was guessing that there was probably only the one guy who'd followed me, but if I got home and there was someone else lurking around waiting for me then I'd have to reformulate. As the taxi drew up outside, everything looked just as I had left it. I figured I would have maybe half an hour before they'd fully realised that they'd lost me and would have to come back to watch the house and wait for me. I had the upper hand, but not for long. If they returned and saw that I was already back, there would be nothing to stop them coming in and beating me up, or worse, here where no one would see. I needed to get a move on and leave the house before they realised I was inside. Once I was back in the open, there would be too many people around for them to try to attack me. Or shoot me. My heart leapt back into my mouth at that thought, and a fresh wave of nausea swept over my body. I didn't want to leave my house, but I had no alternative. I didn't want to end up dead either. I would have to shake them off and find somewhere else to be until it was safe to come home. Hopefully, once I'd met up with Stephen Ibbetson everything would be sorted out and I could return, but I wasn't sure how long that would take. I guessed I'd need to be prepared to be away from the house for a few days at least.

I ran in through the front door, leap frogging over the debris strewn across the floor, trying to avoid any broken glass and definitely trying not to notice John's prized vase; "the only thing in my family that's worth anything," he had said when he had inherited it from his Grandma. It was now laying in pieces across the floor, but I'd have to think about that later; there was no time for sentimentality now. I dashed up the stairs, taking them two and three at a time, then ran into the bedroom. I grabbed a small holdall from the floor. It had been on top of the wardrobe, but was now in the midst of a pile of clothes, bedding, toiletries, and jewellery. I found a handbag that I hadn't used in years and put my current handbag inside it. It was quite garish, made from leopard print faux leather. I had bought it on the beach on holiday one year. It was a terrible copy of a Vivienne Westwood and I'd hardly used it since we'd got back. I'd thought about taking it to the charity shop so many times but it always reminded me of what a good time we'd had on that holiday, and I could never quite bring myself to part with it. It was perfect for what I needed now, so I said a silent prayer to the gods of charity shops, zipped the notebook into an inside pocket, and put the handbag inside the holdall.

Next, I searched through the pile for a tracksuit. I had so many clothes they formed quite an enormous pile in the middle of the room. John used to comment on how often I bought new clothes, but I did like to look nice, and I had been lucky enough to inherit a decent figure, so why not make the most of it? Every now and again I had a blitz, but the clothes I gave away soon got replaced with new ones. The good thing about this was that whoever had pulled everything I owned out of the wardrobe would be pushed to recognise anything in particular.

I located the tracksuit. It was unlike anything else I possessed. It was bright pink and made of velour and had been a really cheap purchase from Primark. A few months before John had died, a friend had invited us to a fancy dress party. After overcoming my initial reluctance on the "chavs" theme, feeling it wasn't terribly politically correct, I entered into the spirit and bought this shocking pink tracksuit. I'd also bought a long hairpiece and some garish makeup and I found these on the bathroom floor, picking them out from the remnants of the bathroom cabinet which now covered the bath, the floor, and also the toilet bowl. I stuffed all these things into the holdall.

I unearthed a pair of black sheepskin Ugg-style slippers which I also took, some massive hoop earrings and some pretend gold bangles. I looked on the floor near the bedside cabinet and picked up some discarded £20 notes. At least the person who'd done this hadn't stolen my money. I found about £200 altogether. I knew I'd need more and I knew I'd have to go to the bank to get it but I hoped my plan would allow for this. Finally, I found my passport on the living room floor and put that in the handbag, inside the holdall.

I studied what I was wearing in the bedroom mirror—this would do, they'd already seen me in these clothes and would be looking out for me. I was wearing leggings and a blue tunic dress. I changed my knee-length boots for a pair of shoes I didn't really like and took a breath. I hoped this would work. I had to disappear from view. I needed to buy some stuff to tide me over the next few days, and I had to lose my tail in order to do so. I had shaken them off temporarily, and I hoped they'd be thinking the house was the best place to relocate me.

I looked out of the window. If somebody was outside waiting for me to come back home, in order for them to be absolutely sure they saw me enter the house they would have to stand at the front. They would either need to wait by the corner which led to Steep Hill or a little bit further down the lane on the other side of the house. I could walk to and from town either way, although I almost always walked past the cathedral and down Steep Hill just because it was more interesting. But they didn't know this. They would have no idea which way I would approach the house from. There was nowhere to hide; if someone wanted to see me arrive, they would have to leave themselves exposed. I prayed that they hadn't realised I had actually noticed I was being followed. I was hoping that they thought they'd just been unfortunate to lose me in the crowd. Because if that was the case, they wouldn't know I was home and would have to think that I'd come back to the house at some point.

And there he was, standing on the corner smoking a cigarette, looking for all the world as if he had just left the corner shop and was having a well-deserved smoke. On any other day, I wouldn't have given him a second look. It certainly wasn't uncommon for people to stand there, leaning against the wall, smoking. But I knew it was him. It was definitely the same guy I had seen peering into the shoe shop earlier. Good, I would take him by surprise when I left the house. I was fairly sure that he wouldn't realise I was inside; I had stayed well away from the windows and he would be expecting me to be walking back home. I gathered my things together, grabbing the holdall but leaving my coat behind. Then, taking a deep breath, I stepped outside.

Chapter Ten

I walked purposefully past my follower and didn't look in his direction. I wasn't sure if it was the right thing to do to pretend I hadn't noticed I was being followed or not, but it seemed the most sensible thing to me. I marched down Steep Hill for the third time that day and headed straight into town. There were no stops off this time; I strode into town as if I had things to do, my quick steps covering up the terror that was brewing inside me. Luckily it was a lovely sunny autumn day and I wasn't cold, especially as I marched along all the way into the city centre. It didn't take long, ten minutes or so, and on a day like this it would normally be a pleasurable walk. Today, however, I had things to sort out.

Firstly, I stopped off at the bank. I had no idea how much money I was going to need. I was rather hoping that I would take a quick trip to London, see Stephen Ibbetson, and then this would all be sorted. I knew I couldn't go back home until I was sure that it was safe, though I knew that after this, I wouldn't be able to withdraw any more cash without potentially giving my location away. I had to overestimate. So, I thought I'd play safe and withdrew £5000. Luckily the payment from John's pension had gone into the bank a couple of weeks before, so I could spare the cash. I had to provide ID in the bank, which necessitated rummaging through my holdall to find the passport in my handbag. It was hard not letting the panic that was rising in my throat take over. I tried to hide my leopard print handbag within the holdall and started worrying that my follower would notice. But when I looked over my shoulder he wasn't there. He had to be lurking outside, waiting. I took a couple of deep breaths and handed over my passport.

I put the money in my handbag, inside my holdall. I put the strap of the holdall over my head and around my arm so that it couldn't easily be grabbed and walked out of the bank and into the sunlight. The guy was there, smoking another cigarette, lurking by the hotdog stand. I caught him out of the corner of my eye, throwing his cigarette onto the ground and hurrying after me. I thought hard. I had my money, I had the notebook, but there were other things I needed and I had to throw him off. I'd got the plan in my head, but now I was going to have to put it into practice. So I steeled myself, took a deep breath, and headed straight for Marks and Spencer.

I deliberately walked through the crowds and tried to blend in. He lost me briefly as I mingled with the people and headed for the stairs. I climbed the stairs and quickly glanced behind me. He was there, turning this way and that, and then he spotted me and came after me, pushing past the shoppers. I scuttled across the first floor and down the escalator again to the ground floor. He came up the stairs just in time to see me disappear down the escalator at the other side of the store. I moved quickly, running down the escalator as fast as I could, and then darted into the changing rooms, which were just around the corner from the escalator. I knew he hadn't seen me go in; I'd jumped off the escalator before he had appeared at the top. Luckily the lady at the entrance to the changing rooms, who should have asked me how many items I had, was turned away, and I ran past and into a cubicle where I shut the door.

"Hey!" She shouted after me. "Are you okay?" But I ignored her and kept quiet.

I very briefly looked at myself in the mirror before taking off my clothes. I thought I didn't look too bad for forty-two—being about 5'5" and a slim size eight helped. I'd left home with no make-up on and without taking too much care I applied a little of a rather bronzy coloured foundation I'd got in a free promotion and had only ever used once. I added my bright pink lipstick and blue eye shadow, before rubbing more rouge than necessary over my cheek bones. I pulled off my clothes as quickly as I could and put on the pink velour tracksuit, then scraped my hair up into a tight knot on the top of my head, securing it with a band. I attached the long false piece, which matched my colour really well, and I now looked as if I had almost waist-length hair. Pulling my hair back so severely changed the shape of my face a bit. It accentuated my cheekbones, which I plastered with a little more rouge. I pulled the black sheepskin slippers onto my feet, put on the large hooped earrings and fake gold bangles, then looked in the mirror. I was almost unrecognisable. Certainly, if you were scanning a crowd and looking for me, you would not have noticed that I was the same person who had run into the changing rooms earlier.

I stuffed my old clothes and shoes into the holdall along with the make-up and left it on the floor. Someone would find it later and assume a customer had left it by mistake. They'd take it to a lost property office for a while and then, eventually, I assumed it would go to a charity shop or be thrown away. I didn't really care. The tunic top was quite nice, but I'd had it a few years and the leggings were wearing out at the waist. The shoes I didn't really like anyway.

I sat on the bench in the changing room and unlocked my iPhone, copying down some of the important numbers. I picked up the leopard print handbag and double checked that the money and the notebook were safe. Taking a few deep breaths, I looked at myself once again in the mirror and then walked out of the changing rooms. I headed towards the exit via the food store and left the shop through the back entrance. I felt incredibly self-conscious, but nobody else took any notice and probably assumed I always dressed like that.

When I reached the outside world beyond the back door, I stood by the wall for a while. After a couple of minutes, the door opened. My heart almost exploded as it hammered in my chest but it wasn't my follower. An elderly couple came out. Then nothing. After another couple of minutes, a very fat man came out. Nothing more. I breathed a sigh of relief. I'd shaken him off, and I didn't believe for one second that he would look twice at the woman in the pink velour tracksuit. I took my iPhone out of the bag. It was fully charged and I turned off all the apps but left the phone on. I glanced around and saw just what I needed. Across the car park was a delivery van, its back door swung open, with the slogan *"We deliver to the four corners of the country, every day"* painted down its side. Perfect. I walked around the back; the driver was nowhere to be seen. I hid the iPhone in the back of the van. The police had my mobile number, and if someone in their ranks was trying to find out where I'd gone by tracking my phone, that should throw them off the trail, at least for a while.

I walked back into the High Street, feeling nervous and forcing myself to not glance around and look for my assailant. I tried to act as nonchalantly as I could. I called in first at Boots. I bought a pair of scissors, deodorant, toothpaste, a toothbrush, some plastic food bags, and some hair dye. Then I went up the High Street to CEX, a shop that bought and sold second hand phones, electrical stuff, DVDs, that sort of thing. I looked at the tablets that they had for sale; they had some iPads, iPad minis, Samsung's, and other makes. I spent some time talking to the very helpful sales assistant, positioning myself so that I could see the door, just in case I needed to run or hide. In the end I bought a second-hand iPad. Maybe it was just my imagination, but I thought I saw a look of suspicion cross his face when I paid in cash. But he took the money without saying anything.

The iPad was similar to my iPhone in terms of operating it, so it wouldn't take me any time to get used to it. I had them set it up for me and show me the basics of how to access the Internet, email, and so on. I knew I would have to be careful and not link it to my iPhone in any way. I'd have to use the email via the Internet, for example; I didn't want to run the risk of being traced even though I had dumped my precious iPhone. I also bought a cheap Sony Erikson phone. I got chargers for the phone and the iPad, as well as some earphones. I then crossed the street and went into Black's and bought a rucksack, some trainers, socks, light trousers and tops, some pants, a zip-up jacket, and two of the only type of bra they had, which was a sports bra. I rushed back down the high street and called in at a phone shop to put £100 of credit on the phone.

I then walked hurriedly over to the Premier Inn, which was the nearest reasonable hotel I could think of, and booked myself into a room under my new pseudonym, Miriam Nathan.

Chapter Eleven

As soon as I was in the room, I flopped onto the bed. I had bought myself some time, thankfully, but I needed to move fast, so I forced myself upright, quelling any notion that I might be in danger, or should be scared. I made myself concentrate on what needed to be done. Firstly, I turned on the iPad and checked my Hotmail account. Little prickles, like hundreds of pins being thrown against my skin, pierced their way up my neck. I'd had a reply from Stephen Ibbetson. Part of my brain urged me to close the iPad, not to look, as if looking would make it more real.

I read on.

From: <s.ibbetson@lbhillingdon.gov.uk>
To: <Sugarandspice328@hotmail.com>
Hello Miriam,
It's interesting to hear from you. I have a slot at 2pm on Wednesday if you would like to meet then?
If you come to the Civic Centre in Uxbridge we can

talk in my office. Just ask for me at reception and
someone will come down to meet you.
Kind regards,
Stephen
Stephen Ibbetson
Assistant Director, Children's Specialist Services
London Borough of Hillingdon: Civic Centre: High
Street: Uxbridge: Middlesex: UB8 1UW
Tel: 01895 254215

Wednesday, wow, that was tomorrow. He had to be quite keen to see me, I thought. I imagined being an Assistant Director to be quite a busy job. I rattled off a quick reply saying that I would see him at 2pm on Wednesday. That meant that I would have to travel to London in the morning, so the next thing I did was open the Trainline page and look at train times. I almost booked online, but then realised that if whoever at the police had accessed my address was trying to trace me through debit card transactions, that would give them an easy trail. Stupid. I needed to keep my wits about me. It would be more expensive, but I'd have to turn up the following day and pay cash at the station. The 7.20am was a direct train from Lincoln, so I resolved to get that one.

By now the light was beginning to fade. I got out the notebook and took some photos on my iPad of every page. I took photos of entire pages, close-ups of the writing, a photo of the outside of the book, the name and address, everything from every angle that I could possibly think of. Then I tore out a page from the back of the book and wrote everything down again on that, only all bunched together and mixed up. I folded the page several times so that it was tiny and zipped it into an inside pocket of the new jacket

I'd bought. It was a pocket within a pocket. Just in case the iPad got stolen. I then put the original notebook in a plastic bag and wrapped it tightly. I put that bag into another bag, and that one into another. I wished I'd thought to buy some Sellotape, but I hadn't so that would have to do.

Without changing out of the pink velour tracksuit, I left the hotel still wearing the garish make-up and pretend long hair. It was dusk now; the traffic had slowed and the streetlights had come on. Although I was sure that no one had seen me, I peered around me before crossing the road. I walked across the road and down by the side of the river, past the Waterside Shopping Centre and along to the steps which led up from the river to the High Street. I bent down behind the steps, checking over my shoulder to make sure that there was no one else around. It was almost dark, and there was hardly any light in that corner. If someone came down the steps from the High Street, they wouldn't even notice me. If someone came the other way, from the river, they would but I'd have to pretend I was ill or drunk or something. I looked again, no one was coming, so I had a good minute or so at least.

I tapped and pulled at a couple of bricks until I found a loose one and I carefully pulled it out. I put the notebook into the hole and then pushed the brick back into place. With the notebook flat against the back of the brick the difference in the level of the wall was barely noticeable. They were all uneven and worn anyway; nobody had replaced the pointing for about three hundred years, so there were several loose bricks. It had been a hiding place I'd used with a friend when we were young. We'd thought it was great fun to leave notes or little gifts for each other in turn in a hiding spot that no one else knew about. Sometimes we would write the letters in code or in invisible ink so that if anyone else discovered them, the messages would stay secret. Sometimes we'd leave a map, or clues, or instructions to find something else and then hide a sweet or a chocolate bar in another location. No one ever seemed to find our notes then, and I was pretty sure no one would think about looking in that particular place for the notebook. I was still reluctant to leave it, though.

When I got back to the hotel I cut off all the price tags from my new clothes and put them in the rucksack. I left out a pair of pants, a bra, a pair of trousers, and a long-sleeved top for the morning. They wouldn't be what I would normally wear, but they would be comfortable and they were very light and easy to carry around.

Then I took off the tracksuit and the hairpiece. I jumped in the shower and washed my hair using the hotel toiletries. When I finished in the shower I wrapped myself in a towel and studied myself in the mirror. I knew I would have to change my appearance if I could, as much as possible. If anyone was looking out for me they would be looking for someone with shoulder-length brown hair. I had to do something drastic. I wasn't going to get away with a hairpiece and terrible make-up for long. I looked at my face in the mirror. It wasn't a bad face; I'd often been described as attractive, although having known every fault in it for so long I wasn't so sure myself. But it was a face I lived with every day, and I was quite pleased with how it looked; I could pass for several years below my actual age. I scraped my hair up and back once again into the ponytail, high on my head, and turned my head upside down. Then I took the scissors and cut off my hair as close to the band as I could. There were a few strands longer than others which I evened out, and after cutting away at this bit and that, I was left with a reasonably neat pixie-style hair-do. The change in my face was startling, and although I'd never really liked my hair short, I thought it quite suited me.

Then I took the hair bleach and dyed my hair blonde. Whilst I waited the required twenty minutes before I could wash it off, I fished out my new phone. It was clunky and difficult to navigate after my iPhone, and I spent the whole waiting time familiarising myself with it and putting in the numbers I had copied from my old phone. I managed to work out how to set the alarm, so I set that for 6am as I didn't want to miss the train in the morning. I rinsed off my hair and stood looking in the mirror whilst I blow dried it. It was amazing. The change was incredible. Even I would have had difficulty recognising myself.

Chapter Twelve

I got undressed and climbed into bed. I took out the iPad and re-read the email from Stephen Ibbetson. *"It's interesting to hear from you."* What does that mean? Interesting? It sounded like he wasn't too surprised. I closed the iPad down, feeling a mixture of frustration, but also an anticipation that going to London might just bring this thing to a close and enable me to return home to my house. My house. My heart sank as I thought about the ransacked place that I used to call home. I wouldn't be able to face going back to it and cleaning it all up on my own. I tried hard not to think about the broken photos; shattered memories of a life that some sleepy lorry driver had snatched from me only a few months ago. I was determined not to cry, not to sink because of this. I had to fight. And getting to London to talk to Stephen Ibbetson was my best hope. The notebook, however, was not coming with me. For one thing, I didn't want to lose it somewhere, and for another I thought it was too dangerous. I'd check out this Ibbetson guy, see if he was the right Stephen and fill him in on what had happened. If he needed the notebook it was in a safe place, and anyway, I had all the photos on my iPad containing the same information.

My mind kept racing back to the house. Once again, I fought back the tears. Clenching my fists into tight balls, I punched down hard on the bed, determined that whoever had done this was not going to beat me down; I couldn't give in. But I couldn't face going back to the house in the state it was in. My eyes stared out into nothingness as I contemplated what I could do, what I could say about everything that had happened, and how I could make sure that nobody else got hurt. Images of Dr Neasden in his final moments filled my head, and I took my time, thinking out a plan that would keep anyone connected with me away from my house. I took out the new Sony Erikson and dialled my friend Robert. He answered on the second ring. Not a surprise—he was seldom more than a couple of feet away from his phone.

"Hello?" The uncertainty in his voice took me by surprise, but of course, I was calling from a different phone.

"Robert, hi, it's me, Verity."

"Oh, hello, darling. How are you? Have you got a new phone?"

"Yes, I do. It's a long story. But… Look, Robert, I need you to do me a big favour."

"Ask away."

I decided to be a little economical with the truth "Well, I've been burgled."

"Oh! My Good Lord. Are you okay? Do you want us to come round?"

The familiar friendliness in his voice caught me, and I blinked back tears that were threatening to spill out. Robert Timpson had been a good friend of mine for years, and together with his partner Keith, and Collette of course, had scooped me up pretty well after John's death. Collette and some of my other friends were amazing but most of them had kids now. Robert and Keith had been there whenever Collette had other commitments. They'd made me do normal things, and even made me laugh sometimes, gradually piecing me back together.

I was so lucky to have them in my life. Robert and I had worked together years ago, but we'd always kept in touch and had remained good friends. I'd already met and married John at that point but Robert had just been coming to grips with his sexuality. When he'd met Keith and settled down a few years later, Keith too had become an integral part of our circle of friends. I knew I could rely on them, but I didn't want them to get involved. There was clearly someone watching my house, and they might not yet realise that I wasn't planning on returning anytime soon. I was sure they'd be keeping an eye on it for any signs of life. If anyone saw either Keith or Robert at the house they might assume they knew something, and I really didn't want anything happening to either of them. I had to tread a careful line.

"I'm not at home at the moment. I've gone to stay with a friend. The house is a bit of a mess."

"Bless you, are you sure you're okay?"

"I'm fine, honestly, but I'm going to stay away for a few days. Listen, I was wondering if you could arrange for a cleaning firm to go in and sort everything out. I'll settle up when I'm back. It's too much of a mess for someone to do it alone, it needs professionals. Can you call someone and ask them to go round?"

"Of course, I'll supervise them myself. I'll make sure it's all spick and span for when you get back."

"Robert, there's something else; it's really important. I don't want to worry you, but the burglars were looking for something in particular and they didn't find it. It's really, really important that you don't go to the house. I don't want anyone seen at the house except a bunch of professional cleaners. Just ask them to pick up the spare key at yours and then let them go on their own."

At this, Robert became quite distressed. He clearly wanted me to be safe and he wanted to make sure the cleaners were honest and did a good job. I managed, with some difficulty, to persuade him that it wasn't a good idea to go to the house right now. I hated not being honest with him, but what could I do? He was worried for my safety. And sanity probably, but we could cross that bridge later. If anyone was watching, they'd think it natural that I'd have the house cleaned up and, hopefully, wouldn't think a cleaning company was involved. I cajoled and persuaded and, exasperated, was on the verge of explaining the doctor's sticky end but then Robert caved in. "Okay, okay, enough! You've persuaded me. Cross my heart and hope to die, I promise I won't go anywhere near. You take care, sweetheart." He was breathing heavily. "And let me know as soon as you're home."

"Rob, can you ask a locksmith to change the lock too?" I didn't know if I needed a new lock; the intruder seemed to have just forced the front door open, but I was taking no chances. "Can you organise for the locksmith to put the keys in the key box? You know the code."

"Of course and don't you worry about anything. I'll pay; we can settle up when you're back home."

"Thanks, Robert, give my love to Keith."

"Sweet dreams, sweetheart. Say 'hi' to Collette."

I didn't put him right when he assumed my 'friend' was Collette and not the Premier Inn. I turned off the phone, feeling a mixture of sadness at having to lead my friend on and relief that the house would be returned to something approaching normal when I got back. I knew everything would be in the wrong place, and I'd have to get new photo frames and probably new crockery too, but that would be the least of my worries.

I went back to the iPad and spent some time searching on the Internet for information that might relate to any of the acronyms in the notebook, but drew yet more blanks. I kept returning to the photo of the page with the word 'Champion!' What did that refer to? I shook my head in frustration. I looked back at Ibbetson's email. *"It's interesting to hear from you."* I played this over in my mind, but couldn't really come to any firm conclusion.

It was then that I noticed his phone number. The last three digits were 215. That corresponded to one of the numbers in the first group of three digits listed in the notebook. I double checked the photos. It was definitely the same. Coincidence? But what use were the last three digits of a phone number? The rest had to be there somewhere. I scanned through the photos again. I looked at the set of longer numbers that Dr Neasden had written a few pages further on. There were eight numbers in each list. Eight plus three made eleven. I counted how many numbers were in Stephen Ibbetson's phone number. Eleven. There had to be a match. I looked at all the numbers again but I couldn't find anything that corresponded. There was no way that any of the numbers in the second list would complete Ibbetson's number. I tried them backwards and scrambled but I could not make any of the second set of numbers correspond to the first three numbers. Maybe it was a coincidence that the number ended 215? There had to be many numbers, hundreds, possibly thousands, that ended with that combination of numbers.

I gave up. My eyes were aching with the effort of looking at the screen; my brain was aching with the effort of thinking about it all. Every muscle in my body was tight with tension, and exhaustion was crushing me. I made a cup of tea using the tiny kettle provided and turned on the TV. I woke up at four in the morning with the TV still on and a half full cup of tea on the bedside cabinet beside me.

WEDNESDAY

Chapter Thirteen

I dozed for a bit, in and out of a fitful sleep, wondering how on earth I had landed in this mess, and missing the calm orderliness of my life. The alarm on my phone went off, although I was already awake so I didn't really need it, and I got up soon after. I showered, then checked myself once again in the full-length mirror; I looked like some relative of mine. The short hair which, overnight, had developed a kind of spiky appearance, and the bleached-blonde look, coupled with the sporty attire made me look like someone on the way to the gym. In truth I hardly ever went to the gym, although I did belong to one. I usually went for the sauna, though, not to actually exercise. Walking up and down Steep Hill kept me quite fit, and I was lucky to have a relatively fast metabolism. It was freaky seeing this strange person staring back at me. The whole sporty, spiky appearance was so different and I was fairly sure that even people who knew me well would walk past me without a second glance.

I put on my zip-up jacket before picking up my

rucksack and slinging it over my shoulder. I stuffed the pink velour tracksuit into a carrier bag along with the sheepskin slippers. I couldn't see that I would ever wear the tracksuit again but I quite liked the slippers. Still, they were too cumbersome to carry around with me, and they had needed replacing anyway. When I left the hotel there was no one at reception, so I left my key card on the desk and walked out. I dumped the carrier bag into a waste bin and found a coffee shop on a nearby corner which was open and, surprisingly, had a small queue of bleary-eyed commuters waiting. I joined the queue, got my usual large Americano and went to sit down, grabbing a newspaper from the rack to read whilst I waited. A steady stream of people came in and out of the café; I was surprised there were so many people up at that time of the morning. Where were they all going? Mostly to work, I guessed. A lot of them had briefcases and seemed like businessmen and women grabbing a coffee to drink on the train.

At 7am I put the paper back where I had found it and then left and headed for the train station. I booked a first-class ticket which, because I was buying it on the day, cost me well over £100, but a standard would have been £78, so I opted for sitting in relative comfort and quiet. I found a seat with a table and hoped that no one would come to join me. I wasn't in the mood for small talk. I glanced around nervously at my fellow travellers, but no one seemed to be taking any interest in me. Although I knew anyone would have to look quite closely to realise it was me, I felt suspicious of everyone. I didn't want to take any chances. I tried listening to people's phone conversations but no one was saying anything remotely interesting. There was a group of giggling middle-aged women who looked as if they might be on their way to a trip somewhere, maybe London for a show or to catch the Eurostar to Paris or something. They all seemed excited and one kept laughing really raucously. *Too much for this time of the morning.* I took my iPad out of my bag, plugged the charger in, and put my rucksack and jacket on the rack above the table. I had a bacon sandwich, some toast, copious cups of coffee, and a muffin for breakfast. I hadn't realised how hungry I was, but then it dawned on me that, what with everything that had gone on, I had barely eaten the day before.

I arrived at King's Cross at almost 9.30, having spent much of the train journey puzzling over the photos of the notebook, still none the wiser. I had briefly spent some time doing the sudoku in the free copy of The Times, but I had found it hard to concentrate. Luckily, it hadn't been a particularly challenging one. I walked across the road from the station and headed down Grays Inn Road. I booked into a small hotel not too far from the station, once again using the name Miriam Nathan. I booked in for a night and paid up front with some of the cash that I had, hoping that I would get things sorted at my meeting with Stephen Ibbetson and be able to head straight back home the following day.

Luckily, they had a room ready. It was on the fifth floor, so I took the lift. It was quite small, but it had everything I needed. There was a small recess behind the door, of about a foot or so, with a hook for coats and a small fixed box for putting your bag on. From the door, a short corridor of about five feet led to the bedroom. There was no need to put a card into a slot to operate the lights, which I liked; I could leave the lights on when I left the room. Off the corridor to the right was a bathroom with a shower over a small bath and all the usual toiletries. A king size bed with an iron frame filled most of the room, and on either side of the bed, lamps stood on sturdy wooden bedroom tables. I flopped down on the bed and got out my iPad, figuring out the route I would need to take to Uxbridge later. It was the very last stop on the Metropolitan line, and I could pick it up at King's Cross, which meant no changes. I looked at my phone; it was now half past ten. I wanted to arrive in Uxbridge a little early to give me time to orient myself. Google Maps informed me that the London Borough of Hillingdon Civic Centre was only a five minute walk from the station. I switched to street view—the Civic Centre looked quite an impressive building, all red brick but an interesting design. I'd sooner get there early and have to have a coffee somewhere than risk being late. I could not afford to miss this meeting. So, I decided to get to the station by midday in order to be doubly sure that I'd get there on time. That gave me an hour and a half and, as there was little else I could do before meeting Ibbetson, I decided to go for a walk.

I hadn't picked the most picturesque area of London to stay, and it wasn't an area I was very familiar with. Normally, when John and I had come down to London for a show, or a weekend break visiting art galleries and museums, we'd stayed in the centre, somewhere near the British Museum. I gathered up my iPad and phone and put them in my rucksack, made sure I had everything safe, put on my jacket, then headed out.

As I left the room, I grabbed the "Do Not Disturb" notice and put it over the handle on the outside of the door. I didn't know why, but I always did this when I left hotel rooms. Perhaps I just thought it would make a rogue staff member think twice before entering the room with a thought to steal something. It didn't really matter in this instance that I had left absolutely nothing in the room, apart from my toothbrush and toothpaste, which they were welcome to; it was more a case of old habits die hard. As I closed the door, the notice blew up and caught upside down in the door. I opened the door and reclosed it, but the same thing happened. I left the notice trapped upside down.

Chapter Fourteen

I turned left out of the hotel and walked for about five minutes, before turning left again and wandering through some streets and past some pretty parks. I ended up on Clerkenwell Road. It had all become incredibly trendy since the last time I had been there which, granted, was probably twenty years before. As I meandered through the streets, I peered in the windows of some of the über-trendy furniture stores and admired the swanky flats for sale in the estate agents' windows. I started wandering north up the Farringdon Road, turning off occasionally and then turning back at the next junction, just seeing what was around. I pulled out my phone, which informed me that it was half past eleven, so I headed more purposefully up the Farringdon Road and towards King's Cross. My stomach was tying itself in knots—a little bit of excitement mixed with a little bit of trepidation. I hoped that by meeting Stephen Ibbetson I would be able to quickly return to my normal routine. But I wasn't really sure what to expect and I didn't have a clear strategy, other than to see how it went. *"Trust no one."* I had to be cautious.

I found the right platform for the Metropolitan line, bought a trashy magazine at a W.H. Smith, and a cup of coffee from a Costa stand. At midday the train was not too busy, and I easily found a seat, so I sat in the corner and flicked through the magazine I'd bought. There were pictures of celebrities I didn't know, articles about TV programmes I didn't watch, and stories about film stars I knew of but didn't really care about. I read about high-street fashion and laughed inwardly at some of the pictures of "fashion-able" members of the public dressed in outrageous, clashing clothes. *Good to be an individual.* I glanced at an article on hair styles. Apparently, the pixie cut was "in." I studied my unfamiliar reflection in the train window and wondered if my self-administered haircut would count as fashionable. I somehow doubted it.

It was almost one o'clock when I emerged from Uxbridge station. I wandered down the High Street and into the shopping centre, finding a space in a café upstairs inside one of the department stores. The large windows looked out over the entrance to the Civic Centre on the opposite side of the road. I ordered a coffee and a ham and cheese toastie and sat in the window watching the people coming and going. It was a busy place. People with identity badges hanging around their necks came in and out, mostly to stand on the pavement and have a cigarette, chatting to colleagues before heading back inside. A whole host of other people—couples, families with small children, older people—came and went. Some disappeared and I never saw them again, but others entered and re-emerged within a few minutes. Everybody busy going about their business.

At ten to two, I walked across the road and into the reception. A curt receptionist gave me a visitor pass and asked me to wait in a room through some double doors. I sat on a chair watching BBC News 24 on a silent TV on the wall. Pictures of unrest somewhere played on the screen, with rebels and government forces firing weapons at each other and civilians running for cover. *Nothing changes.* After a few minutes Stephen Ibbetson appeared. I recognised him from his staff photo. He was shorter than I'd expected, just a few inches taller than me, and also fitter; his physique obtained only by spending several hours a week in a gym. His expensive-looking suit was a little worn at the edges, and he'd paired it with an open-necked shirt and tan coloured shoes. He smiled and held out his hand. Creases appeared around his eyes as his cheery, friendly face broke into a smile.

"Miriam, good to meet you," he said, as I shook his hand.

It took me a while to register my pretend name and I hoped he didn't notice my hesitation. "Likewise," I replied.

We walked to the lifts and he pressed the button for floor four. When we emerged, it became apparent what a bizarrely designed building the Civic Centre was. The sign on the wall near the lift said "Centre Core." I followed Stephen along the edge of a room marked "East," full of busy people sitting at desks. To our left was another room full of busy people, but at a half-room level lower. It was all open-plan and the people would have seen our feet walking past but not our top half. Also visible to our left was a room a half level higher, but you couldn't really see much of this, as it was above head level. Weird. We turned a corner and along the edge of another identical open-plan room, this one marked "North," and it also had the strange half-level rooms to one side. Stephen led me down a few steps and towards a small office, where he held open the door and gestured for me to go inside.

"Can I get you a drink? Coffee? Tea?"

"Just a glass of water would be good, if that's okay?" I'd had enough coffee to float a boat and couldn't face another.

He went off to get a glass of water, and I sat down. As the reality of having to talk to him struck home, nervousness gripped at me like a screaming child that won't let go. My legs shook against the seat of the chair; my dry, sandpaper mouth crying out for the water. I didn't know how to play this. I was completely out of my depth. The doctor had implored me to find this man, although I wasn't really sure why yet, but the words *'trust no one'* resonated through my head like a beat on a drum. *Trust no one, trust no one.* I was reserving judgement.

Chapter Fifteen

Stephen Ibbetson came back into the room, carrying two plastic cups full of water. He put them down on the desk and closed the door before sitting down at the opposite side of the desk and smiling his crinkly faced smile again. After the usual niceties about the weather, the tube journey, and the relative merits and demerits of public transport, his smile dropped and a more serious look clouded his face.

"So, tell me, you have had some dealings with Dr Neasden?"

"Yes, he asked me to come and visit you." I picked up the cup and gulped in most of the water.

"I see." He smiled again. "In relation to…?"

I lied. "He told me about the work you were doing together." They must have had dealings with each other, so I thought the term "work" would cover a range of options and I was hoping for the best.

"The paper?"

Writing a paper together, of course, an academic exercise.

"Yes. I think he thought you might be able to help me out."

"Help you out, in what way? What do you do then?"

I remembered about Dr Neasden's work with those who had no recourse to public funds. *Quick, Verity, think of a lie, a lie, a believable lie. Shit, shit, shit.*

I carried on without a blink. A smile. "Yes, I work at the local college in Lincoln, and we have some young people who needed help. That's how I met Dr Neasden." Well, part of that was true. A lie is easier to maintain, surely, if it is based in truth. I surprised myself at how believable I sounded. And Dr Neasden, unfortunately, was no longer around to refute the point that we had met in those circumstances.

"And why did Dr Neasden suggest you came to see me?"

"He thought you might be able to help." *I'm being too vague, I've already said that.* I decided to take a leap— if he was writing a paper on something, whatever it was, he had to know something about the subject. "You being something of an expert in the field, he said you were highly regarded." *Careful, Verity, don't push it.* But flattery will get you everywhere.

A tilt of the head in recognition of the compliment. "Yes, well, with Heathrow in our patch, becoming an expert is, unfortunately, something that is hard to avoid. It's a relatively common occurrence and some of the children and young people—" He paused. "And vulnerable adults too, who are brought to this country are subject to terrible abuses. Well," he looked off to his left, "I'm sure you've read about some of the cases in the newspapers." He arched an eyebrow and I thought he was going to carry on, but he just stopped.

I nodded. He was making an assumption that I

knew what the paper was on. My mind whirred and I hoped he couldn't see me trying to figure it out as we spoke. I had to keep up the pretence or I thought he'd stop talking to me. He thought I knew more than I did. *Think. Heathrow, children and adults being brought into the country. Dr Neasden's voluntary work. Shit. I was reading about this the other day. What is it called? What is it called when people are brought here against their will, or under some pretence?* Trafficking. I dragged the word up from the back of my brain somewhere. It suddenly dawned on me. He was talking about trafficking, and he thought I knew something about what they had been working on. Or what Dr Neasden had been working on, at least. *Should I mention the notebook?* I thought about this quickly, before carrying on. I still couldn't remember if Dr Neasden had asked me to talk to Ibbetson or take the notebook to him. What I could remember was the desperate *"trust no one."* I decided discretion was the better part of valour, and I carried on; I was in enough shit as it was, I couldn't afford to dig myself into more danger by being indiscrete.

I had read about cases of trafficking in the news-papers; it was only a couple of weeks ago that some poor young woman from Romania, or Bulgaria, or somewhere had been rescued from a family after years spent as a domestic slave, since she had been brought here aged about ten.

"Would it be possible to see the paper you were working on?" I asked.

He straightened up in his chair. His attitude shifted. He seemed cautious, almost suspicious. "It's confidential, I'm afraid. Still in draft form. There's plenty of stuff on trafficking on the Internet if you want generic information. I'm not quite sure how Dr Neasden thought I could help."

I'd pushed it a bit, and he was closing up. I paused. Then he seemed to realise he had sounded defensive and he instantly loosened up once more. That smile again.

"The young people at your college. Where are they from?"

A stab in the dark. "Eastern Europe." Time to bite the bullet, I thought. "Dr Neasden said you could help, and now he's dead. And I'm not sure what to do now."

He stared back off to the side. "That's very sad, I agree. Dr Neasden and I had worked closely together for some time. He was a good man, very dedicated to helping people that no one had ever bothered to help. Not everybody wants to help people who are brought to this country, or realises that they are often made to come, against their will. Many people would prefer to punish them for being here in the first place." He stopped and looked up at me. That hint of suspicion had come back. "The work that Dr Neasden did wasn't popular with a lot of people. We'd published a couple of papers together, but they weren't universally applauded." He paused again, softened. He returned his gaze to the table. "But I didn't realise he'd died until I got your email. When did it happen?"

It seemed like about three years ago. "Monday," I said.

He appeared a little surprised, so I went on, "Mr Ibbetson, Dr Neasden pointed me in your direction and now he is dead. I don't know what to do, so I've come to you as he suggested. It's more than the young people at the college." I decided I had to lay a few of my cards on the table. "On Monday somebody murdered Dr Neasden. He was shot in his home. And he asked me to find you."

A shift. I noticed a shift in his eyes; it was subtle and he tried to hide it. I guessed it was the shock—he clearly hadn't known that Dr Neasden had been murdered. He closed up again.

"I'm really sorry, Miriam, but I don't know what I can do to help."

Miriam; the pretend me with the blonde spiky hair and new found ability to lie through her teeth. "I was there just after Dr Neasden was shot. I tried to keep him alive but I couldn't."

Ibbetson said nothing, just shook his head.

I carried on, "I gave a statement to the local police."

I wasn't getting anywhere. I sighed. There was no way I could go home. This was so far from being solved. I thought about the notebook, the acronyms, the fact that I had got Ibbetson's name from the notebook. He hadn't mentioned anything about it, and so neither did I. I still had the notebook and somebody badly wanted it, but I decided to play a bit dumb. I needed to get things sorted, and I desperately wanted to go back home, but I wanted to do that alive. It seemed that someone would do anything to get their hands on the information I had, even though I had no idea what it all meant. *"Trust no one."*

"Mr Ibbetson, after Dr Neasden suggested I came to see you. He was murdered, and then my house was turned upside down. I have absolutely no clue why that was." Okay, not strictly true, but Miriam seemed quite good at maintaining a lie. "But I followed his advice and came down to see you. I'm worried about what this is all about." I paused. "I'm worried for my safety and I don't know what to do. Why do you think he asked me to come and see you?"

He was still silent. Lost in thought. The smile had gone, replaced by a glum stare off to the left.

"Please, please help me. The only people who knew where I lived after Dr Neasden's death were the police. I can't go to them. I think someone in the police used the information in my statement to come to my house."

His gaze shifted back to mine. He looked profoundly sad. I felt for him; if he and Dr Neasden had worked closely together, it had to have been a shock to find out he had been murdered. It also dawned on me that perhaps there was an element of worry for his own safety, if this was anything to do with the paper he and Dr Neasden had been writing.

"I work very closely with the police here in London, the National Trafficking Unit." He raised his eyebrows and gesticulated towards his computer as if to indicate where the information he needed was held. "I can put you in touch with a good policeman I know. I could arrange for you to meet and you can explain your situation to him. He might be able to help make sure you're safe when you get home. This has nothing to do with you, right? You weren't involved in Dr Neasden's death in any way?"

"Absolutely not."

"Then there's no reason for you to not go home and be safe. If the local police are using information in a way that they shouldn't, this guy will be able to help, I'm sure. He'll make sure they're exposed."

I nodded. "Can you email me the details? You've got my email address." Disappointment wracked my body. My much-hyped meeting with Ibbetson had turned into a crushing anti-climax.

"Sure. Where are you staying?" The smile was back. A sense of self-assurance had crept back into

Stephen Ibbetson's demeanour. He stood up and opened the door.

"Over near King's Cross." I hoped that was vague enough. I wasn't about to give my location away to anyone.

We walked to the lift together. I would never have found the way out of that maze of a building by myself. Everywhere looked exactly the same. It felt like something out of a Kafka book. I wondered how on earth the people who worked here knew where they were. At the lift we said our goodbyes and shook hands.

"Good luck," he said. "You'll be fine, don't worry."

Chapter Sixteen

I left the Civic Centre and turned onto Uxbridge High Street. The weather had shifted whilst I'd been inside and I shivered in the cold. I crossed the road and went into the shopping centre, dipping into Dorothy Perkins to pick up a scarf. As I looked at the display, the red tartan one caught my eye, but I decided instead on a plain grey. I didn't want to be wearing anything distinctive. I also bought a grey woolly hat, partly to keep out the cold—my neck was feeling it since I'd cut my hair—but also in case I needed to cover up my blonde hair at any point. A grey hat would blend into a crowd nicely. I paid in cash and headed for the tube station.

I spent the forty-five minutes heading back to King's Cross deep in thought. Dr Neasden and Ibbetson had been working on a paper to do with trafficking. Child trafficking I assumed, given Ibbetson's position; I didn't really know much about the crime, apart from what I'd read in the newspapers. I knew that people had been brought into the country to work as domestic slaves, as prostitutes, and as pick-pockets, but that information was well known. Would it be worth killing someone over? It didn't make any sense. I thought of the people involved in bringing the people into the country and spiriting them away when they arrived. Perhaps Dr Neasden had been about to expose someone? Perhaps there was someone fairly high-profile involved? Would someone kill so that they escaped justice? People had killed for less, I decided. My stomach sank at the thought that, rather than things resolving themselves after my visit to Ibbetson, they had become more complicated. Disappointment drove through me and I hung my shoulders low as I slouched into my chair. Nothing was resolved, far from it. I didn't want to be in the middle of all this. It had absolutely nothing to do with me. But I knew that I couldn't extricate myself from it now. There was no one I could turn to for help. I was floundering, out of my depth and drowning under a sea of helplessness. Hopefully, meeting Ibbetson's police friend would give me a way to get back home and back to normality.

I wasn't quite sure why I hadn't mentioned the notebook to Ibbetson. It just hadn't felt right, somehow. He didn't seem aware of it, and if it had to do with the paper they were working on, then surely Ibbetson would have asked about it? He had become a little guarded when I'd asked him if I could see the paper. But surely if he knew there was an important notebook around, he would have at least alluded to it. Perhaps Neasden had wanted me to show it to Ibbetson and he would have been the right person to deal with whatever information it contained, but it just didn't seem that way. I was sure I'd done the right thing. Ibbetson had seemed nice enough and maybe I was being a bit too careful. Dr Neasden had wanted me to find Ibbetson, which I had now done, but he had told me to trust no one. He hadn't said trust no one but Ibbetson. I thought back to Dr Neasden's blood-soaked body, the bullet wound, the impassioned look on his face. No, I couldn't be too careful.

When I got back to King's Cross it was almost five o'clock, so I walked straight to the hotel and took a shower. I dried my hair with the hotel hairdryer, getting used to my appearance in the mirror now. I grabbed my rucksack, jacket, scarf and hat, then headed out to find some dinner. As I pulled the door closed, the "Do Not Disturb" notice did its flippy thing and ended up trapped in the door again. This time I didn't even bother to try to untrap it.

I walked for about ten minutes before finding a lovely pub-cum-restaurant and I ordered a large glass of rioja and some fish and chips. Whilst I was waiting for my dinner, I fired up the iPad and checked my emails. Nothing yet from Ibbetson. The rest of the inbox of my Hotmail account was full of junk because it was the address I always gave when I knew I would be bombarded with offers and unsolicited crap. When my fish and chips arrived, I picked at them whilst browsing the online daily papers and catching up on national and international news. Nothing of note really; uprisings in the Middle East, protests about government cuts. It was all becoming a bit predictable. When the waitress came to take my plate away, I ordered another glass of wine.

I Googled "trafficking" and instantly felt overwhelmed at the volume of results; well over forty million. That would take some sifting through. I concentrated initially on the hits that were more specific to child trafficking, as that seemed most likely to be Ibbetson and Dr Neasden's focus. I then scanned a few bits here and there, not reading anything in depth. People trafficked other people for all sorts of reasons, sexual slavery being the most common. They also trafficked them for the removal of kidneys for kidney transplants, or for use as a surrogate for childless couples. They trafficked children for child pornography. *Jesus.* Could Dr Neasden's work have had anything to do with that kind of thing? I couldn't understand why he would keep a separate notebook, though, if he was writing a paper about it. Perhaps he was working on something that Ibbetson didn't know about? That would make sense. Ibbetson had seemed shocked to hear of Neasden's murder. Although, why would he have implored me to talk to Ibbetson? Maybe he was the only person Neasden thought would be able to figure it out. Maybe I should have told him about the notebook. I was going round in circles and getting nowhere. I went back to the Google search.

According to Wikipedia, the human trafficking industry was worth $32 billion per year. *Bloody hell.*

But there were whole areas of the police dedicated to dealing with trafficking, and they were all well aware of the sort of activity that took place. Why hadn't Dr Neasden reported what he was working on to the police? Maybe he had tried the local police. I knew there had to be some corruption there because at least one of them had used my address details. But why not go through Ibbetson to the Met? If the people were coming through Heathrow, as Ibbetson had suggested, that would make more sense. I was getting lost trying to think about it all.

A "bling" sound interrupted my thoughts; an email had arrived. I opened Hotmail.

From: <StephIbb54@gmail.com>
To: <Sugarandspice328@hotmail.com>
Miriam,
My colleague Sam Charlton, DI will meet you at the
Urban Kitchen on Farringdon Road at 7.30pm
tomorrow.
Good luck
Stephen

He'd sent it from his personal email address, not work. I had a look on Google maps—the Urban Kitchen was only fifteen minutes' walk from my hotel. I sent a quick email back acknowledging receipt.

I packed up my belongings and walked back to the hotel. I booked in for tomorrow night and was told I could keep the same room. I paid cash up front and no, I still didn't want to use a card to set up an account. If I had any extras, I'd pay for them as I went. I took the lift up to my room on the fifth floor and cleaned my teeth, got undressed, and climbed straight into bed.

THURSDAY

Chapter Seventeen

I didn't wake up until 10am on Thursday morning, something almost unheard of since John had died. It was light outside, although it was dull and windy. I took my rucksack and left, leaving the "Do Not Disturb" sign in its usual upside-down position. It was chilly out, and several degrees colder than it had been recently. I zipped my jacket up under my chin and pulled my scarf tightly around my neck. I fished out the grey hat and pulled it over my ears. I walked up to the Euston Road and found an Internet café where I could browse and print stuff if I wanted to.

To begin with, I Googled Detective Inspector Sam Charlton who, surprisingly I thought, had a LinkedIn account. I knew, or suspected, it was the right guy as I didn't think there could be that many Sam Charltons working for the Met, although the profile didn't mention that he worked for the Human Trafficking Unit. I couldn't view the full profile as I only had the free version and I wasn't "connected" to him, but the short version had a photo showing a forty-something, attractive black man. He had worked for the Metropolitan Police for twenty years. Apart from that there was little information. I looked at the Met website but they didn't have information on individual members. That wasn't a surprise, I supposed.

Moving on, I did another search for information about trafficking.

I found a recent report from the Children's Society called *Still at Risk: A review of support for trafficked children.* I printed off the full report.

I had a brief look at the United Nations' report *Global Report on Trafficking in Persons*, but decided not to print it as it had been written in 2009 and there was a lot more recent stuff.

I printed off Andrew Boff's two hundred twenty-nine-page tome *Shadow City: Exposing human trafficking in everyday London* as it was both recent and local.

Lastly, I printed off the *Second Report of the Inter-Departmental Ministerial Group on Human Trafficking.*

Then I Googled "Neasden and Ibbetson trafficking," and I found a reference to a previous paper they had written in 2011. It was entitled *Child Victims of Trafficking: Victims, not Illegal Immigrants.* I could only read the excerpt, though, as it had been published in a journal where you had to be a subscriber to read the papers. However, the brief told me little more than the other papers I'd printed off, and I noticed that some of the citations were from the reports that I'd been able to access, so I hoped that if there was anything significant it would be summarised in them. I paid up for all my printing and put it into my rucksack.

Next, I found a Phones4U shop and bought another pay-as-you-go phone. I wasn't quite sure why, but I just wanted to be really careful and also have some options. I stuck to the same model Sony Erikson so I knew how to use it. Once outside the shop, I sat down on a bench and copied the few numbers I had across from the old phone to the new one. I took the battery and SIM card out of the old one and put them in my rucksack. Then I walked down to the British Library and found a spot to sit and read through everything. I made notes on my iPad as I went, and although I wasn't sure how it might be relevant to my current situation, by 2pm that afternoon I had learnt an awful lot.

I had learned that nobody seemed to know exactly how many victims there were due to the hidden nature of the crime, but certainly there were many victims of human trafficking in the UK, with around a quarter of these being children.

I also now knew that many of the child victims, if found, were placed in care, but they often went missing from their care homes because of being scared or coerced by the people who brought them into the country. Others were met by people who will spirit them away for whatever purposes they want. Some of the young people who had been inter-viewed for the research gave reports of feeling terri-fied and suspicious of everyone. Often, they said, nobody properly explained to them what was happening. I thought about these poor young souls without anyone to care for them, being used for sexual servitude, or working on cannabis farms or undertaking other illegal activity. Many said that they were brought to the country with promises of jobs or an education, or had been forced to come here to work to pay off debts that their family owed and which they would never be able to repay. Some of the young people they had talked to had escaped but then had run back to the people who had been maltreating them. They believed that they had nowhere else to go.

According to the various reports and charity estimates, there were between one and twenty-seven million victims of trafficking worldwide. The government report I read stated that there were an estimated almost twenty-six hundred victims of trafficking in the UK. Non-government organisations working with the victims of trafficking stated that this estimate was a tip of the iceberg. Yet according to Boff's report, there were only eighteen convictions across London for trafficking offences in 2012-13, and this had been the most for the last three years.

Chapter Eighteen

I was hungry when I left the British Library, and feeling empty and sad after reading so many horror stories. I walked across the road and found an Eat Cafe to sit in, and bought a slice of carrot cake, a banana, and a cup of coffee, taking them off to sit down on a spare sofa. I took out my iPad once again and looked at the photos of the cryptic numbers. I tried to imagine what Dr Neasden would have been thinking if he'd wanted to keep a few key phone numbers but didn't want them being instantly recognised.

I spent some time trying to work out how he might have hidden the numbers within his notebook. If they were indeed phone numbers, then he had written the last three digits separately. I decided to work on the principle that Ibbetson's number was definitely here, somewhere, and that I might as well spend the next couple of hours trying to figure it out. I didn't have much else to do and wouldn't be in a worse position if I couldn't find it. If I could, then I might well have two other phone numbers to give me a clue as to what this was all about. A sinking feeling of despair clutched at the base of my stomach; I wasn't going to be able to rely on Ibbetson or anyone else to get me out of this mess, and I had to do something myself. So, working on my principle that Ibbetson's number was in there somewhere meant that it had to be in some sort of a code; at least the first part. Dr Neasden, I guessed to make them look less like phone numbers, had split them into two lists. Well, that had worked. I hadn't realised that's what they were until I had actually seen Ibbetson's sign-off and realised that the last three digits were the same as one of the numbers in the list. In fact, I wasn't one hundred percent convinced still, but that didn't fit with my principle, so I soldiered on.

If I was going to be working out a code, I figured it would be easier to do this with a proper pen and paper rather than on the iPad, although it did occur to me that, if I knew where to look, there was probably an app for that somewhere out there in the ether. I finished my cake and walked a little further down Euston Road until I found a small newsagent's shop. I bought a small spiral bound pad and a couple of ball-point pens and took them off in search of somewhere to sit. When I found another café, I opened up the photos of the numbers and copied them into the notepad.

I started work; if the last three digits of Ibbetson's phone number were 215, I had to find the beginning of it in amongst the three numbers in the first list, the list with eight digits. I knew that none of the numbers corresponded to the actual phone number, even when I had tried scrambling them up, so I had to assume that they were in some kind of code. I guessed that this would have given a bit of added security, as the formula for phone numbers with the 01 or 07 prefix is fairly easy to spot. I imagined it wouldn't need to be a hard code, just enough to prevent the list looking like a list of phone numbers. And as they all began with a different digit I assumed that, once coded, Dr Neasden had shuffled them all around a bit. That meant I would need to figure out how they'd been mixed up, too. That would obviously be easier if I could work out which of the three was the code for Ibbetson's number.

Okay, so I started with the first eight digits of Ibbetson's phone number, 01895259. I sorted these into a list.

99
55
8
1
2
0

Then I looked at the three coded numbers and wrote them out in similar lists so that I could compare.

00	88	99
9	77	33
7	9	66
3	5	2
6	2	1
4	0	
8		

That told me that the coded number for Ibbetson was 72709588 as it was the only one with two sets of double digits and four single digits. I looked at all the lists. The only digit common to all the numbers was 9. So, 9 must correspond to 0. All the numbers would have to start with a 0. So I began my decoder.

Real   Code

0   =   9

It was a start.

Next I knew that either 9 or 5 in the real number had to be equal to 8 in the code, and either 9 or 5 in the real number had to be equal to 7 in the code. Ibbetson's number contained two 9s and two 5s, and the coded number contained two 8s and two 7s. I started with what I knew; 0 = 9, so how did you get from 0 to 9? That looked like it could be a fairly simple manoeuvre. If you looked at the numbers as if they were on a circle, you could minus 1 and then 0 would equal 9. That would be a really simple code, just moving back one each time. Would that work for the other numbers? It would for 9, if that was equal to 8. Nine minus one equals 8. But that would mean that 5 would have to equal 7, and even with my limited maths I knew that 5 minus one didn't equal 7.

I tried all sorts of ways of getting from 5 to 7. Add two. That didn't work for getting 9 to 8 though. I could double 5; 5 x 2 = 10 then minus 3. But if I did the same sum with 9, it came to 15.

Okay, I thought I'd try it from a different angle. What if it was 5 that became 8 in the code? How could I get from 5 to 8? Well, I could double it; 5 x 2 = 10 and take away two to equal 8. Or I could minus one; 5 − 1 = 4 and double that and that would also equal 8. That was essentially the same sum. Would that work for getting 9 to 7? 9 x 2 = 18 then 18 − 2 =

16. Hmmm. Sixteen didn't fit the code at all. And you couldn't have two digits replacing one. But what if I added those two together to get back to one number? 1 + 6, that would equal 7. And doing the sum the other way, got me the same result, $9 - 1 = 8$ then $8 \times 2 = 16$ and $1 + 6 = 7$. But the 0 presented a problem. 0 $\times 2 = 0$, and even if I went back two from 0 on a cycle I'd come to 8 and not 9. I tried it the other way. $0 - 1$ would equal 9 on the continuous cycle. $9 \times 2 = 18$. Then if I added $1 + 8$ that brought me back to 9.

I smiled. I had it. I did the same sum with all the numbers from 0-9 until I had the finished code and I added them all to my list.

Real		Code
0	=	9
1	=	0
2	=	2
3	=	4
4	=	6
5	=	8
6	=	1
7	=	3
8	=	5
9	=	7

It was a simple code, but effective. The coded numbers did not end up being sequential, but the sums all produced a different code for each number. I compared my code to Ibbetson's number and also the way it had been written in the notebook. I wrote them one above the other.

01 895259
REAL

90578287
CODED

72709588
SCRAMBLED

I looked and my heart sank a bit. Because of the double numbers, the order of scrambling could be done in a few different ways. The first seven could have been moved from the end of the number or the middle. There was no way of knowing. That would mean when I decoded the other numbers there would be several potential scrambled combinations. I'd end up with a list of *possible* numbers rather than two definite ones. More work.

Chapter Nineteen

I packed everything away again in my rucksack, feeling a little depressed both about the amount of work I would need to do to decode the phone numbers, and also about the plight of trafficking victims. I headed back to the hotel. I showered and changed into clean clothes. They were almost identical to the ones I'd taken off, but at least I felt fresher. You didn't have to walk around London for long without feeling as if you were covered in grime and dirt.

I thought about the person I was going to meet. Ibbetson had introduced us. Ibbetson had been Dr Neasden's research partner and had been the person he had implored me to contact. But a police officer? Would the police in Lincolnshire have contacted the Met? No, I didn't think so; I didn't think they knew I was down here for a start. Could the Met be involved in whatever it was Dr Neasden had uncovered? Again, I didn't think so, but I couldn't be sure. The Met seemed to be involved in lots of trafficking related issues, but if whatever Neasden had been working on had anything to do with the London police, I thought

Ibbetson would have been aware of it, and he didn't seem to be. Unless he was bluffing? He could have been. But I hadn't had the sense that he was. To be honest, I hadn't had the feeling that Ibbetson would have been bright enough to have bluffed about it. He had given no hint that he knew anything about the notebook. He hadn't asked if I had anything that belonged to Dr Neasden, or tried to make me give him any information. He'd seemed shocked. Shocked at Dr Neasden's death and shocked at what, perhaps, he might be involved in by proxy. Perhaps he was worried for his own safety?

I decided that, if I wanted to get home and leave all this behind me then I really only had one option and that was to meet this Detective Inspector. I hadn't actually done anything wrong; and if he was involved? Well, I thought I would have to deal with that when it arose. I would have to take my chances. What was the alternative? To stay in a hotel in London forever, afraid to go home?

I left the hotel at about 7.20, knowing that it would take me fifteen minutes to get to the Urban Kitchen and hoping that DI Sam Charlton would get there first. I closed the door, smiled at the upside down "Do Not Disturb" notice, and walked briskly down to the pub.

I recognised DI Charlton straight away from his LinkedIn profile picture, although his hair had grown quite a bit since then. In his picture he'd had a really short buzz cut, now he had inch-long dreadlocks covering his head. He was tall, about six feet, and slim. I walked up to him. He smiled as I approached— Ibbetson must have described me to him and he clearly recognised the description. He gave a broad smile and tilted his head back as I approached.

"Miriam?" He held out his hand.

"DI Charlton?"

"The same," he said. "But, please, call me Sam." He gestured towards the bar. "Want a drink?" He was holding a beer glass. The fact that it was almost full told me that he hadn't arrived long before I had. He was wearing a suit; I couldn't tell in the dimly lit pub whether it was dark blue or black, but I could tell it was reasonably good quality. He wore a pale blue striped shirt with silver cufflinks and a red tie, which he was loosening. He removed it from round his neck and put it in his pocket before undoing the top button of his shirt.

"Red wine, please; a small rioja if they have it."

He signalled for me to go and sit down. I found a seat at one of the old style kitchen tables, snug in one of the corners, and glanced out of the window. I couldn't see a lot, it was mostly obscured by the window boxes outside, which contained still-flowering geraniums and overflowing ivy. It was a cosy, traditional place. There was a blackboard on one wall with "today's menu" written in a fancy chalk script, and a log fire midway along the wall, underneath the blackboard. The log fire hadn't been lit; I guessed it was a bit too early in the year. But there was a stack of logs next to it, looking as if they had prepared well for the inevitable cold snap.

DI Sam Charlton came over to the table, carrying his pint and a glass of red wine. "No rioja so I got a tempranillo. I hope that's okay?"

"That's fine," I said, taking the wine and trying a sip. It was, it was lovely. I liked Spanish wine.

"Now, how can I help you?"

"Well," I said, thinking. If I was going to ask this policeman to help me with going home and sorting things out, there was no point in him continuing to believe that I was Miriam Nathan. I'd thought about this over and over. The mantra *"trust no one"* had played round and round my head. I'd have to blow my cover, but I desperately wanted this to be finished and to get back home. And he appeared to be my best hope. If he knew anything then he would know it wasn't my real name anyway. I thought I could suss him out whilst I was being a little cagey, see if he fished for any information, try to get a sense of where he was coming from. I bit the bullet. "I ought to tell you first that my name is not Miriam Nathan."

"Not Miriam Nathan?"

"No."

He raised one eyebrow and smiled before running the fingers of one hand over the corner of his mouth, giving off an air of mild amusement. He looked up at me, raising both of his eyebrows this time, as if soliciting an explanation.

"I was scared," I spluttered, unexpectedly thrown by his attitude. "My home had been ransacked. I felt like I was on the run."

"And now?"

"Well, I'm hoping that's where you will be able to help me."

"Okay, well I suppose you ought to start by telling me your real name."

I hesitated. *"Trust no one."* Oh, hell. I had to do something. "Verity," I almost whispered it, "Verity Spencer."

"Okay, Verity. So tell me what happened."

I started on the story of what had happened, except that I stuck to the version where I had found Dr Neasden's wallet rather than his notebook, and I also, without explicitly saying it, carried on the impression that Dr Neasden had suggested Stephen Ibbetson would be able to help me in some way. That way I wouldn't have to reveal that I had his notebook, or that it even existed. I rather hoped that my story was a good enough blend of truth and fiction that if Charlton were able to access the police records then he wouldn't notice any discrepancies. But I was still hiding the fact that I had the notebook and that I was fairly convinced that there was something in there which someone badly wanted. I wasn't going to give that piece of information to anyone.

It was half an hour later, and we had both finished our drinks by the time I'd finished my story. It was my turn to buy, so I went and reordered before returning to the table a few minutes later with replenished glasses. Just as I was putting the glasses down, Charlton's phone rang. He looked at the number, pressing "answer" whilst simultaneously gesturing that he needed to take the call. He stepped outside, pushing buttons on his phone as he went. He stood, just visible in the dark of the beer garden, huddling by the door, pulling his jacket up around his ears.

Whilst he was gone, I thought about what I'd told him. Once again, I'd been suitably cagey about what I knew. I wasn't giving any information to Charlton apart from the very basics. I was playing it a bit dumb, but I thought that's what I needed to do. I'd guessed if anyone was suspicious that I had the notebook they would try to get the information out of me. But Charlton, like Ibbetson, seemed blissfully unaware of its existence, let alone the meaning of its contents. He had asked questions and given prompts throughout my narration of what had happened, and he had given no indication that he was aware of the notebook, or for that matter, Dr Neasden.

Charlton was only gone two minutes before he came back, apologised, and sat down. He sighed and took a swig of his beer. "I'll be honest," he said, "I'm not sure I'll be able to help you."

I must have looked crestfallen because he quickly followed that statement up with, "But I will do what I can."

I nodded, but said nothing.

"I should be able to access the police records on the national database, so I can have a look and see if there is anything in them that might give us a clue." He took another slug of beer. "If not, then I can ring up the investigating officer. What did you say his name was?"

"Mike Nash. But, like I said before, I'm a bit suspicious about how the house-ransackers got my address. It must have been through the local police. I don't want to make it worse."

"I'll be discreet. You said that Dr Neasden and Ibbetson were working on a paper? About child trafficking? Anything else on that?"

"No, Ibbetson was quite cagey on the details. I know they've published at least one paper in the past, in 2011, but I couldn't print it off because it was in a journal." It struck me then that I'd been in the British Library all morning and could have more than likely looked at the journal there. Damn.

"Well, I can always use that as a shoe-in. If I need to ring this Nash guy I can always use that as an excuse."

I kept quiet about the research I'd read on how poor the Met were at picking up cases.

He carried on. "It also provides a legitimate excuse to be looking at the local records. If I think there might be a connection to local trafficking it'll be a good enough reason to look."

I gave him the number of my new mobile phone. We chatted a little whilst we finished our drinks. He seemed like a pleasant man and I asked him about working for the Human Trafficking Unit and the kind of work that he did. He was easy to talk to and he had a good sense of humour, making me laugh out loud on more than one occasion. It was good to forget the mess I was in. Then he looked at his watch and apologised that he would have to dash off. He asked if I was okay to walk back to my hotel, which I assured him I was, and then rushed off into the night.

It was heading towards 9pm. I thought about sitting and having another glass of wine but decided against it, and instead walked the fifteen minutes back to my hotel, leaning into the wind and wondering when it would start raining.

Chapter Twenty

I took the lift to the fifth floor, turned the corner to the right outside the lift and walked towards my room. I had my key card out and ready to use but as I lifted my head to use it, I stopped. A horrible tension rose in me, gripping me from the legs upwards. *Oh my God, oh my God, someone has been in my room.* In fact, they had to still be in there because I knew it was almost impossible to close the door from the outside without the "Do Not Disturb" sign turning upside down. How the sign had managed to right itself when it was closed from the inside was a puzzle I wasn't about to try to work out. All I knew was that when you closed it from the outside, it always flipped itself over. And yet there it was, the right way up. *Shit, shit, shit.* I started to run away, back towards the lifts, but halfway along the corridor I stopped. Where would I go? I sank to the floor, leaned against the wall, and considered my options. I didn't have many—face whoever it was in my room, or run. Maybe it was the couple of glasses of wine that were giving me extra bravado, maybe not, but one thing was for sure, I couldn't face running anymore. If they were after me, whoever they were, they would most definitely keep coming.

I stood outside the door, trying to think, trying to imagine what it was they were doing. *Waiting for you to come back, you idiot.* They still thought I had the notebook, of course. Well, they were right there but they couldn't know for sure. I hadn't mentioned it to anyone. No one, not even DI Charlton. Nobody knew for certain that I had the notebook. I visualised the layout of the room. Where would they hide if they were waiting for me to return so that they could ambush me? The bathroom wouldn't work, because the main door opened so that when you walked into the room you could see into the bathroom. There wasn't room to hide behind the bathroom door because it was too close to the bath, and it was frosted glass anyway, so you'd notice anyone behind it. In the bedroom, the massive mirror on the left hand wall meant that you could see almost the entire bedroom from the door. Anyone hiding round the corner would be noticeable in the mirror as soon as you came in, meaning someone coming through the door would instantly be able to back out and run away. Unless they hid under the bed? But that would make no sense either because by the time they'd crawled out I'd be able to run away.

The only logical place I could think of that made any sense at all, if you were waiting to pounce on someone, would be in the recess behind the door. My breaths were coming quick and fast, matching the beats of my heart, and I leant against the wall in the corridor for a minute, trying to slow everything down, trying not to alert anyone to my presence. I'd have to be quick and sharp. My build wasn't up to much in terms of strength, so I'd need to make up for that by being fast and decisive. I put my rucksack properly on my back without making a sound. I could have put it on the floor near the door to give me a little more agility but I was reluctant to leave it. It had everything in it; all my notes, the photos, everything. If anyone ran out of the room before I got to it, they could easily pick it up and run away. No, it was safer on my back. I looked at the door and took a deep breath, counting to ten as I let it out through pursed lips. I reminded myself that I had an advantage—they didn't know about the "Do Not Disturb" sign, and they wouldn't realise that I knew they were in there. I put the key card in the door. That would mean they would be aware of me returning. Then, as swiftly and as hard as I could, I smashed the door back into the wall with all my force and weight. An aching thud and a pained groan assured me that I had done some damage; something crashed to the ground and skittled across the floor. I grabbed the door again, adrenaline pumping through my body, and smashed it another time into the wall. Except it didn't go as far as the wall this time, as something, or rather someone was in the way. I grappled along the wall for the light whilst yanking the door towards me as I swung into the room and took a wild kick into the space beyond.

What had been stopping the door was the man's foot; he'd wedged it there to prevent another blow to the head. Blood was pouring down the side of his face from a deep gash; he had clearly hit the coat hook when I smashed the door open the first time. His face was contorted into an angry grimace and as I swung my leg to kick him, he grabbed my ankle and twisted me round sharply. A stabbing pain pierced through my ankle and I fell on the floor with a thud. I had no time to put my arms out to stop me. My chest hit the ground and for a second I was winded completely. All the air left my lungs and a searing pain ran through me as I gasped to refill them.

He dug his fingers into my skin as he yanked me towards him by the ankle. "Where is it?" he shouted. "Where is it?" He continued to pull me towards him as I struggled to regain my breathing. "Cow, I'm talking to you."

I twisted round as quickly as I could and kicked backwards at his hand with the heel of my other foot. I caught him sharp on the wrist with the bottom of my trainer. It wouldn't have done much harm but it was enough to make him shout out. He let go of my ankle, and I scrambled away towards the bed. I saw then that what had rattled across the room was a gun, a small handgun, and as I crawled across the floor I pushed it under the bed and to the other side of the room as far away from my assailant as I could.

"Bitch!" he shouted and he came at me again, kicking me in the back, just below my rucksack. His foot hit the small of my back with such force that I fell forward onto the ground and crashed my face into the floor. A pain exploded in my mouth from my tongue, or my lip, I wasn't sure. I pushed myself to my knees and watched through my legs as he geared up to attack me again. As he ran towards me, I kicked my leg back as hard as I could and caught him in the stomach. He was a big but pudgy man with pasty white skin and a reasonably fat tummy so my kick didn't do much damage, but it slowed him down enough for me to stand up. He immediately came at me again and punched at me, hitting me hard in the shoulder. He pushed me onto the bed, the rucksack digging painfully into my back. He rushed at me and I slapped him across the face, but it barely touched him, although it stung the palm of my hand. He grabbed me by the throat with his left hand and started to squeeze. He slapped my face with his right hand, hitting me with such a force that for a second the room went completely black. A wave of nausea washed through me; I wished I hadn't had two glasses of wine to drink.

He put both hands around my throat and squeezed even harder. I struggled to breathe as pinpricks of light exploded in the corner of my eyes. I clawed at his hands, gasping, desperately trying to get air through a non-existent gap in my throat. I clawed again at his hands, trying to pull them off my throat. I was feeling dizzy from a lack of oxygen and tried in vain to pull his hands away.

"What have you done with it?" he shouted. "Bitch! Tell me what you've done with it."

I couldn't have answered even if I had wanted to. I couldn't breathe. I was clutching at his hands, but there was no hope I could pull them away from my neck. I didn't know what to do. I struggled to move, but he had a tight grip. From the depths of somewhere I vaguely remembered a self-defence course I had attended a year or two ago at work after the college had become worried about female staff walking home late and in the dark. The male instructor had talked about jabbing people in the eyes as this was an area that would really hurt. I lifted my right hand and jabbed my thumb into his left eye with as much force as I could muster. He cried out, reaching up to his face and grabbing my hand to pin it down on the bed.

The release on my neck was a relief; with only one hand around it there was enough room to just about breathe. The air rushed in, feeling like fire against the sides of my throat. I glanced up at his flabby body looming over mine. He was on all fours on top of me. I was lying beneath him, my legs beneath his body. I looked at my leg and took aim. I pulled it up, with all the force I could muster, sharply between his legs. There hadn't been enough space to get a full swing but I caught him straight between the legs with my shin and it was clearly enough to hurt. He let go of me, clutching his balls and writhing on the edge of the bed.

"I'll teach you, whore," he screamed through gritted teeth, his lips curling into an agitated snarl. He reached behind the bed for the gun. It was inches from his grasp. I moved as quickly as I could and grabbed one of the ceramic lamps. It was a solid square, hard enough to do some damage, but not too heavy to get a good swing. I yanked the plug out of the wall as he bent down to pick up the gun and crashed the lamp down on his head with as much strength and force as I could gather.

It worked. He sank to the edge of the bed and then rolled off and onto the floor. He was overweight and he was wearing slacks and a tracksuit top which had risen up revealing his flabby tummy hanging over the top of his trousers. I aimed another kick at his balls, and this time my foot connected with a mighty crunch.

It was only when his response to my kick was little more than a soft moan that I realised the man was actually unconscious. He was bleeding from the head but breathing rhythmically and softly, so I figured he would be okay. Hopefully, when he came round, the pain would be enough to keep him occupied for a while. To be honest, the adrenaline was flowing so freely at that point I could quite easily have smashed his skull with my bare hand and not worried, but I restrained myself. My foot felt as if it had exploded on impact with him—there was a searing pain in my toes but I ignored it. My lips and face were also swelling up, but I didn't have time to worry; the adrenaline appeared to be numbing any pain.

I looked around the room. Things had been turned about a bit; he'd clearly been looking for something, although there was a limit to the damage that could be done in a hotel room, I supposed. My heart was thumping as a fresh wave of adrenaline rushed through my body. I reached past the unconscious man and picked up the gun, calmly aiming it at his head. The main thing preventing me from pulling the trigger was that I thought it would alert people. Besides which, my hands were incapable of holding it still. Despite the shaking, I kept the gun pointed at his head in case he came round and I bent down to fish in his pockets. I pulled out a phone and a wallet which I put in my jacket pocket. He had some handcuffs attached to his belt, clearly meant for me, so I took those, put one end round his right wrist, pulled his arm high above his head to the top of the bed, and attached his arm to the iron frame. I rummaged through his pockets again for keys, which I located in one of his tracksuit jacket pockets along with several £20 notes, which I also took.

I checked the gun. I had no idea what sort of gun it was, and I wasn't about to fiddle with anything. I took my rucksack off and placed the gun inside. In a rather paranoid fashion I made sure the barrel was pointing at the ground and away from my back, just in case guns were capable of firing themselves without anyone pulling the trigger. After hurriedly gathering my things together, I took a last quick glance at the podgy man still sprawled on the floor. He was breathing gently. He'd no doubt have a sore head and sore balls in the morning, but he'd be fine. I guessed it would be a surprise for whoever found him, though. It would take him a while to work himself free, and I figured he'd rather pretend that he was trying a kinky game or something than admit to the real reason he'd ended up handcuffed to a bed. I turned off the light and pulled the door closed, leaving the "Do Not Disturb" sign back in its normal upside down position.

Just as I was leaving the room, a woman wearing a receptionist's outfit came, almost running, out of the lift and up the corridor. "Is everything okay?" she said, gasping. "Someone rang and said they thought there was a disturbance."

"No, it's cool," I said, keeping the swollen side of my face away from her. My voice was thin and scratchy from being strangled and I tried my best to sound as normal as I could. "Sorry, I must have had the TV on a bit too loud. There was some fighting in a film. I'm sorry. I'm off for dinner now."

"Okay." She peered back over first one shoulder then the other so I engaged her in polite and sparkly conversation all the way back down to reception. I waved her a cheery farewell and left the hotel, just about managing to stay upright until I reached the outside world. I paused and leaned against the wall to keep myself from falling over, my legs buckling underneath me. Images of the man's face so close to mine, and memories of his heavy breath played in my brain as I tried to steady myself. I wanted to lay on the ground, to curl up and hide, to escape the memories of those hands still clutching at my throat. But I knew I had to get as far away from the hotel as I possibly could.

Chapter Twenty-One

I didn't know where I was going. My foot was throbbing from the kicks I had administered, my ankle ached from being twisted, and my legs would barely hold me up they were shaking so much. I was sure I must have broken a bone at least. I walked and walked, resolving to take up self-defence lessons when I got home. The swelling in my face and lips was getting worse, and my throat scratched every time I swallowed, as if I had drunk acid. I'm not sure how long I was walking for, but I ended up some-where near Covent Garden station. I walked with a furious pace, fuelled by the adrenaline and unable to think clearly, just wanting to put as much distance between me and that creep as I could. Maybe it was the same guy who had turned over my house, or perhaps this was a special London hit man. I walked up and down streets, turning this way and that, making sure that it would be impossible to follow me just in case anyone had been waiting outside the hotel. It was pouring with rain and my clothes had plastered themselves to my skin; even my weatherproof jacket proved to be inadequate against the driving rain. I had no umbrella, but even if I had it would have been little use anyway. Water was bouncing off the pavements, drenching everybody's socks and jeans. I shivered as the wind howled against my soaking clothes, freezing me as I walked. At some point, as I was wending my way back and forth through the streets, I hit Oxford Street and walked past Primark. It was still open, despite it being almost ten o'clock. I went in, adding my drips to those that were already on the floor. It was almost closing time, and the place was pretty much deserted. I went to the "sleepwear" section and quickly chose the warmest, cosiest pyjamas I could find and a pair of woolly socks. The young girl at the till took my money with an air of utter indifference, as if she were already sitting on her sofa in front of the television, mentally if not physically, and then I rushed out once more into the cold, wet evening.

After some time, I found a smart hotel in Covent Garden and checked in for the night, this time dreaming up a name from nowhere, Carrie Davenport. I stood dripping in the foyer and the receptionist took pity on me, offering to tumble dry my clothes once I'd changed out of them. I went straight up to my hotel room on the ninth floor. It was a comfortable room, much more in the traditional style than the last one. A king-sized bed filled most of one wall, opposite a little work area with a modern desk and chair. The lamps in this room were screwed to the walls, so I hoped I didn't need to hit anyone over the head. The wardrobe had a full-length mirror on the inside of the door, but I kept that shut. I looked dishevelled, my lip misshapen with the swelling, although the rain had rinsed all the blood away. My foot ached, my ankle ached, my throat ached, and I was shivering quite dramatically.

I stripped off my wet clothes and left them on the bathroom floor. There was no bath, but the shower was a big one with an oversized shower head. I stayed there for what felt like hours, letting the hot water warm up my frozen skin. Eventually I emerged, feeling calmer and warmer. I assessed the damage to my foot. It would bruise, but there didn't appear to be any broken bones. My lip had a mark where my teeth had driven into it, and the swelling was pulling it to one side. An angry red mark circled my neck; I looked exactly as if I had been in a fight with a pudgy, pasty man.

I put on my new, soft, fluffy pyjamas and socks. I hardly ever wore pyjamas; John and I had always slept naked. In fact, pyjamas had been the cause of one of our most spectacular arguments. We didn't argue often, but when we did we didn't hold back. I couldn't really remember how it had started now, but it had had something to do with me deciding to wear a pair of pyjamas in bed one freezing winter evening and John deciding that this was a sign I didn't want my skin against his. At least that was my memory of what had been said; John would probably tell it differently if he could. Anyway, we'd screamed and shouted and I'd thrown a shoe at him, which had caught him on the head and caused a gash that bled profusely. We had made up and ended up snuggled in bed, both wearing pyjamas as something of a compromise, I supposed. I glanced down at the fluffy pastel hearts covering my body and smiled. Even remembering the bad times didn't seem to dull the ache of missing him.

I scooped up my wet clothes, put them in the laundry bag, and left it in the corridor outside my room. I shut the door and made sure the deadbolt was engaged. Then I flopped down onto the bed. It was only then that I started to slow down; the adrenaline leaving my body and tears appearing unbidden in my eyes. Instead of fighting them back, I let them flow, building up as the emotions erupted within me. I wasn't sure if I was crying for John, or for my house, or for almost being strangled. Or maybe it was for all three. I sobbed, great heaving sobs, tears pouring down my face and I lay hugging one of the pillows for a while until my body calmed down. Eventually I got up, made a cup of tea, and then picked up my rucksack and sat on the bed.

I emptied the contents of the rucksack onto the bed. My clothes had got a little wet through the fabric, but it had proven surprisingly water resistant. I draped my clothes and shoes around the room so that they would be dry in the morning, and examined the items I'd taken from the intruder. I put his phone to one side and looked through his wallet. His credit and debit cards named him as Kevin Lambert but there was no driver's licence and nothing to suggest where he came from. His wallet also contained a couple of loyalty cards for coffee shops but they were chains like Caffe Nero, so nothing there to indicate a location. There were a couple of ten pound notes, a fiver, and some change. Nothing personal at all. Where had he come from, and how had he known where I was?

I picked up the gun. I'd never held one before, and I was cautious with it. It was a stubby looking black gun. Along the side of the barrel it said Sig Sauer P229 so I guessed that was the make and model. There was a small lever just below the barrel and another at the top of the handle. I left them well alone. Another lever at the back looked like you would pull it down with your thumb when you were holding the gun. I had no idea what any of these things did, and I wasn't about to start experimenting. I picked the gun up in both hands, still worried that it might fire itself, and put it in the drawer under the television.

Next, I looked at his phone. It was an old fashioned one, similar in style to my little Sony Erikson, but made by Nokia. There was no passcode entry so I turned it on and scrolled through the list of calls. He had received a call at 8pm that night. *Shit.* That was about the time that DI Charlton had gone outside on a call. For a brief moment I entertained the idea that they'd been talking, with Charlton giving a description or my location. But no, it couldn't be that; both of them had been received calls. And, looking back, I was fairly sure that I had seen the photo of a smiling, attractive blonde pop up on Charlton's phone when it had rung.

The number that had called at 8pm was listed as unidentified, so there was no way I could ring it but there were other numbers in the call list. I struggled to keep my eyes open as exhaustion overwhelmed me; I'd have another look tomorrow.

I lay back in bed, staring at the ceiling through the dim light that filtered past the curtains. However I played it, I didn't think it could have been Charlton that had alerted anyone to my whereabouts. He didn't know where I was staying, plus he really hadn't had enough time. That only left Ibbetson. It had to be something to do with him. Perhaps he had used Charlton as a decoy, but it had to have started with him. He had asked where I was staying, and although I hadn't told him, I'd said near King's Cross so it wouldn't have been too difficult to ring around hotels. And I'd used the same false name I'd given him when

I checked in. Stupid, stupid mistake. Tiredness clouded my memories; the rain, the hands on my throat, the wine, the gun. Weights dragged at my eyelids, pulling them together.

And then I'm walking round the Civic Centre in Uxbridge with the gun that I took from Lambert. I stride calmly round the building, holding the gun out in front of me. No one is taking any notice of it, or me, they are just carrying on with their work as if it is a perfectly normal occurrence. I find Ibbetson's office easily and walk straight in. He's sitting there, his head bowed over some paperwork, but he looks up as he hears me enter. As he sees the gun he starts to panic, scrambling to get away from his desk. I don't say anything to him, I just aim the gun and shoot him through the head. I walk out of the office, carrying the gun down at my side, but I can't find my way out of the building. I start running but I'm going round in circles, and every time I take a turn it leads to a dead end. I turn another corner and I'm back at Ibbetson's office. He's still there with a hole through his forehead, and panic rises inside me. I run faster and faster, past all the workers, up and down the strange half level floors but I'm going nowhere. I can hear the blood thumping in my ears and bile is rising in my throat. I open my mouth to cry out, but nothing comes.

FRIDAY

Chapter Twenty-Two

My arms and legs had tangled themselves in the sheet, and my body lay perilously close to the edge of the bed. I opened my eyes and a flood of relief passed through me as I realised I had been dreaming. A smile crept unbidden across my face and I jumped out of the bed, leaving the memory of Ibbetson behind. I was actually in a bit of a sweat, not just because of my night-time shenanigans, but as I reached the bathroom I realised the heating was on full blast. I'd been so cold the night before that I had turned it up. At some point in the night I must have taken off my pyjamas, but I didn't remember it. They were lying in a heap next to the bed. I went through to the bathroom and examined myself in the mirror; the red marks were still visible around my neck, although the swelling in my lip had gone down a little. I gathered up the clothes that I had placed around the room and were now, thankfully, dry and glanced out the window whilst I put them on. The rain had stopped but the trees bent almost horizontal in a fierce wind, and people scuttled along the road with their collars pulled up round their necks. I put my scarf on, which I wrapped tightly round my neck to cover up the red mark, and pulled my hat down over my ears. Then I remembered the gun. What was I going to do with that? I didn't want to take it with me, but I also didn't really want to leave it in the hotel room. I took a chance. I wrapped my pyjamas round it and stuffed it back into the drawer. If anyone came to clean my room, despite the "Do Not Disturb" sign, and opened the drawer they would just think it was clothes. Hopefully.

I left the hotel and went to buy coffee and a pain-au-raisin at a local café. I limped a little as I walked along, with the cold air biting into my tender throat as I breathed. I sat down in a corner and ate my pastry. Between mouthfuls, I got out my phone and called Ibbetson's number. It was early, about 8.30, but I figured an Assistant Director would be there at that time. It answered on the second ring.

"Good morning, London Borough of Hillingdon, Dorothy Chambers speaking, how can I help you?"

"Could I speak to Stephen Ibbetson please?"

"I'm afraid he's in a meeting. Can I take a message?

"Yes, please. It's Miriam Nathan. Can you ask him to call me as soon as his meeting is finished? Please let him know that it's urgent." I gave her the number of my new mobile phone.

"I'll give him the message," she said curtly, and I imagined a piece of paper with only my name and number being passed to him or put into a tray with several others, never to see the light of day.

I disconnected and turned on my iPad, going straight to the photo of the eight-digit numbers. I wrote down the numbers, as they were in the lists and began to use my decoder on them. I started with the top number, just because it seemed logical. Once I'd decoded the numbers, I sorted them according to the way Ibbetson's number had been scrambled up. Because there had been two sets of double digits in Ibbetson's number, this meant that there were four possible ways of scrambling, which led to four combinations that the number might end up being. I wrote them all down.

```
01974513
01931547
01971543
01934517
```

Plus, there were two possible three-digit endings, 762 and 879, so that would leave me with eight possibilities.

I moved on to the last number and went through the same process, coming up with the four possibilities. I added these to my list.

```
02076744
02044767
02074764
02046747
```

They could also be attached to either of the three-digit endings. So far, then, I had sixteen possible combinations of phone numbers.

An hour had passed and there had been no response from Ibbetson, so I tried again. The same, rather officious woman answered; his PA, I assumed. I told her who it was.

"I passed on your message but I'm afraid Mr Ibbetson is in another meeting now."

"Well, can you tell him I called again? It is really urgent that I speak to him."

I hung up and ordered another coffee. This time, with a slice of coffee cake. I went back to the numbers. I knew that 0207 was the code for inner London. I Googled 0204. *Hooray*; *something helpful at last.* Without even having to open any of the links I read the first result *"There are no numbers in the UK that start with the prefix 0204, although there are plans to introduce this as a new prefix for London area numbers later in the year."* That meant it was currently not in use, so I could cross out some of my numbers. It at least got me closer. And because that meant that the scrambling method I had used to make the 0204 numbers was wrong, I could cross out two of the other numbers as well. I revisited the list.

01974513
~~01931547~~
01971543
~~01934517~~
02076744
~~02044767~~
02074764
~~02046747~~

I knew 0207 was a London prefix, so I left those for the time being. I Googled the area code 01974; it was for a place called Llanon in Wales. That made no sense. Why would anyone from a tiny place in Wales be involved? I tried Googling 01971; this came from Scourie, a place I had never heard of before but which was, according to Google maps, almost as far north in

Scotland as you could go. This was making no sense at all.

Then my phone rang. I answered without even looking at it.

"Verity, it's Sam. Charlton."

That threw me a bit; I'd been expecting Ibbetson. "Sam. Hi." My voice still sounded a bit ropey from the night before and I hoped it wasn't too obvious.

"I've only done some of the work, but there is definitely something strange going on. Someone has added something to the record of your account of Dr Neasden's death."

All the hairs on my back stood up and goosebumps appeared down my arm. I said nothing.

"You didn't speak to anyone else, did you, after leaving Dr Neasden's house?"

"How do you mean?"

"Did a police officer come round to your house and talk to you?"

"No. I haven't spoken to the police since Monday." They'd have a job, I thought, and wondered how many missed calls my iPhone had received on its trip round the country.

"The record shows that a Detective Inspector Adrian Darnold came to visit you on Tuesday morning. I won't bore you with the details, but he has more or less discredited you as a witness. Says you were hysterical and that as you were recently widowed..." He paused. "Well, basically, in not so many words he is saying not to believe a word you say."

I breathed out sharply. "No shit." I wrote the name down; Adrian Darnold DI. "A DI; so he's superior to Nash, yes?"

"Yes, but hang on. There's more."

"More?" What more could there be?

"I read the report on Dr Neasden's death. It's not far off what you said to me. Except…"

"Except what?"

"There's no mention of a bullet wound. Nothing at all."

I didn't know what to say. Bloody hell. Someone had changed the account of what had happened.

Charlton continued, "I don't know if that is the way the report was written, or if it has been altered by this Darnold person after Nash filed his report. You need to be careful, Verity."

"I'm not going anywhere very soon." Then I filled him in on the events of the night before, although I didn't mention that there had been a gun which I had taken from the scene and was now in my new hotel room. There was a limit to what you could say to a Detective Inspector. He asked questions about the man, so I told him what I knew, which wasn't much more than a name and a description.

He sounded duly concerned for my well-being.

"I'm okay, honestly. It's all superficial. My foot hurts a bit, but, you know…" I tailed off as I caught my reflection in the window. The swelling in my face was reducing a little but there was a nasty gash on my lip and an angry red mark around my neck.

"I can find you a safe house to go to whilst I carry on investigating."

I was touched by his concern, but I stayed silent. I probably would have leapt at the chance of a safe haven only a couple of days ago, but determination had gripped me now. I had come this far, and I was desperate to find out what was going on.

"I'll be fine, Sam. I really will. I'm sure my hotel is as safe as anywhere."

"Just let me know if you change your mind, okay?"

"I promise."

I hadn't told him about the notebook, and I wasn't about to. I had to figure that bit out myself. *"Trust no one."* This Darnold person had discredited me as a witness and I needed to stay sharp. Charlton was trying to help, I was sure, but police could talk to each other and I felt safer out here, where no one knew where I was. I could stay on my toes much more easily if I was in control of what I was doing. He gave me his mobile phone number.

"Be careful and don't do anything rash. Stay in touch."

I put the phone down on the table, but then a fiery anger took hold and I snatched it straight back up again. I stabbed in Ibbetson's number. When the woman answered again and said he was still in a meeting, heat seared up through my cheeks and I clenched my teeth tight. I didn't believe that he was in a meeting. I thought she was lying. I closed my eyes and paused, taking in a long, deep breath. Keeping my voice calm, determined, and flat, I said, "Well, go and get him out of his meeting. I don't care how important it is, if he doesn't phone me back *instantly* I will personally come in and drag him out myself. Okay?" I hung up.

Ten minutes later, the phone rang again. I recognised the number. I jabbed at the answer button with my finger.

"Ibbetson, you *prick*. You nearly got me killed."

"What are you talking about?" He was trying to sound as if he knew nothing. He wasn't being very convincing.

"You know damn well what I am talking about. I'm talking about the *twat* who was hiding in my hotel room when I got back from seeing Charlton last night."

He sounded uncomfortable. "Miriam, what is it?" He was stuttering. "What…what happened?"

"*You* happened. That's what happened. I come down here to get help and you send round the moron flabby hit-man to wait in my room and *shoot* me. *That's* what happened."

"I had nothing to do with that." His attempt at bravado was almost amusingly feeble.

"So why did you send the fat man round to my hotel room?"

"I didn't…I didn't…I didn't do anything like that. My God. Are you alright? I rang Charlton, that's all… I didn't send anyone round. I don't know people like that." He sounded so nervous; he sounded genuinely shocked and disturbed, but he had clearly done something other than just ring Charlton. I could tell it in his voice. Something that had led them to me.

"Ibbetson, you're lying. I can tell," I said through gritted teeth. My mouth curled into a snarl. I would not let him get away without telling me what he had done. "Who else did you tell about our meeting? Did you ring anyone other than Charlton?"

He said nothing but his breathing became increasingly fast and the heaviness of it carried down the phone.

"Ibbetson, stop behaving like a twat and tell me who you told. That pudgy bastard that came for me last night is still chained to the bed with a bedpost up his arse." Okay, not strictly true, but I wished I'd thought of doing that. My cheeks burned and I pulled at the neck of my top, flapping it to create a draught. "I took his gun. Which I still have. I didn't shoot him, but I am quite warming to the idea of coming after you and trying it out on you. Now. Tell me. Who did you tell?"

"I'm sorry....I didn't..." He was gibbering. "I didn't mean..."

I changed tack a bit, quietening down my tone, not least because people were glancing in my direction and paranoia bubbled through me, rising to the surface. "What's this all about, Stephen? What have you got involved in?"

"I don't know," he said. I genuinely thought he really didn't know. "I don't know. Neasden was doing some extra research. He said he'd found something big, scarily big. But I don't know what. He wouldn't tell me. He didn't tell me what, and now he's dead." He was scared, it was all over his voice.

"So, you were worried? After I'd been to see you?"

"Yes. And then..." he swallowed several times, coughed, and tapped what I assumed was a pen against the phone. "I called Charlton, but then I...I didn't know they'd...I mean...I didn't mean for..." His voice was barely a whisper now. "I was scared."

I slowed right down and tried to sound as sympathetic as I could. "I understand that you didn't mean for me to get killed. Luckily for you that hasn't happened, because I've kept copious notes which would now appear to implicate you if I did." Another lie. They were becoming easy now. "Just tell me what you did." I lowered my voice even further and said calmly, "Ibbetson, just tell me what you did. I know you didn't mean to do anything bad, but please, just tell me."

He took a deep breath. I could tell he was struggling. I didn't think he'd be returning to work that afternoon. "I didn't think...I didn't think it would hurt. I mean, I didn't think it would matter to call them. I just thought they would know what had happened to Neasden. I was just trying to find out."

"Who, Stephen? Who did you call?"

"The police."

"Other police? Other than Charlton."

"Yes." He was almost inaudible. "The Lincolnshire police."

"The police I told you I didn't trust?"

Silence.

"The police I told you had been round and ransacked my house?"

"Yes."

Jesus. I closed my eyes and sighed. "Who? Who did you talk to?"

Nothing.

"Ibbetson. It's important. Was it Darnold? Did you ring Adrian Darnold?"

Nothing. Just heavy, anxious breathing.

"Ibbetson. Was it Darnold?"

Click. The line went dead. I looked at the phone. Great, now Darnold would have my pseudonym too. And possibly a description of what I looked like with bleached hair. Thank God I'd used a different name to check into the hotel this time.

Chapter Twenty-Three

I gathered my stuff together and went for a walk, wandering through Covent Garden towards Holborn and then back along Oxford Street, where I dipped back towards Covent Garden and from there to Seven Dials. A little independent coffee shop seemed like a suitable place to stop. It was in a secluded little yard off the main shopping area. I ordered a decaffeinated coffee this time and another cake—a strawberry confection with loads of cream and icing sugar, thinking that the sugar boost was just what I needed. Hopefully no one was tracking what I had been eating for the last few days. I didn't think I'd be getting any awards for a healthy diet. I seemed to have been existing mostly on cake.

Once I'd settled, I fished out my iPad and the notes I had been making, then grabbed the phone and started ringing the various number combinations. I worked my way down the list of numbers, trying each one twice, once with the 762 ending and again with the 879 ending. The first three were met with the familiar rising *beep, beep, beep* and a woman in a posh voice telling me that the number I had dialled had not been recognised and to please check and try again. The fourth number actually rang. Somebody answered on the fifth or sixth ring. What I thought was a man answered and he spoke with the thickest Scottish accent I could ever have imagined.

"Scourie Birdwatching."

"I'm sorry?" I struggled to understand what he was saying.

"Scourie Birdwatching."

"Sorry, are you are a nature park?"

"No, lassie. We organise trips to the nature reserves. To watch the birds."

"Okay, thanks. I think I must have dialled the wrong number."

"Nae worry." The man, or possibly woman, said and put the phone down.

I made a note next to the number and moved on. Only one of the other numbers rang. It was one of the London numbers. The lady who answered it sounded about a hundred twenty-six years old and kept asking me to repeat what I'd said. After two attempts at apologising, I just disconnected the call.

I slumped into my chair and let out a heavy sigh. After having eventually worked out Neasden's code, I was no further forward. I reached for Lambert's phone, putting the battery and SIM card back in and opened the call list. Then I wrote down every call that had been made or received in the last two weeks. Some came up only as names, so I noted down the name and then cross referenced the names to the contacts in the address book. I wrote down all the other numbers in the address book. There were only a few. I guessed that this was a work mobile, as there were only a couple of calls made and not that many received. As well as the address book not containing many numbers, there were no familiar numbers, no women, no "Mum" and no "home."

I cross checked the list of numbers I had with the decoded list from the notebook. None of them matched. Although…I looked again. There was one number that was almost a match, except one digit was different. I checked again. One number, which had been a received call on Tuesday, was identical to one of my decoded numbers, except that instead of starting 01 it started 07. Prickles of excitement played along my spine. Perhaps Neasden had added an extra decoy in case someone else, like me, had figured out his code. He'd disguised the number as a landline, when in reality it was a mobile. It was probably just a complete coincidence that the same landline number had led to a tiny village in the north of Scotland.

I pondered which mobile to use. If I used one of mine and it was an important contact, then they would have one of my numbers and I'd potentially have to ditch the phone. On the other hand, they would, in all probability, be aware that I had taken Lambert's phone and if I rang would know that I was on the trail. I wasn't sure if that would be a bad thing, but I guessed it probably might be. I decided to use the new phone. It was only cheap and I could buy another SIM card for next to nothing if I needed to.

I picked up my phone and dialled the number. Somebody answered before the second ring.

"Darnold."

Shit, shit shit. I was suddenly shaking violently. I pressed "end" and almost threw the phone across the table, as if Darnold might climb out of it and finish the job Lambert had started. Some of the people in the café turned to look at me. I took some deep breaths and calmed myself down. It was a break-through. Neasden had written Darnold's phone number in his notebook. He had to be significant. He had to be involved in this, and not in a good way. It was, after all, him who'd changed the information in the police report. What was he trying to cover up? Was it just the fact that Neasden had been shot, or was there something else? He clearly wanted to discredit me. I could imagine them in court suggesting I was distraught, confused, mistaken; that I'd just imagined that I'd seen the bullet wound. My brain whirred; there was something. Something that I knew was important, but I couldn't quite figure out. Whatever it was, it was deep in the recesses of my mind and my brain was not grasping hold of it.

I looked back at my list of numbers and under-lined the number and wrote "Adrian Darnold DI" next to it. Another strange sense of recognition swept over me and I stared into the air, hoping for inspira-tion. I jerked back to reality with a jump as Lambert's phone vibrated its way across the table. Darnold's number showed up on the screen and I stared at it as my heart pounded away against my chest. After some hesitation, I pressed answer and held the phone to my ear, trying not to breathe.

"Lambert? Lambert, what's going on? Where are you and why didn't you call me yesterday?" His voice was gruff and deep, as if he'd smoked twenty ciga-rettes a day for the last thirty years.

A brief pause.

"Lambert. You are in deep shit." The phone went dead.

So, Darnold didn't know that Lambert hadn't succeeded in his mission. And they didn't know I had Lambert's phone. It suddenly dawned on me that this was a very good thing as I had just put the battery and SIM card back in and if they had realised, and they had been tracking Lambert's phone, then I would have just given away my location. I kicked myself; I couldn't afford to make stupid mistakes. I'd taken the SIM card out early on, but hadn't thought when I'd put it back in—I had been so keen to look at the numbers, lost in what I was doing. *Stupid, stupid.* But I had no time to wallow, and Darnold, at least, thought that Lambert still had his own phone. I wasn't sure if Darnold had intended for Lambert to kill me, or if he was just going to use the gun to intimidate me into telling them where the notebook was. Either way, he was clearly supposed to have let Darnold know. I wondered if it was Darnold who was in charge of everything, and if so, what it was he was protecting. Lambert, assuming he had escaped by now, had either not wanted to tell Darnold he'd messed up or not been able to. I quickly took the battery and SIM card back out of the phone and put it in my rucksack.

Chapter Twenty-Four

I had outstayed my welcome at the café. I could sense the woman behind the counter glaring at my empty cup. I couldn't face another cup of coffee, so I gathered my things together and headed back to the hotel. As I walked, I remembered the sense of recognition when I'd written Darnold's initials down. I couldn't quite bring to mind what it was that had given me that feeling, but I thought I'd ponder it a bit more from the hotel. I took the lift up to my room, and outside the door, in a laundry bag, were my clothes all clean and dry. I picked them up and took them into the room.

The first thing I did when I got inside was to check that the gun was undisturbed. There it was, still wrapped up in my pyjamas. I breathed a sigh of relief. I sat down at the desk and took the first phone I had bought out of the rucksack. I put the battery and the SIM card in and switched it on. The display told me that I had missed thirty-two calls. *Bloody hell; what was going on?* Twenty-six of them were from Robert. The others were mostly from Collette's number, and there were two from an 0845 number, which I guessed would be unsolicited marketing calls. I had six voice-mail messages, so I listened to them. The first one was from Robert.

"Verity, it's Robert. Just to let you know that I've organised for the cleaners and the locksmith to go round. I've stayed away." He paused. *"Honestly, I haven't even peeked. Anyway, the house will be sorted by the end of Friday so you'll be able to come back then. Okay? See you. Bye."*

The next one was from Robert, too.

"Verity! I know you are not staying with Collette because I saw her in town today. You were supposed to be meeting her for coffee but didn't show up. Are you okay? Verity, let me know what's happening and where you are."

Damn! Of course, coffee with Collette. I'd completely forgotten that I'd said I'd meet her on Thursday morning. My mind drifted for a moment to an alternative reality, one where I'd been on time for coffee on Monday and not even seen Dr Neasden. A life where I hadn't noticed the dropped notebook at the bottom of the hill. In that reality I would have carried on unawares, meeting Collette on Thursday morning and hearing all about her meeting with the head teacher. *Bugger.* Collette had been so good to me and I hadn't even let her know that I couldn't make it. A wave of guilt washed over me. I blinked hard to stop tears that were forming in the corners of my eyes, wiping them away with the sleeve of my top. I was a long way from home, and so far away from everyone I loved; a ball of pity tugged at my chest. I had a strong urge to dive under the duvet and curl up on the bed to try to escape from it all for a while. I wanted one of Robert's reassuring hugs.

I stood up and made myself a cup of tea, deciding that I couldn't afford the time to sink into a mire of self-indulgent sadness. I took a few deep breaths, picked up the phone and carried on listening to my concerned friends.

In the next message Robert actually sounded a little exasperated.

"Verity, it's me again. Where are you? I'm getting worried."

Then one from Collette. She spoke in a high, shrill voice and gasped between words.

"Darling, how are you? Are you okay? Oh my God, Vee, everyone is worried about you. Rob gave me this number, he said you were burgled! Vee, what happened? What are you doing? Where are you? And why did you tell Rob you were staying with me? What's going on, Vee?"

My guilt deepened.

The next one was nothing, just the sound of a phone being put down. The last one was Robert again.

"Verity, darling, we are worried about you. Are you okay?"

I sighed. It was nice that my friends were concerned about me, but I could have been a million miles away from them at the moment. And I knew I couldn't be distracted by trying to keep other people happy. I didn't want to ring them; I couldn't face all the questions and I knew I'd have to lie, which I didn't want to do. I didn't want them to be worried about me, though, and mostly I didn't want them going round to the house. I tried not to linger on the feeling that I had somehow let them down by getting involved in this situation and running away without even attempting to explain. I picked up the phone and wrote a quick text to Robert.

Everything ok. Lots to explain. Pls tell C all is fine. Will be back soon. Lots love V xx

I pressed send and then removed the battery and SIM card quickly before I got a reply which I knew would set the guilty feelings off again.

I took out my iPad and looked through the photos again. I wasn't sure why I was bothering; I knew them all off by heart and I was sure there was nothing new to be seen. But then it jumped out at me. The list of acronyms. The bottom acronym was ADDI. Adrian Darnold, Detective Inspector. Not an acronym after all. It was a name and a position.

I scoured the list again. Did this mean that the other letters on the list were also initials and jobs? RSDI. Could that be another Detective Inspector? And what about KTMD? MD? Doctor of Medicine? There were too many questions and my head was spinning. I thought about Darnold again, ADDI. But there was something else. There was something niggling in the back of my head, which would not come forward. I shook my head as if to try to free it, then went back to the photos and my notes. What did "Champion!" mean? Once again, I shook my head. I had no clue.

I revisited the phone numbers, looking again at the second decoded number. The one that had started 0207. It had led me nowhere and I wondered if

Neasden had used a 2 in that number in place of a 7. It would make sense to use a 2 because it would make the number look like a London landline. Once again, I searched the numbers that I had noted down from Lambert's phone but still none of them matched anything in my list. So, using my new phone I started dialling them all again, but this time using a 7 instead of a 2. The first and second drew a blank, but when I dialled the third one on the list it rang. It rang about six times, then stopped. I thought someone had picked up so I held my breath but instead there was a click and a pause, then a deep, male voice said,

"This is Richard Sanderson's phone. Thank you for calling. I'm sorry I can't take your call but if you leave a message, including your name and number, I will return your call as soon as I can."

I hung up without leaving my name or number, or a message.

Richard Sanderson. Could that be RSDI? Perhaps I might be getting somewhere. I rang the other number combinations just to be sure but they were all "incorrect" or "unavailable." It took me by surprise how many number combinations you could ring that didn't belong to anyone. It seemed that there were so many mobile phones and landlines in the country that I'd have thought every combination possible had been taken. It appeared not.

Chapter Twenty-Five

Next, I tried calling Sam Charlton. He answered almost immediately.

"Charlton, it's Verity. I think I might be onto something. I'm not sure what, but you may be able to do some checking."

"Go ahead."

"Well, it was definitely Darnold who sent Lambert over to my hotel last night."

"Okay."

"And it was definitely him who Ibbetson rang. Or someone, but I think it was Darnold, which is what led him to me. I don't think Ibbetson really knew what he was doing. He sounded really flustered when I told him what had happened."

"Any idea what it is all about?"

"No, Ibbetson was really nervous, almost gibbering, and he wouldn't say. But I have another name. I think it's another policeman."

"From Lincolnshire?"

"Well, I guess. That's what I'd thought, but actually I don't know for sure."

"What's the name?"

"Richard Sanderson. I think he is a DI too."

Charlton whistled through his teeth. "Okay, I'll check it out and get back to you if there is anything. How are you holding up?"

"I'm okay," I said.

I suddenly felt weary, and not at all okay. My throat still hurt, as did my lip and my foot. I looked around at my hotel room and instantly felt very homesick. The messages from my friends had brought home to me how much I had been relying on them lately, and I missed them.

"I'll be fine. Let's get this sorted out, though." I gave Charlton the contact details I had for Sanderson and hung up.

I looked at the time on my phone. It was just after 6.30pm. I couldn't believe where the time had gone. I felt exhausted. I undressed and got into the shower in the hope that it might revive me. I considered getting straight into bed; I was so tired I thought I would easily sleep through until the morning. But I was hungry again, so I put on my freshly laundered clothes and headed out. I had wanted to work through the texts on Lambert's phone but I didn't want to turn it on again, just in case. I was looking around for a likely place to eat dinner and then it struck me; I bought a ticket and went down into the depths of Covent Garden tube station. There would be no signal down here. I sat on a bench, double-checked that the 4G network hadn't reached this station yet, then fished out the phone and put the battery and the SIM card in. There was absolutely no signal at all. Good. I worked through the texts, noting them all down in two lists—those that had been received, and those that had been sent. I wrote the date and time down next to each message, as well as the number it had been sent or received from; these were mostly the same couple of numbers, so I shorthanded it to a, b, c and so on. There weren't that many texts, which was lucky as it was laborious work and, because it was an old style phone, it didn't keep texts as conversations like an iPhone did, which would mean cross checking sent messages with received messages when I later came to read them in more detail. That was something to look forward to, then.

It took me the best part of an hour, but at least I could feel that I had avoided at least one way of being traced. I emerged from the station, headed towards Shaftesbury Avenue and into the nearest decent-looking restaurant, which turned out to be a quirky French bistro on a corner just a few minutes' walk away. The waitress was French, or she was effecting a very good French accent, and I ordered a large glass of bordeaux and a bowl of beef bourguignon. It was a small restaurant; there couldn't have been more than eight or nine tables. About half of them had people sitting at them, even at this early hour, although many of them were dining alone. People in London on business, I assumed. All the tables were covered in gingham tablecloths, and the menus for the day, with today's date, were all handwritten on headed pieces of A4 paper. The kitchen was off to one side of the room, with the chefs on full display, preparing dishes and talking to each other in French. The whole place had a homely, and very French, feel. It reminded me of the places John and I had been to when we had been holidaying in France. Not the more sophisticated and upmarket restaurants of the south coast that catered for moneyed, international tourists; more the rustic, country restaurants in proper French villages used by the locals. Those had been the places we had preferred to go to.

The waitress came back with my wine and some bread. I took out my notes detailing all of Lambert's texts. The texts only went back about six weeks and many were just very short messages giving a time, a date, and a location. That had to have been for a meeting, or a rendezvous of some sort, or to pick something up, or drop something off. Maybe Lambert was dealing drugs? Maybe this was all to do with drugs. There was huge money to be made there and, I guessed, people would be involved who wouldn't stop short of shooting someone in the stomach. I imagined there would be some police officers who would accept a bribe to back off too and then turned a blind eye to certain "goings on" in their area. Could Neasden have stumbled across something involving child trafficking and drugs? I remembered from my research that dealing drugs, tending cannabis farms and so on was one of the major reasons that people were trafficked to the UK. It was a possibility, and would make sense in the context of Dr Neasden's specialism.

My dinner arrived, so I pushed the texts to one side whilst I ate. The food was amazing. It was fresh and tender and delicious. I was starving. I'd only eaten a couple of pieces of cake today. Probably very calorific, but not very substantial. I wolfed down my bourguignon and vegetables and all the sautéed pota-toes, then wiped the plate clean with my bread. Then I ordered a bowl of tiramisu. Not very French, but homemade. I had a glass of French brandy with my tiramisu, which was creamy and divine, and just what I needed. I hadn't had a proper meal in days, and I felt better for it, less weary as well.

I ordered a cup of peppermint tea and sat and

drank that in peace, watching people coming and going. Most of the business diners had gone and been replaced by groups of friends, couples, and families. The place was full and I wasn't surprised. I paid my bill in cash, leaving a sizeable tip, then walked back around the corner to my hotel. I opened the door cautiously, but there was no one in the room. I went in with the intention of working further on Lambert's texts, as I needed to find out what the connection was between him, Darnold, and Sanderson. I put on my pyjamas and cleaned my teeth, then took my iPad and the notes out of the rucksack and got into bed.

SATURDAY

Chapter Twenty-Six

I woke with a start. I was lying across the top of bed, my neck aching from being at an angle it wasn't intended to stay in for a prolonged period. I glanced at my phone; it was 4am. I had clearly fallen forwards from a sitting position and gone to sleep where I had landed. The light was still on and the iPad and notes were still on the bed. I moved them to the bedside cabinet, turned off the light, and went back to sleep.

I woke again at 9am, feeling well rested and alert. I got showered and dressed, then gathered all of my stuff together ready to go out and find some breakfast. I caught sight of myself in the mirror. The swelling on my lip had all but disappeared, and the red mark around my neck had faded. I wondered if I should dye my hair a different colour. Maybe red? I thought about whether Ibbetson, or Lambert, had given Darnold a description of what I looked like now. I had got quite used to the blonde, though, and I didn't think I would achieve much by dying it again. It might throw them off for a while, but what I really needed to do was figure out what was going on and stop them from wanting to chase after me. I couldn't just keep running away and changing the colour of my hair. Looking at myself in the mirror, I wondered what John would think about my new appearance. A wave of sadness crept over me as I realised he'd never see it. I missed John so much. His death had come as such a shock. It wasn't like there had been anything to prepare us. One minute he'd been driving, alive, down the road and the next minute he'd been dead. Memories of our time together tumbled into my mind; the ups and downs, the arguments and shoe-throwing, the good times and the bad. It had been a normal marriage, full of trials and tribulations like anyone else's. But now he was dead, snatched so suddenly away from the life he should still be living.

Hang on. The niggling was back, but this time the thoughts were bubbling to the surface. I pushed the sad images away as I struggled to hold on to the bubbles before they dissipated once again. Death, something to do with death. Dying, somebody dying. The cause of death. A certificate. A death requires a death certificate. The police could alter their record of what had happened at Dr Neasden's house but the death certificate would state what had been the actual cause of his death.

I zipped up my jacket and put my grey hat on my head. I quickly re-wrapped the gun in my pyjamas and left it in the drawer under the television. Then I grabbed the rucksack, slung it over my shoulder and left the hotel to find a different cafe to work in. The man behind the counter instructed me to sit down and said he would bring my coffee and croissant over to me, so I paid him and then went and found a sofa. I was just taking my rucksack off my back when vibrations in my pocket indicated that my phone was ringing. It was Charlton.

"Morning, Sam. How are you doing?"

"Hey. You sound a bit brighter this morning. Listen, let's meet up this evening. I'd like to catch up on stuff but I don't want to talk too much on the phone."

"Okay." I wondered if he was worried his phone was being listened to. "There's a cool little French restaurant near here. I went there last night and it was great. If that's okay?"

He agreed that it would be.

I told him the name and location. "Oh and, Sam?"

"Yep."

"Dr Neasden must have had a death certificate."

"Well, yes, but…"

"It will state his cause of death. Which was clearly a bullet in the stomach. It might help prove that Darnold is tampering with the records."

"I'll do a little digging. See you later."

My coffee and croissant arrived. I fished out my copies of Lambert's texts and studied them in more detail. I went through them all, checking the number they had come from or been sent to, and cross-checking this against the time and date they had been sent or received. It was boring work. There were no real conversations; in fact, almost all the texts seemed to concern arrangements to meet. There were some vague references to "pick ups" and I, once again, wondered if there was some drug connection. It seemed that, looking through the messages, it was Lambert who was telling others where to be and at what time. Most of the replies were "ok" or "got it" or "message received." It was all very bland.

I checked the numbers. All the texts relating to these meetings had been sent to just two different numbers. Only two. This phone was clearly only used for making arrangements. I cross checked the numbers against the list of calls that Lambert had made and received. One of them was on the list. Lambert had called it a few days previously. I picked up my phone and dialled. After a couple of rings, someone picked up. *Shit, I should have thought about this before dialling.* I didn't know what to say; I was completely unprepared. Then a deep, resounding male voice said, "Yeah? Who is this?" I couldn't think of an answer to that, so I hung up.

Damn. I'd thought someone might have answered, giving me their name when they picked up, and that the loose ends would all neatly tie up. But things weren't working as smoothly as that. I went back to the texts. It was then that I noticed the date. The date on the last text. I'd completely lost track of the days and the dates over the last week, but the text said:

Sunday 5th. Toddington. Northbound. 2pm.

Shit. Sunday 5th. That was tomorrow. I ticked off the days in my head; it took me a while but, yes, today was Saturday. The text had been sent to the number that Darnold had never called. He'd received an answer only a few minutes after he'd sent it.

Got it. C.

Who was C? None of the initials in the notebook had a C in them. I considered ringing and taking a stab in the dark "hello is that Charlie?" but it could be Clive, or Chris, or probably a hundred other names that started with a C. It could be a Catherine or a Charlotte for all I knew. Whoever it was, I knew I needed to be there, at Toddington at 2pm. I'd think about whether I needed to ring the number later, but now I had to get prepared. I made a list of things I would need.

Top of the list was a hire car; I'd need a car to drive to Toddington—it was miles up the M1. If I hired a car, I'd need a driver's licence. I had mine in my bag, but did I really want to use it? I sat and thought of a plan for stealing someone else's licence, but it all seemed a bit speculative. What if I nicked someone's purse and they didn't have their licence in it? Plus, I'd have to choose someone who was vaguely the same age as me, or with a picture that could possibly pass for me. In the end, I decided that the best thing would be to just go for it and book it in my name. I figured that as long as I paid cash and didn't use my debit card, it shouldn't be too risky. Someone would have to be actively looking for me renting a car, and why would they suspect I'd do that? And they would have to ask every car hire place in the country, surely? I could see that they might be looking for debit card transactions, and it would be stupid to use one of those, but as long as I paid in cash I didn't think using my driver's licence would be too risky.

I Googled car hire firms in North London; I figured I didn't want to have to drive through central London if I could avoid it. A couple started off with a helpful tone, but they wouldn't let me pay cash, they said I'd have to pay in advance with a credit or debit card. I even tried telling them a sob story about having my handbag stolen and all my cards were in it, along with my train tickets and I just wanted to go home. They must have thought I was trying to scam them, so I gave up and moved on. Eventually I found a firm in Highgate with an extremely helpful assistant who said it would be okay to pick up a car in the morning and pay in cash when I arrived. I fished out my driver's licence and ordered a medium-sized family car. I wanted something that would blend in.

Then I paid for my coffee and croissant and went on a search for all the other things on my list.

Chapter Twenty-Seven

I started by walking to Oxford Street. I headed westwards along the south side of the street. The weather had warmed up again, to the point where it was almost unseasonably warm. I stopped and took off my jacket and hat. I folded my jacket and put it into my rucksack, along with my hat, but I kept the scarf round my neck. Then a few hundred yards further down the road I found exactly what I was looking for; Ann Summers.

I had never been in an Ann Summers shop before, and I sauntered past the rows of fancy bras and pants towards the back of the shop, glancing around, trying to look as if I was an old hand at this. The assistants looked me up and down as if they were appraising my outfit; my outdoor wear didn't really chime with the notion of sexy underwear. Still, maybe I had hidden depths that my clothes didn't betray. I smiled, thinking of the big pants I had on that I'd bought in Blacks. I held my head up and headed further into the shop. To my left a bank of racks held clothes to dress up in, including nurse's outfits, French maid outfits, and one for a dominatrix. All for women to dress up in, I noted. Most of them appeared to be PVC and didn't look very comfortable. In the middle of the room there was a circular display that you walked into. I looked at the array of objects in amazement. Boxes of vibrators filled the shelves; different sorts, of all sizes and colours, some with variable speeds and some with several add-on pieces. There were also clamps, rings, and anal plugs, as well as a weird looking vibrator with two prongs. I picked it up and was reading the back of the package when an assistant came up and asked me if I needed any help.

"No, that's great, thanks," I said sheepishly. "Just looking."

I put the strange double vibrator down and carried on through the display to the other side of the room. Here there were whips and leather bondage gear and copies of "Fifty Shades of Grey" next to paddles and shackles. I marvelled at the vagaries of human proclivities; John and I had had a fairly active sex life, but it had been strictly normal, under the covers stuff. Should we have the lights on, or do it in the afternoon, or on the kitchen floor was about as risqué as we'd got. Then I saw what I needed; handcuffs. I bypassed the pink fluffy ones and those you could attach to feet and hands at the same time, and went for the boring metal ones. I picked them off the display and studied them. They weren't as sturdy as the ones I'd used to attach Lambert to the bed in my hotel room, but they would definitely do; they would certainly hold someone up for a while if the need arose. I wondered when Lambert had been discovered and by who, and what he had said by way of an explanation. Maybe he was still there, shackled to the bed.

I picked three pairs of handcuffs off the hook and

took them to the counter. The shop assistant smiled but said nothing as she put them in a bag for me.

"You never know when you might need to tie up more than one person," I said with a smile.

She just laughed, as if she was well used to the idea of handcuffing several people in one go and said, "Quite."

I walked further along Oxford Street, looking down side streets for second hand bookshops. After walking for half a mile or so, I found a likely looking street off to the North side of Oxford Street. There was a quirky little book store a couple of hundred yards down the road on the right-hand side. I stepped inside and perused the shelves. Instantly a thin and wiry man came over and asked me if I was okay. He didn't look at all as if he should be working in a second hand bookshop. I always imagined bookshop owners should wear corduroy trousers and sleeveless sweaters with collarless shirts and have shaggy, curly hair and wire-rimmed glasses. A bit like the Irish guy that had been in Black Books, whose name I could never remember. This guy would have looked more at home as a villain in a Harry Potter book. He had a hooked nose, thin lips, and he rubbed his hands together when he talked. He reminded me of the child catcher from Chitty Chitty Bang Bang.

"Just looking thanks," I replied and carried on, scanning the shelves.

"Were you looking for anything in particular?" he asked, slicking his straight black hair over a bald patch, then wiping his greasy hand down the side of his oversized suit jacket.

"No. No thanks, just browsing."

"Any genre you especially like reading?" He rubbed his hands together as if miming washing them.

I turned to look at him. I had a serious urge to shove him backwards into his bookcase and drown him under a pile of falling books. Instead I smiled curtly, said, "I'm fine," then turned away and carried on perusing the shelves.

He didn't say anything but I could sense him hovering behind me, hopping from foot to foot and rubbing his hands together.

I couldn't see what I wanted so, against my better judgement, I turned to the shop owner, or manager, or assistant, or whatever he was.

"Do you have a section for dictionaries and encyclopaedias?"

"Of course." He nodded and kind of bowed in the direction he wanted us to go. I followed him to the back of the shop, where he indicated with a sweep of his arm a bookcase full of enormous books. I pulled a couple from the shelf and held them, weighing them in my hands. The hovering man seemed to find this incredibly curious.

"Any particular kind you were after?" he asked in his thin voice. It matched his thin stature. And his thin hair.

"No, no." I kept pulling books off the shelf until I found one that was perfect. It was bound in that stuff that was like a cross between a paperback and a hardback; was it called softback? Heavy enough to really hurt if you swung it at someone's head, but soft enough not to kill them. I didn't want anyone's life on my hands if things got tricky.

I took the book to the counter and paid. Then I returned to Oxford Street, turned right, and walked almost to Marble Arch to find Selfridges. I went up the escalator to their homeware department and through to the kitchen section. I walked around for a while before finding an assistant and asking about the various knives they had on sale. It was Saturday, and I wondered if the young man helping me was on a Saturday job and still at school. He looked about fifteen and, according to his name badge, was called Liam. Maybe it's me growing old, I thought. Anyway, Liam seemed to know his stuff. I explained that I wanted a knife that was not very long, but that could cut through really tough meat and wouldn't break easily. He selected a few and described the relative merits of each. I chose some that were made from Japanese steel—apparently really strong but also very sharp—I took two paring knives with 3.5" blades and two 6" chef's knives. That set me back almost £200, but I needed to be prepared. Liam wrapped the knives carefully and put them in a bag with the receipt, and I thanked him and left.

I went through homeware to find the curtain section. There I selected several yards of clear curtain wire. Having had an intruder in my hotel room, I thought it might come in handy in case I needed to booby trap another room. I went back down the escalators and returned to the street.

I headed along Oxford Street towards Covent Garden and called in at Jessops. There I bought a powerful torch and a pair of binoculars. I got the assistant to show me how to use them properly, how to focus them and change the focus for nearer or further away objects. I thanked him and left, carrying on along the road until I found a food store. There, I bought three lemons, some ground black pepper, some cayenne pepper, some extra-hot chilli powder, some Sellotape, and some Tabasco sauce.

As I continued my trip back towards the hotel, I passed an outdoors store. I paused; shoes hadn't been on my shopping list, but I remembered how my foot had hurt after kicking Lambert, and I veered in. A young girl came to help and fetched a variety of styles to try. She asked what activities I would be using them for. I felt like telling her I was planning on using them to kick people in the balls, or on the shins, but I thought better of it. After trying on several pairs I settled on a pair of sturdy walking boots. I knew I would have to drive the hire car whilst wearing them, and so I didn't want anything too clumpy, but at the same time I wanted something that would protect my feet and also hurt any adversary if I needed to swing my foot between anyone else's legs. Momentarily, I wondered what my long-haired self from a week ago would have thought about me preparing for kicking people, hitting them with heavy books, or handcuffing them to beds. I imagined she would have taken a very dim view. I smiled at my reflection in the mirror as I left the shop; not just physically different now, but mentally too. Whilst I knew that I was getting involved with some very dangerous people, I had discovered a determination that hadn't existed in me for some time, and I would not give in without a fight. I knew they were going to keep coming for me and I was not going to sit around and wait. I had to take the fight to them.

Finally, I found a Boots and called in there. I wandered around until I found the holiday section, and there I located some empty plastic bottles that you can fill with your favourite toiletries when you go away without falling foul of the "no more than 100ml" rule. I chose a couple that had a spray pump-action top and took them to the counter. I joined a long queue of people and eventually made my way to the front of the queue and paid. I walked out into the autumn sunshine and headed back to my hotel.

Chapter Twenty-Eight

When I returned to the hotel, I assessed my purchases. I spread everything out on the bed. The new shoes were good. If I kicked anyone wearing those, I didn't think my foot would hurt quite as much as the last time. The pain had now subsided in my toes, and I really didn't want to experience that again. I took the binoculars out of their box and put the box back in the carrier bag. I walked over to the window and surveyed London from the hotel window. There was a reasonably good view down the Thames if I peered between the buildings and, once I got the binoculars focused, I could see one end of Tower Bridge quite clearly. I tried moving quickly to look at something closer and practised refocusing as fast as I could. I practised it a few times, moving and refocusing, until my fingers knew exactly where the dial was without me having to think about it.

I then got out the torch and went into the bathroom which had no windows. I shut the door so that it was in darkness and turned on the torch. I surveyed the bathroom with the beam of light, noticing a couple of spiders that had escaped my attention until now. I let them be; spiders had never bothered me. Not like earwigs, or maggots; I hated those things but spiders were okay. The beam was sharp and focused, not spreading too far out either side. Perfect. I went back into the room and sat back down on the bed.

Then I gathered together the items I'd got in the food store. I unwrapped the cellophane from around the spices and grabbed one of the mugs that had been left next to the little hotel kettle. Using the mug as a mixing bowl, I poured some of the black pepper, extra-hot chilli powder, and cayenne pepper into it, and stirred them all together. When I was satisfied, I tried a taste, just a little on the tip of my tongue. I could stand hot food; in my opinion, the hotter the better. Whenever John and I had gone out for curry, I would order the hottest meal on the menu. If it brought tears to my eyes, that was the sign that the heat was about right. As I tasted my mix of spices, tears welled up in my eyes; not from sentimentality, but from the heat. Wow, that was quite a hot mix. My tongue was on fire. I added a little more of each to the mug, just to be sure. Then I unwrapped one of my new knives, cut into one of the lemons and squeezed it into the mug. I did the same with the other two lemons and then added quite a bit of tabasco sauce to the mix. I stirred the whole thing together, with one of the hotel teaspoons to get a really good mix and then went into the bathroom. I fished out the plastic bottles and, over the sink, I carefully filled both of them with the lemon, tabasco, and spice mix. I tried both bottles to see if the spray action worked. It wasn't quite MACE, but it would be a suitable substitute.

I put all my new purchases, except the walking

shoes, in the drawer under the television with the gun. Then I had a shower, dried my hair, dressed, and got ready to meet Charlton. I looked at myself in the mirror wearing my outdoor trousers and long sleeved top; pretty much the same outfit I'd worn the last time I'd met him. I thought, briefly, that maybe whilst I was out I should have bought a dress so I would at least look like I'd made an effort. Then I told myself not to be stupid; it wasn't a date, for heaven's sake. Besides, I still had a cut on my lip and a faint red mark around my neck. I wasn't at my most attractive.

Charlton hadn't got there when I arrived, so I asked for a table for two. The same waitress who had been there the night before pointed to a couple of empty tables and I chose one tucked away in the corner. I ordered a glass of wine whilst I waited and perused the menu. All the items were different from the night before, which indicated that they had to make them fresh each day. Just as the waitress came over with my wine, Charlton arrived. He ordered a French beer and sat down, surveying his surroundings.

"I've never been here before," he said as he glanced at the menu. "Looks okay, though."

I told him I'd eaten here the night before and had been impressed.

"Are you okay?" he said, staring at my cut lip with a frown of concern.

"I'm fine. You should have seen the other guy," I joked. But it didn't really sound funny when I said it out loud, and I was not sure Charlton was too impressed. The waitress brought his beer over, along with some bread and olives, and so we ordered. He asked for the escargots to start, followed by Sole with lemon; I had soup of the day and chicken fricassee. We nibbled the bread and exchanged niceties. Hadn't the weather improved? What about current politics in America? We chatted away as if the death and mayhem that had surrounded me for the best part of a week didn't exist. The conversation came easily, and before I knew it we'd finished our starters and were waiting for the main courses. He was good company, an intelligent and thoughtful man. The time slipped easily by.

"So what have you been up to today?" he asked after a brief pause in the conversation.

"Shopping," I replied with a bright smile.

"Oh, that's a good idea. It's good to try and relax when you're in a bit of a stressful situation."

I nodded. A bit stressful? That was an understatement.

"Did you get anything nice?"

A few homemade weapons, I thought, but I kept that to myself. I hadn't mentioned anything to Charlton about the texts on Lambert's phone or the arrangements for tomorrow. Or the fact that I planned to hire a car and see what I could find out. I thought that he might be less than enthusiastic about my plan and try to talk me out of it. "I got some new shoes," I said brightly.

The main courses arrived, and the conversation moved on. Once we had finished our food, declined desserts, but ordered coffee and brandy, I said, "Anyway, lovely as this is, shall we compare notes on how we are getting on with things?"

Charlton kicked off with what he had found out earlier that day.

"Richard Sanderson is a Detective Inspector with Nottinghamshire police," he explained. He told me about his digging around and how he had found this out, double checking with the phone number I'd given him to make sure it was the same guy.

I nodded. That made sense; Nottinghamshire bordered Lincolnshire so it wouldn't be a surprise if people from that force were involved too. It might even have made it easier to cover things up.

Charlton carried on, "There is a connection between Sanderson and Dr Neasden."

"Oh, really? Interesting."

"Yes, it is." He paused to take a slug of his brandy. "Dr Neasden was doing some work with a young man who was being prosecuted by Nottinghamshire police."

"I think he did voluntary work with people who had no recourse to public funds."

"He did. This young man was an illegal immigrant. His name is Ndeye Ndawayo. He came, originally, from Rwanda. Sanderson was in charge when the young man was arrested for burglary. He claimed to be sixteen years old, but that was disputed, because apparently he had papers saying he was twenty-one."

"What happened?"

"He was convicted of burglary and he was sent to an adult jail."

I thought about that, but said nothing.

"What I did find strange was that there were no other police involved in the arrest."

"Is that unusual?"

"Well, it's not completely impossible, but it is unusual for a Detective Inspector to be the arresting officer for a burglary. I'm a Detective Inspector myself. I know that these days I spend most of my time doing managing and administrating. Obviously I get involved, but more as the chief investigating officer, I'm not often out on the front line."

"Maybe he got lucky? Just happened to be there when the lad ran out with a bag of swag over his shoulders?"

"It's a possibility," he conceded.

"And what was Dr Neasden's involvement?"

"He was helping the young man access medical treatment."

"Medical treatment?"

"Yeah, not sure what for though."

"Blimey."

We sipped our coffees and brandies in silence for a while.

"So, tell me a bit about the other guy. The one who ended up looking worse than you." Charlton pursed his lips and rubbed his finger along his jawline, as if he wasn't sure whether to be concerned, impressed, or amused with my hotel room antics. He asked a few more questions; what had he looked like, what had he sounded like, how I had managed to overpower him, and so on. I somewhat overplayed the effect that crashing his head into the coat hook had had, and rather underplayed me kicking him in the balls when he was unconscious. I still made no mention of the gun. We asked for the bill, paid, and then Charlton got up. He offered to walk me back to the hotel, but I was reluctant to give away my location to anyone, even this charming man. *"Trust no one."* I let him leave first, making the excuse of needing the bathroom. He promised to be in touch if he had anything relating to Dr Neasden's death certificate. He had put some feelers out, he said, but had got nothing back yet.

I waited ten minutes after he'd gone. Without really knowing why, I walked around in circles for fifteen minutes, through the streets of Covent Garden, which were still teeming with people, before returning to my hotel. I was pretty sure that nobody had followed me, and that if they had I would have lost them by darting in and out of the busy little streets.

It was half past ten when I got back to the hotel. I took the lift up to the ninth floor. I'd had a pleasant evening. Despite the circumstances, and despite the danger I knew I was in, I'd had an enjoyable few hours in the company of Detective Inspector Sam Charlton. I cautiously opened my bedroom door, double checked that there was no one there, made sure the gun was still safe, put the deadbolt on the door, and then got changed and went to bed.

SUNDAY

Chapter Twenty-Nine

I got up early on Sunday morning, so that I had plenty of time to prepare. I put the heavy book in the carrier bag that had come with the spices and lemons and I laid it down sideways. I wrapped Sellotape around the bag, just above where the book was so that it wouldn't slip, and tried swinging it a few times to check it was secure. Everything stayed in place. *Good.* I placed the two bottles of my homemade pepper spray in one of the front pockets of the rucksack and put two of the knives in the other front pocket and two in the side pocket. I put the handcuffs on top of all my clothes. As I was wearing the walking boots, and there was no more room in the bag, I left the trainers on the floor, by the bed. I looked at the gun, but I hadn't a clue what to do with it. It wouldn't be safe to leave it in the hotel room. I picked it up and, after carefully trying a couple of the levers, I figured out how to take the handle apart so that I could take the bullets out. This fascinated me. How could you put the bullets in the handle and yet they came out of the barrel? I assumed there had to be some mechanism for pushing them round the corner but I wasn't going to investigate. I stuffed the bullets into a zip-up pocket in the back of the rucksack and hid the gun in amongst my clothes. I gathered up all the packaging from the purchases I'd made and also the spices, lemon peel, and everything. I distributed them across a couple of the carrier bags and took everything with me.

I went to reception, settled my bill, and checked out; even though I had had no extras on top of the room rate, the bill was eye-watering. You couldn't stay cheaply in London. As I left the hotel, I picked up a free copy of the "i" newspaper and walked to Tottenham Court Road tube station, grabbing a cup of coffee on my way there. I dumped the carrier bags in different litter bins as I hurried past. Perhaps I was being a little overcautious, but you never could tell. I recalled that when I hadn't been too careful, like using the same pseudonym twice, it had backfired. No, there was no such thing as being too cautious, and I didn't want anyone figuring out that I had been making pepper spray in my hotel room, even if I had used a made-up name to check in that even I couldn't remember. *"Trust no one"* had become my mantra, and I repeated it as I walked along, to the rhythm of my steps.

I took the northern line all the way to Highgate, which took just under twenty minutes; almost enough time to read through the paper. I arrived at the car hire place as they were opening at 8.30 and hung around whilst they brought the car to the front, took my money, checked my driver's licence, explained the terms and conditions, and so on. I paid extra for the super damage waiver insurance and took the keys.

It was a slate grey Vauxhall Insignia. Pretty bog standard and nothing special at all. It was perfect. It was alright to drive, although I really didn't like the press button handbrake. I felt suddenly incredibly nervous, and it dawned on me that I hadn't driven a car since John had died. Ours had obviously been written off, and although the insurance firm was going to pay me a decent amount for the loss of it, I hadn't even thought of buying a new one. In the first weeks after John's death I wouldn't have been capable of driving, and if I'd needed to go anywhere recently I'd usually got a lift off Collette. I hadn't done that often, as the thought of being in a car had scared me. It felt strange and unnatural to be behind the wheel. I couldn't stop myself from thinking about John's last moments, driving along, not knowing what was about to happen. I'd often wondered what his last thoughts had been, and whether he'd realised the lorry was heading for him. The police had assured me that he would have died instantly as the lorry impacted with his car, but there must have been a few seconds when he'd seen the lorry heading his way and had known there was no way out. I wondered what had gone through his head at that point. I shook my head, trying hard to concentrate on the here and now, and pulled out gingerly before heading up the Archway Road and joining the M1 just after Brent Park.

The motorway was reasonably quiet as it was relatively early on a Sunday morning and I made good time getting to the services at Toddington. I turned into the northbound service station and parked in the furthest corner. I looked around. It would be a good spot. I could stand behind the car and remain relatively hidden, but I could see the entrance and the whole of the car park. I took out my binoculars and scanned the car park. I watched a few cars coming in, people getting out and going in to use the services, people coming out and driving off. I was fairly sure that I could cover the majority of the car park from where I was standing. The only problem would be if it got busy and there were too many people milling about. I went into the services and bought a coffee and a cake and sat down by the window. I was early, but it gave me time to think.

I pulled out my iPad and checked the copies I'd made of the texts that had been on Lambert's phone. I double checked the message and double checked the date. I was definitely in the right place and on the right day. It was only half past ten, so I had three and a half hours to wait. I hoped the weather stayed fine.

My phone rang; it was Charlton.

"Verity, are you in your hotel?"

"No. I'm not. I'm a bit busy today, actually." I cursed myself for sounding so on edge. I hadn't meant to sound quite as abrupt as I did.

"What are you doing?" He paused. "Verity, what are you up to?" He had obviously picked up on the anxiety in my voice.

I wouldn't tell him. "I'm just checking something out. Don't worry, I think I might be onto something and I'm just doing a bit of digging, that's all."

He sounded unsure and kept urging me to be careful. I got the sense that he thought I might be getting into something that was well over my head. He was absolutely right.

"I probably shouldn't be telling you this, but I got hold of a copy of Dr Neasden's death certificate."

"Oh, well done. And?"

"Apparently he died from cardiac arrest caused by advanced heart disease."

I was stunned. "What? But that's…"

"Also a cover up. Yes, I know."

"I think the cardiac arrest was more likely brought on by having no blood left."

"Verity, be careful. I'm telling you this because we are dealing with some dangerous, and clearly quite devious, people. Think very carefully about what you are doing, won't you?"

I tried to push his concern to the back of my head. I needed to find out what was going on.

"But how will that tie up with the police report? The report that said there was a break-in?"

"I imagine the report will now conclude that the stress of the break-in, coupled with Dr Neasden's 'advanced heart disease' was what caused his death."

"But what about the investigation?" I asked.

"If Darnold is in charge, then it will probably be quietly dropped. How many burglaries do you know where the burglar is never caught? I'm sure he will have manipulated this so it doesn't show up as manslaughter or murder. It'll be an unsolved burglary that unfortunately led to the death of a man who was very ill anyway, and not much longer for this world."

I remembered Dr Neasden striding up Steep Hill, looking anything but very ill, and as if he was going to be in this world for a long time to come.

"Do you know who signed the death certificate?" I asked.

He paused. I got the sense that he was weighing up what he should and shouldn't tell me. He sighed at the other end of the phone and I imagined him running his finger along his jaw as he thought about whether it was more dangerous to answer my question or to keep me in the dark. I resisted the urge to push him for an answer, and after what seemed like a lifetime, he responded. "Yes, it was a doctor called Kenneth Townsley."

Kenneth Townsley. Why did that ring a bell? I struggled to grab hold of the memory that was pushing its way to the front of my brain. The acronyms. *Oh shit. KTMD. Kenneth Townsley Medical Doctor. The last of the acronyms.*

"Verity?"

"Yes."

"Whatever you are doing, be careful. Don't get involved in anything you can't handle. These people are clearly dangerous and not afraid to cover up whatever it is they're doing. A woman, alone, with nothing…well, I mean no exp…well, all I'm saying is to be careful. Okay?"

I thought about the makeshift armoury I was carrying with me, but didn't tell Charlton I was heading out equipped and ready to cause some damage if I needed to. That would definitely give him the impression that I was getting into something over my head. Probably I was, but I had to carry on now; if I didn't get to the bottom of this, I'd never be safe. So, I just mumbled, "I will, I promise. You too."

Immediately after I had put the phone down, I got out my iPad and Googled Kenneth Townsley, MD. It turned out that the initials MD were a bit of shorthand on the part of Dr Neasden, as Kenneth Townsley—or should I say *Professor* Kenneth Townsley —had many initials after his name including BM, BCh, PhD, FRCP and FMedSci. I hadn't a clue what any of those meant. Bachelor of medicine, I guessed. But BCh, what was that? Bachelor of something. But what, chemistry? Chemotherapy? Could you get a degree in chemotherapy? PhD I knew was Doctor of Philosophy, as I had thought of studying for one of those myself in the past. Then Fellow of something or other. Professor Townsley, it appeared, was a very well-qualified doctor at Lincoln County Hospital and was a specialist in cancer. I went onto the hospital website and read his biography.

It appeared that the professor had qualified in the mid-seventies and had undertaken several specialist qualifications. I guessed that would account for all the letters then. He had worked in the states for a period in the early nineties, where he had been undertaking research on how cancers grew and changed in the body. He had worked at Lincoln since 2000, and apparently was "currently leading on a number of national trials for cancer treatment development."

But why had he signed Dr Neasden's death certificate? Unless Dr Neasden had been suffering from cancer and had been seen by Townsley recently, I couldn't think why a specialist at a hospital would sign a death certificate. Dr Neasden had died at his home. Surely they wouldn't have taken him to A&E at the hospital? When John had died, he'd apparently been rushed to Hull Royal Infirmary and had been declared dead on arrival at the hospital. Because his death had been sudden, it had been reported to the coroner for an investigation. It hadn't really needed much of an investigation—his death had been caused by the massive trauma of being hit head-on by a lorry. So the coroner had agreed to issue the death certificate reasonably quickly. But with Dr Neasden, there had clearly been no hope of reviving him. They had done all they could in the house. They hadn't even turned on the sirens when they'd left with him in the ambulance, but his death was certainly sudden. I assumed they would have taken him straight to the mortuary. Surely they would have done a post-mortem? So who would have certified his death? And why would a cancer specialist have been involved? Townsley had to be involved in the cover-up. His were the last initials in the notebook, along with Sanderson and Darnold. They had obviously been covering this up together. If Neasden's death was explained away as being due to natural causes, then perhaps the coroner wouldn't have been involved. There would be no investigation. Maybe they hadn't even done a post-mortem. What the hell was going on?

Chapter Thirty

Dr Neasden had written Townsley's initials in his book. Townsley was a cancer specialist; I couldn't conceive of a connection. I searched a little more on the Internet and found a couple of articles about, or by, Townsley. The ones written by him all sounded very medically oriented and were mostly to do with the rate of the growth of cancer within the body. There was one article I discovered in a newspaper archive, but it gave me no clues. It was from two years ago, almost to the day. It was about the research that Townsley was doing at the hospital. He had won some kind of prestigious award from the Royal Society of Medicine, and had been given grants from the European Research Council and the Medical Research Council to enable him to continue his research, which was described in the article as "ground breaking." The article was full of platitudes from hospital staff, both managerial and lowly, as well as from the Royal Society. There even pictures of him with patients, all full of both smiles and gratitude. It seemed that Professor Townsley was not only well qualified but also well renowned and well respected.

What could the connection possibly be? I stopped trying to think about it, and instead I did some research on Sanderson and Darnold. I started with Sanderson. I dug around for about half an hour but I couldn't locate much on him. There were a couple of very brief articles in the local press reporting trials at Nottinghamshire Crown Court, and a little piece about the Christmas drink-driving campaign from a couple of years ago. There didn't appear to be a picture.

I went and got myself another coffee and then started on Darnold. I got luckier there; I learned a bit more about him. He seemed to like getting his picture in the paper. There was one very clear picture of him at a fundraising event for Children in Need. It had been for the previous year and the local police had apparently been "rowing around the coast" in a rowing machine, taking turns to do so many miles each. There was a picture showing a young man rowing and another man standing next to the machine. The caption said,

"Detective Inspector Adrian Darnold watches PC Ian Lenton complete his stint at the rowing machine."

Darnold was standing next to the rowing machine, looking into the camera and smiling broadly. He looked about average height, judging by the things around him, and was a stocky build. I guessed he was around forty-five, but could have been five years either side of that. He had a full head of short hair with a little quiff at the front and was wearing shorts and a stripy polo shirt. His rosy cheeks and the hint of a double chin gave the impression that he struggled to keep excess weight off.

I flicked through a couple more articles. Darnold seemed to enjoy courting the local press. Maybe part of his job was to engage with the public. There was another shot of him, standing with an elderly lady, accompanying an article about home safety. He looked sturdier in this photo. I checked the date; it was more recent than the rowing picture. Maybe he'd put on some weight this year. I scanned through some reports that didn't have pictures and were about local crimes where the police were appealing to the public for more information.

I was getting bored. I had an idea of what he looked like now and was about to call it a day, but then something caught my eye. There was an article about an award ceremony for local youths. I read through it.

"Detective Inspector Adrian Darnold of Lincolnshire police was joined yesterday by Lincs FM presenter Stewart Calder, to hand out awards to local young people. The annual 'Get Real!' Awards Ceremony for local youth was held in the ballroom of The Lindum Hotel, which was donated to the event without charge. Recipients of awards are chosen each year by a panel of young people, who also organised the event. Awards were given to local heroes, such as James Dawlish, 16, who rescued his elderly neighbour from a fire. Others were for succeeding against the odds, such as Emily Wilkinson, 20, who has just been accepted to do a law degree at Cambridge University following a period in a drug rehabilitation centre."

The article went on to list other award winners.

There were several photos; photos of Darnold and Calder shaking hands with various award winners, beaming at the camera, their smiles not flagging throughout the ceremony. There were photos of people holding their awards and photos of the young organisers. Then, at the bottom of the article, there was a photo of the young people who had organised the event with a man; a very tall black man who towered over everyone else. He must have been 6'4" at least and looked as if he was in his late twenties or early thirties. He had very dark black skin and was flashing a huge, sparkling smile. He was wearing a T-shirt and had his arms spread around the shoulders of those closest to him. Arms that sported muscles that could only have been gained by spending long periods lifting weights. And possibly taking steroids. His long, braided hair fell over his back and shoulders. He was leaning down and over the young people, some of whom were looking up towards him and smiling. The caption underneath said,

"The young organisers of the Get Real! Awards with Young People's Advocate, Champion Obote, who helped them bring their ideas to life."

"Champion!" The word in Dr Neasden's note-book. I laughed out loud and sat back in my chair. *Champion!* It was a person. I wasn't sure why Dr Neasden had put the exclamation mark there, perhaps because it was an unusual name, or maybe because he couldn't believe this young person's advocate was involved. Maybe he wasn't involved. Ibbetson's name had been in the book and I doubted he knew much. I looked back at the smiling face of Champion Obote. He looked for all the world like a friendly, outgoing person; exactly the sort of person who would be great as a young person's advocate. I could imagine they would easily get along with him and looking at the eager faces smiling up at him, I didn't doubt for one minute the trust in their faces.

Chapter Thirty-One

I looked through the iPad and reviewed all the photos of Dr Neasden's notebook. I knew now, or was fairly sure that, the word "Champion!" referred to Champion Obote, the young people's advocate. He clearly had a connection with Darnold, working with some of the same young people. I had all the names to go with the initials. I had figured out the phone numbers, and I had found Stephen Ibbetson. I had worked it all out. Yet, somehow, I felt hardly any further forward than I had when I'd first looked through the notebook and understood none of it. I had no idea how Richard Sanderson and Kenneth Townsley fitted into any of this. I didn't really understand what Darnold was doing. I knew that between them they were covering up the fact that Dr Neasden had been shot, but I had no idea why. I had figured out who the players were, according to the notebook, but I didn't have any idea what it was they were playing in. I was shooting in the dark. Dr Neasden had given no clues as to exactly what was going on, just the people involved. Did they know what was in the notebook? Had Dr Neasden confronted one of them, maybe? And told them he had made notes? Clearly they wouldn't want their names to be connected with each other as that could lead a trail, a trail I was following. But perhaps they also thought that there was more in the notebook than just the names?

I went back to the counter and bought a revolting motorway service station sandwich. I forced myself to eat it, against my better judgement, as I hadn't a clue when the next time would be that I would get to eat, and I needed to have my wits about me. I needed the energy. I still had an hour to wait, so I picked up a tabloid that someone had left on the table to my left and read that. That was a distraction; flicking through the pages to see which group was being vilified today for not being white and middle class. I flipped past most of the propaganda and went more or less straight to the Sudoku and completed the easy one and the hard one. I left the really difficult one on the basis that I probably wouldn't finish it in time. I went off to the toilets, then steadied myself against the sink as I washed my hands and looked in the mirror. Nerves were eating at me; shivers shook my body and I struggled to focus on my reflection. I had no idea what I might be getting into, where I might be going, or what I might see; everything was an unknown. Breathing in deeply, I stood for a minute or two and let my heart rate slow down, and the shaking subside. Then I headed out to my spot at the top of the car park.

It was a good day for staking out. Well, I had never staked anything out before, but I assumed it didn't get much better than this. I looked up at the clouds. They didn't look like rain clouds but they also didn't look like they were going to clear away at any point that afternoon. Perfect.

I stood behind the car and wondered what someone would think if they saw me scanning the car park with a pair of binoculars. I was fairly well hidden behind the car. At 5'5" I was taller than the car, but just enough so that I could rest my chin on the roof and not be too conspicuous. I put my grey hat on and pulled it down over my ears. That way I would blend in even more with the car and the grey sky behind me. I took out the binoculars and focused on the entrance to the car park. Cars were coming in at a reasonable pace, but there was generally a gap between each one. I practised watching certain cars, watching them empty out and watching the driver, and sometimes passengers, getting out and going into the services. I tried it by looking through the binoculars and I tried without. I discovered it worked best if I watched the entrance without the binoculars to start with and then focused in on a particular car as they drove around and found somewhere to park. That way, I had time to note the registration number whilst they were finding a space, and then pick them out again with the binoculars as they were parking. I practised doing this with several cars until I had the timing down to perfection.

I wasn't really sure what I was looking out for. I could miss something completely. It could be that they, whoever they were, would go into the services and I would be none the wiser. I'd thought about this whilst I had been inside eating my horrible sandwich. I had thought about watching from the window of the services. I'd decided against that on the grounds that it would be much harder to be inconspicuous inside. I was also fairly sure if there was a "pick up," which was what I thought was going to happen, that it would happen in the car park. If they were handing over a package of drugs, they would be far more noticeable inside, and people would be much more likely to remember them. People chatting in the car park would be easily forgettable; people didn't really look around them as they hurried from their cars to the inside. The petrol station had CCTV so I had also ruled that out as a possible location. I decided to remain where I was. I could miss something but I was far more likely to see whatever was happening out here. I stayed put behind the hire car.

My other problem was that I had no idea who I was looking out for, nor what it was they were going to "pick up." I assumed that if there was some kind of exchange happening that I would notice a person, or persons, from one car approaching someone from another car. I decided that was the behaviour I would have to look out for. I knew the time of the meet was 2pm and I wondered if either party might arrive early so I was also keeping my eye open for anyone arriving in the car park and just waiting. It seemed that quite a few people took a while to get out of their cars. Perhaps they were putting sat navs out of sight, making sure they had their wallets or handbags, unbuckling their children or something. Down in the middle of the car park a man was sitting in his car for what seemed like ages. I started to get excited, scanning to the entrance, then back to him again. But then he got out, locked his car remotely, and marched off into the services.

I looked at the time on my phone; it was ten minutes to two. I started watching with more interest. A couple of cars pulled in together. They made for opposite ends of the car park. The doors of one car opened and a family got out—a surly teenager, a small child, and a screaming toddler. The mother dragged the screaming toddler along, eventually scooping him up and carrying him. The other car had a couple inside. They walked arm in arm into the services.

Another car had entered the car park. This one had a white lady driver. She parked as close to the entrance as she could and ran into the services. Probably desperate for the loo, I thought. I returned to the entrance. A black car was just pulling in, and I could see behind the wheel a black face, but the dull light from the clouds obscured it, reflecting on the windscreen. I quickly reached for my binoculars and my heart leapt, beating faster and faster. My legs buckled beneath me and I pressed onto the roof of the car with my elbows to stop myself from falling over. All my instincts were screaming at me to get out, go back to the services and hide, that I was in over my head and I should leave all this to the experts. I steadied myself and stood firm. *Shit, shit, shit. This is it, Verity. Keep your wits about you.* Without a shadow of a doubt, the man who was just pulling into the car park in a black A Class Mercedes was Champion Obote. Then it dawned on me. The text; *"Got it. C."* C for Champion. He was a few minutes early and he came through the car park towards me. I peered through the binoculars, and it felt as if he was looking directly at me. He seemed so close. I scribbled down his number plate and watched intently.

Chapter Thirty-Two

I t was only a couple of minutes and a few cars later that he stepped out of his car. I was trying to keep an eye on everything, looking backwards and forwards between Obote and the entrance. It was not an easy task. A grey BMW 5 Series had just pulled into the car park and parked a couple of lanes away from him. I'd noted down the number plate as it had entered the car park, as I had with the other cars that had entered in the last few minutes. Champion Obote got out of his car and answered a call on his phone. He was so tall it seemed as if he was unfolding as he got out of the car, like a beach umbrella being pushed up to full height. He looked round; clearly on the phone with whoever he was due to meet. A slim white man got out of the BMW and headed towards him, also on the phone, and Obote dropped the call, going over to meet him. I quickly scribbled out all the other number plates I'd written down so that I would know I had the right ones, Obote's and the slim man's.

The two men met in the middle of the car park and shook hands. The white man gently held Obote's elbow as they did so. A gesture of familiarity. They looked for all the world like a couple of friends, or business partners exchanging greetings. They stepped to one side next to an old red Ford Fiesta as another car pulled past them. Obote dwarfed the slim man, although I guessed he must have been about 6' tall. His smart suit flattered his slight frame. I scanned them from head to foot through the binoculars. Obote clearly worked out; he had the build of a boxer with his big arms and trim waist. His long hair fell down his back, tied at the nape of his enormous neck. The man he was meeting was a squirrel in comparison. He was facing my way, staring directly into the binoculars with his puffy, swollen face, his thick lips protruding above a small, round chin. He exuded an air of superiority, despite being several inches shorter than Obote, and I got the impression that whatever they were in together, he was higher up the chain.

I watched them as they exchanged words. Their hand gestures and smiles suggested friendly greetings. There didn't appear to be any disagreement or argument going on. After a couple of minutes, the white man returned to his BMW and opened the back door. My heart thumped loudly, pounding against the car with every beat. It surprised me that they didn't hear it, and turn round to look at me. What was he going to get? Perhaps he was reaching in for a packet of drugs. Maybe I should take photos on my iPad camera, but I didn't feel I had time to get it out of the rucksack and I wanted to carry on watching. I couldn't afford to miss anything.

I was expecting the man to lean into the back of the car, but he stood back and held the door open. I didn't know what I was expecting to see, but it hadn't been this. Two young boys, or they might have been girls, it was difficult to tell, climbed out of the back seats. They both appeared small and thin, but I guessed they were about fourteen. Their short hair made them look like boys, but their faces were soft and childlike and gave no clues. They were both white, and they stood nervously near to the car. They were wearing jeans and long-sleeved hooded tops and clutching something in front of them. Bags maybe, or another top. They looked lost, and neither man spoke to them. The white man merely gestured towards Obote, and the boys, or possibly girls, followed him.

The whole group went back to the Mercedes and the boys got in the back. Obote locked the car with the children inside whilst he exchanged a few more words with the puffy-eyed guy. This exchange had a less friendly feel than the initial conversation they had had. The white man was holding up a hand, and Obote was nodding and raising his eyebrows as if to say "yeah, I know," and the white man made an emphatic, palms down gesture with both hands. Obote nodded again, raising his hands and shrugging his shoulders. They stood there talking for a little while longer, and then they shook hands again. The white man went back to his BMW, and Obote watched him until he had driven away. He unlocked the car and folded himself back inside, closed the door, then drove off.

I dashed around the car, threw the binoculars onto the passenger seat, along with the number plates I'd scribbled down. I watched Obote pull out, and then I followed behind him. I repeated his number plate over and over so that it was indelibly stamped on my brain. I followed him towards the exit of the car park, staying a little way back so as not to look too suspicious. And then, just as I was passing the petrol station, an elderly woman driving a Nissan Micra pulled out in front of me, obscuring my view. At first, I thought that was not so bad because it would hide me from Obote and make it less likely that he would spot me in his rear-view mirror, but then the woman drove painfully slowly towards the exit.

Obote sped up and pulled into the traffic on the M1, but the Nissan Micra held back. I was getting anxious but there was no way to get past; the exit slip was only made for one car at a time. The traffic on the motorway sped past and the Micra pootled along nervously looking for a gap to pull into. I was jittering in my seat, willing it to pull out, or at least pull far enough along the slip road that I could move past. Cars were passing by in their dozens and I was feeling a sense of despair. After what felt like hours, the Micra eventually reached the part of the slip road that opened out slightly. I didn't care what the driver thought of me or my driving skills; I put my foot down, sped around the side of her, and shot onto the motorway to the blaze of a horn from the lorry that I had just cut up.

Chapter Thirty-Three

I got up to full speed as fast as I could. I wasn't
sure how long I had been waiting or how many
minutes Obote had on me. Neither could I
remember how far it was to the next exit, and I
needed to catch up with him before then or I wouldn't
be sure if he had turned off or not. I put my foot
down and pulled into the outside lane, overtaking
about four cars. I continued to repeat Obote's number
plate over and over like a mantra as I sped along,
trying to catch up with him. I prayed that he wasn't
driving really quickly; I imagined his Mercedes was
capable of much greater speeds than my Vauxhall and
he could have got away from me. I spotted what I
thought was a black Mercedes up ahead, but it was
some other model and I hurtled on past.

I was nervous and almost in despair. I couldn't
believe that I had let him pull away from me before
even the first hurdle. I was a rookie at this and I was
kicking myself that I hadn't waited until we were on
the motorway before putting some distance between
us. *Stupid woman.* Then, I spotted him. He was driving

along on the inside lane. I slowed a little and checked the number plate. Not that I needed to; the outline of his long hair and enormous body were clearly visible behind the wheel, but I wanted to be sure. I pulled into the inside lane, leaving a couple of cars between us. I was surprised that Obote was driving along at around seventy miles an hour, signalling clearly each time he overtook or pulled back in. But then, of course, if he was travelling with two young people who had been trafficked, I guessed he really wouldn't want to be pulled over by the police. He was doing everything perfectly legally and was driving so as not to draw any attention to himself.

I settled in behind him. Sometimes letting a couple of cars come between us and sometimes just one. I didn't want him to notice me. There were other cars about that had been driving along leapfrogging each other for a few miles too, so I didn't think he would have any cause to suspect that he was being followed. Even if he noticed a car behind he would just assume, as I did, that it was merely someone heading in the same direction as him.

We continued up the motorway for about sixty miles before we turned off at junction 21a, just past Leicester. I managed to follow him and stay a few cars behind. Luckily it was quite an easy junction so it wasn't too hard. I was thankful that there wasn't a large junction or traffic lights to negotiate after my last debacle. We were now heading up the A46; back up to Lincoln, I thought. It seemed feasible that whatever was going on was going on in Lincoln, so it didn't surprise me to be heading back that way. We kept on along the A46 for miles, driving impeccably. It was a hugely boring drive but at least there the odd roundabout to break up the monotony. It was getting hard to concentrate and I had to keep reminding myself, every time we came to a junction, to keep focused. Obote could turn off at any moment and I would need to be prepared to follow.

But he didn't turn off. We followed the A46 all the way to Lincoln. As we drove along the dual carriageway from Newark, I felt suddenly alert and interested, the boredom of the journey falling away. We had to be nearing our destination, so I'd have to keep my wits about me. I'd come all this way and I couldn't afford to lose him now. I overtook a couple of the cars I had kept between us and pulled in with just one car separating us. I sat up in my seat and really concentrated. We turned up the bypass, past Whisby Nature Park, the magnificent cathedral looming into view. It looked massive from this distance, dominating the city from the top of the hill with the houses tumbling down below it. On the second stretch of dual carriageway, Obote pulled into the right-hand lane and I followed, pulling in right behind him. I wasn't going to make the mistake I'd made in the service station and have someone hesitate in front of me. If the need arose I was prepared to jump a red light to keep up with him.

We turned off the bypass and drove into the city past the old racecourse. We negotiated the lights at the end of the road, turned left, then right, along past the Council Offices and through the city centre. As we approached the pedestrian crossing, I revved up my engine; people were about to run across between us and I sped up, narrowing the gap, not wanting to risk losing sight of the car when the road spread out into three lanes a little way further on. Some of the pedestrians no doubt thought I was being a bit reckless but I could live with that—I hadn't knocked anybody over.

The lights up ahead were red so I hung back a little, swung the sun visor down as far as it would go and pulled my hat down almost to my eyes. If Obote looked in his mirror he wouldn't be able to get a clear view of my face.

As the lights turned green, we carried on past the college. I didn't even glance at my place of employment. We drove on past the arboretum and then, a little further along the road, Obote indicated to turn right. I slowed down a little. I wasn't going to risk being too obvious. He drove about halfway down the road and parked on the left-hand side. There were one or two spaces on either side of the road, so I let a couple of cars go past me, and then pulled across and parked on the right.

Obote got out of the Mercedes and opened the back door. The two young boys got out, and he ushered them towards one of the houses, hustling them along the pavement and grabbing one of their arms as they got close. The houses were mostly terraced, with groups of five or six to a terrace and then a gap between the terraces. Obote took the boys down the side of the house at the end of the first set of terraces. The house had a slightly bigger garden than the other houses and a wall along the front. To the far side of the wall, at the front of the house, there was a gap that led to a path which ran along the side of the house and, presumably, to the back door. Obote took the boys down this path and disappeared from view.

Chapter Thirty-Four

I got out of the car, but didn't lock it. I figured that if I needed to get in it quickly and drive away, I didn't want to be fumbling for the key. I walked along the road and passed the house, peering down the gap between this one and the next. Obote and the children had disappeared, presumably inside. There would have been enough room to pull a car into the gap, but perhaps it belonged to next door. The wall that surrounded the house Obote had gone behind encompassed a path of about three feet that went around the side and to the back. There was no garage.

I thought about going round and having a look but I didn't want Obote to see me. I returned to my car and waited. I was feeling quite hungry now, my tummy letting out deep rumbling noises every few minutes. I had eaten nothing since the service station sandwich and that was about three hours ago now. I couldn't risk going to buy something to eat, though, so I sat and waited. It wouldn't be long before it got dark and I hoped Obote wouldn't be too long. Hopefully, he would be hungry too and want to get home and eat something.

A car further up the street pulled out and I parked in the empty space. I could get a good look at the house from there. I looked around, trying to take in every detail. Most of the houses had front doors which were next to each other, alternately on the left and right of the house as you looked at them. I assumed that each house would be a mirror image of the other. This house was at the end of the terrace and the door was on the left of the house; as it was the end house, it had no partner door like most of the others. It looked as if it might be slightly bigger than the others. There was a bay window in the front room to the right of the door and also on the bedroom above. The window directly over the front door was smaller and the windowsill was falling away in places. The whole house looked in desperate need of renovation. The paint was peeling off the window frames and many of the bricks had worn away. A piece of guttering hung from the corner of the roof and missed the top of the drainpipe so I imagined when it rained, the water would pour directly off the gutter and down the side of the house. Every window at the front had the curtains closed, and those in the front room were hanging off the rail in several places. I glanced around at the other houses in the street. Many of them were in a poor condition and this one didn't really stand out particularly. I didn't think anyone would notice that it looked neglected. My tummy rumbled as I sat in the car and waited. It was also getting colder as night was beginning to fall. I didn't want to start the engine just yet as I didn't want to attract any attention. So I sat there, shivering, waiting and looking.

Eventually, Obote emerged from around the side of the house. He didn't turn his head to look up the street; he just ran across the road and jumped into his car, driving to the end of the road where he indicated that he was turning left. As he pulled away, I turned on the engine and then waited until he had disappeared around the corner before pulling out and following. I was just in time to see him disappear left again up the street which ran parallel to the one we had just been on. I followed, hanging back a little and watched him turn right back onto Monks Road. I crept to the junction just in time to see him turn left again a few hundred yards further along. I knew those roads led nowhere so there was no rush.

The road went steeply uphill. It had a wall at the end with trees and waste ground beyond. There were terraced houses on both sides and everyone had their wheelie bins outside. Each house had a small yard at the front. Many had a wall along the edge of the yard with a gap leading six or seven feet up to the front door. Most of the walls were much deeper at the bottom end than the top as the road had such a sharp incline. Some people had rendered and painted the walls, others had knocked them down all together. Some of the gaps in the walls had had gates put across them of varying designs. Almost all the houses looked fairly well cared for, with plants in their front yards, or trees and shrubs. There was the odd "For Sale" sign. It was a pleasant residential street.

Obote drove about three quarters of the way up the hill, parked his car, and got out. He opened the boot and removed an overnight bag, or a sports bag, before locking the car with the remote control and disappearing into one of the houses on the right-hand side, close to the top of the hill. Once he was in the house, the lights at the front came on, leading me to presume that no one else was in there with him. I made an assumption that this was where Obote lived. I parked at the top of the road and walked back down to have a look. The wall around his house was a bit deeper than some of the others and it had a gate to the left which was open and pushed against the dividing wall with next door's. There were no plants in the yard, apart from the odd weed coming up through the concrete. The hallway light shone through the glass above the front door, but the front room was now in darkness. If Obote had any sense he would be in the kitchen getting himself some food.

There wasn't much to see, so I got back in the hire car and returned to the house Obote had taken the boys to. I must have only been gone for twenty minutes or so, but the road had filled up with cars in my absence and I had to park just around the corner. I grabbed my rucksack and put it on my back. I pulled my hat down over my hair and walked towards the house, thankful that my dark clothes would hide me a little. It was quite dark now and many of the houses had lights on. Quite a few had drawn the curtains but as I walked along the street towards the house, I caught a glimpse of several couples and families watching television or playing on video games, living normal lives. Envy gnawed at my stomach; I wanted to go to my own house only a short distance from here and watch something boringly normal like The X Factor Results. I'd never watched The X Factor before John had died, but since his death I had become quite obsessed with it and followed it every week. I never voted, although I got really cross when the public voted off the decent singers over the good looking ones. I'm not sure what John would have thought; he had an inherent loathing of all reality TV. I pushed that thought to the back of my brain; I couldn't afford to drop my guard and I certainly couldn't afford to be getting maudlin for home.

Chapter Thirty-Five

I got to the house and stood in front of it. It was all in darkness. For a moment I considered the idea of calling Charlton and letting him know where I was, but I couldn't think of how to phrase it without sounding like I was in a heap load of shit. I was, after all, definitely in a heap load of shit and was getting more nervous by the minute. I was fairly sure that he would tell me not to get involved any further, but I really didn't want anyone to talk me out of things now. A confusing mix of emotions swirled around inside me, anxiety and fear but predominantly curiosity and a need to see this through. If I had any chance of helping the children Obote had taken inside I couldn't hang about waiting for the cavalry to arrive.

I walked up the short path and tried the front door, probably unnecessarily pulling my sleeve over my hand just in case anyone came dusting for fingerprints later. What I hadn't noticed before, when looking from a distance, was that the front door had several locks keeping it firmly closed, at least three or four. It was well and truly shut and there was no way of getting in. I walked past the bay window and tried to peer through it and into the front room. The curtains had a small gap in the middle where they had come away from the curtain rail and didn't meet up properly but I couldn't see much; the room was in complete darkness. I carried on round the side of the house and into the back garden, which was completely overgrown, although it was hard to see properly in the dark. It wasn't large; it was about twelve feet to the fence at the end, and the lawn was about a foot high. The fence that separated the garden from the one next door was broken and falling down in places. There were a few shrubs and trees at the end of the garden and several bags of rubbish strewn about.

Everything was dark. I had expected there to be a light on somewhere in the house; I assumed the two boys that Obote had brought here were still inside, but the house was utterly black. I tried the back door. Again, as with the front door, several locks kept it firmly shut. It was a solid wooden door, so I went over to the window and peered in through that. The curtains at the window, unlike those at the front, had not been closed, so I got out my torch and turned it on. I held it flat against the glass so that the light would shine through. The kitchen was almost empty. The remnants of a fitted kitchen—cupboards and drawers—clung to the walls but there didn't appear to be any appliances. Paint was peeling off the walls, and the different shades of fading indicated where the fridge, washing machine, or maybe a cooker had once been. Bare electrical wires stuck out of the walls above dusty worktops. A serving hatch above the cupboards led through to the next room. It was closed and, although I couldn't see it clearly because of the angle, appeared to have a grill of some sort covering it. On the floor in the middle of the kitchen, a broom and a shovel lay discarded next to what looked like bits for an electric drill. The door at the far side of the kitchen, which presumably led to the hallway, was closed and across the top, middle, and bottom were industrial-strength bolts with locks that were keeping it that way. *Jesus, what is going on here?*

I moved on to the next window. This one was close to the fence of the next-door house so I turned the torch off until it was pressed against the window. I guessed that this room was supposed to be a dining room, but it looked as if it hadn't been used for ages. A table was folded up and shoved into one corner of the room. There was a step ladder in the middle of the room and in the corner what looked like tins of paint, or varnish, or something. The door through to the hallway was, once again, bolted shut with three massive locking bolts. I thought about the logistics of achieving this; someone must have put the bolts on this side of the door, then climbed through the serving hatch and into the kitchen, then put the grill over the serving hatch. I took a step back and let out a deep sigh, unease filling my body as I fought to prevent panic overtaking me. What on earth were they doing? Why bolt *children* into an unattended house?

The sound of voices jolted my attention away from the house. *Shit.* Voices that were getting closer, coming down the side of the house. I turned off the torch and ran to hide behind the shrubs in the corner of the garden. It was in complete blackness and thanks to my dark clothes, no one would be able to see me. There were two deep voices, and they sounded as if they were in a heated argument.

"Don't be stupid, there's no way you can do it, no way," said one of the voices and, as the men rounded the corner and approached the back door, I saw that this one belonged to Champion Obote.

Following Obote round the corner was a much smaller man who I recognised immediately from his photos as Adrian Darnold, and between the two of them was a young black girl. She looked about fifteen, but could have been younger. It was hard to tell with so little light. Obote fiddled with the locks on the door, undoing at least three, I lost count, before pushing it open. The kitchen light went on, and I moved forward a little. A bare bulb, one of those old-fashioned, high-energy types, hung from the ceiling. I had a perfect view inside the kitchen and I was sure they wouldn't be able to see me amongst the darkness of the garden. The girl was small and had long hair braided really closely to her head. She stared forwards into the dark, her pretty, petite face betraying no emotion at all. She stuffed both hands into the pockets of her trousers, bunching up her shoulders as she did so, and made no effort to move or speak. Obote locked all the locks on the back door behind him and then gave Darnold a glare. He grabbed the girl by her upper arm, unlocked and undid the bolts on the door to the hall, and then disappeared with the girl. Darnold pulled the bolts again once the girl and Obote had gone through the door. He paced around the kitchen, his lip drawing tighter together with each step. No lights came on further inside the house. Apart from the kitchen, the place was in darkness. I crept forward a little more, crouching behind a low shrub.

A few minutes later, a loud knock sounded from inside the house. Darnold unbolted the door and let Obote through, who then bolted and locked it behind him. Obote's brows knotted together, creating deep lines across his forehead. His lips curled back into a snarl. The two men turned to face each other. They were shouting but I still couldn't quite hear what they were saying, and I strained to catch the gist of the conversation. Both men gesticulated wildly; their faces contorted as they argued. It was clear that they were both furious. They were raising their hands, pointing, shaking their fists and their heads as they moved in a slow circle around the room.

Obote was screaming, "…can't just walk away… not as simple…" but each time he turned his head slightly, I lost a few words.

Darnold was bright red and spitting as he spoke, "…not his gofer…too big for his own…just ring me up…bring his kids back…"

I couldn't really follow what they were saying, but as the conversation got more heated their voices got louder. Obote looked even bigger as he pulled himself up and stood to his full height. Darnold was a good six inches shorter but he was shouting just as loudly. Their words were coming clearly through the glass now.

Obote snapped round to face in Darnold's direction. "You're in too deep already, you can't get out now."

"I don't care," Darnold spat the words out.

"You'll be ruined, you know he will see to that."

Darnold was so red I thought he was going to catch fire on the spot.

"Listen to me," he shouted. "I don't care. I've had enough. Covering a few things up, that's one thing, but these kids! They're *ill* for God's sake." He threw his hands up in the air in a gesture of despair. Whatever it was they were doing, he clearly didn't want any further part in it. He was getting louder, "I'm sick of him, thinking he can tell me what to do, expecting me to jump whenever he says."

"He *can* tell you what to do," Obote shouted back. "He's the one paying you to do it."

"Not anymore. I'm not doing it anymore. I won't make trouble for him. I'll resign from the force; I'll come up with a story. I won't implicate any of you sick bastards. Don't fret about that." Darnold made to go to the back door.

With one stretch of his massive arms, Obote caught him by his collar and dragged him back into the room. He said something to Darnold, but his voice had quietened down and I couldn't hear him.

Darnold span round on his heels so that he faced Obote, jabbing his finger in the air and shouting at full volume, "I'm out. I don't care if I lose my job. I don't care if I lose the money. This"—he gestured around him at the house—"is not worth it." And once again he made for the door.

"Get back here," Obote barked at him.

"No," Darnold shouted. "Tell Townsley from me, I'm out."

Darnold fumbled at the locks on the back door but he wasn't quick enough. Obote grabbed him and pulled him back into the room. Darnold tried his best to punch Obote in the face, but it had minimal impact. He pulled his arm back to punch him again, but Obote saw it coming and danced to one side, grabbing Darnold's arm as it swung past his face. He twisted the arm sharply as Darnold cried out in pain and pulled it up behind Darnold's back. Obote pushed him forward across the room, smashing his face into the corner of one of the work surfaces. He pulled him back up to standing, blood pouring out of a gash just above Darnold's eye. Obote crashed Darnold's face into the worktop again, and this time when he pulled him up his nose was twisted sideways and his face was covered in blood.

Obote let him go, moved away and circled round. He looked like a boxer preparing to strike. Darnold shook his head, trying to reorient himself ready for the next attempt, but he was being too eager, like a yappy little dog facing up to a Rottweiler. He kicked Obote in the shin, and it looked as if this might have worked. Obote seemed to lose his focus momentarily, and Darnold took advantage by punching him again, this time in the shoulder. Obote, however, quickly regained his control and charged at Darnold with his shoulder, pushing him back against the cupboard. Darnold appeared to be completely winded—he struggled to breathe and his hand went up to his chest. He staggered onto his feet and stepped forward a couple of paces. But Obote had been quick. He'd bent down and picked up the shovel. As Darnold approached, Obote took his arms back as far as they would go and swung the shovel with all his massive force against Darnold's head, which twisted horribly on his shoulders. An arc of blood spurted out from somewhere, his ear or the side of his head, and he dropped to the ground like a felled tree. I lost sight of him as he fell but Obote went over to him and swung the shovel once more at his head. It seemed to me that this was probably an unnecessary precaution given the angle that his head had twisted round to with the first blow. I shocked myself at the coldness of my thoughts, but I felt disconnected, almost as if I had been watching a movie. As the reality of what I had just witnessed kicked in, bile rose in my throat and I had to fight to keep concentrating and not give in to the urge to vomit. Obote stood up, looked as if he kicked Darnold on the floor, and then threw the shovel to one side. He wiped his hands on his jeans, undid the locks on the back door, switched off the light and then calmly left, locking the back door before scurrying down the side of the house.

Chapter Thirty-Six

I waited a moment to check that Obote had gone. I listened to the sound of a car engine start up and pull away, and then I gave it a couple of minutes to make sure that he wasn't coming back. I crept up to the house, lifted the torch up against the window and scanned the floor of the kitchen. Darnold was lying there, his feet hidden beneath the window but his body clearly visible. His head was twisted round in the most unusual way. My stomach churned when I saw it. I took a moment to catch my breath, moving away from the window and leaning my hands on my knees. I looked back into the kitchen. Darnold was staring lifelessly to one side, a pool of blood collecting beneath his head. There was no doubting that he was dead; not that I could have got in the house to do anything about it if he hadn't been. I went to the back door and tried it, but there was no way of opening it with all the locks and bolts it had. I peered once more through the window and Darnold was still lying there, staring off at nothing with his head at a bizarre angle.

I stood back and scanned the building. The house was quiet with no sounds coming from inside. I shone my torch up at the upstairs but there was no light and no signs of any life at all. I was more confused than ever. I knew there were people inside but there was no sign of anyone. What on earth could be going on? I knew that the only way to find out was to get inside, but there was no way I could get in without the keys. Even if I smashed a window, I wouldn't be able to get through the door into the hall. I presumed all the downstairs doors would be the same. *God, I hope there isn't a fire.* I had to get the keys, and to do that I had to get at Obote. I sighed at the thought and leaned against the outside of the back door. He was a foot taller than me and probably about a hundred pounds heavier. I would have to plan, and I would have to be careful. The thought of ending up in a pool of blood like Darnold made me shiver with fear.

I sat on the back step and thought about what to do. I needed to make sure that I knew what Obote was doing. Would he come and try to clean up? It was dark, and that would give him cover, but maybe he would figure that there was little chance of anyone finding the body during the night. Desperate as I was for a rest, I didn't think I could take the chance. Reluctantly, I got up and walked to my car. I slung the rucksack into the passenger seat and drove off back towards the city, parking in one of the small car parks. It was Sunday, and after 6pm, so there was no need to pay. I walked to Tesco Express and bought a few supplies—a take-away coffee, some sandwiches, crisps, sweets, some fruit, a couple of small bottles of no-calorie lemonade, and a couple of Snickers bars. I looked in my basket; having never staked anywhere out overnight before, I wasn't sure what I would need.

I thought about it and put the lemonade back. I wouldn't have access to a loo for a long time and I thought dehydration seemed preferable to wetting the seat of the hire car. Glancing around me at the people carrying on with their everyday lives, I watched them as if I inhabited a different dimension to them. The reality of what I had just witnessed hung over me, weighing down my shoulders. At the back of the shop somebody laughed, and I stared at them, observing what was happening without being a part of it.

After paying for my things, I walked over to the pub opposite and sneakily used their toilets. I grabbed a couple of handfuls of loo roll, just in case I needed to find a bush somewhere during the night, and stuffed them in my pockets. Then I walked back to my car and drove back to Obote's road. I drove at a crawling pace past his house. The light was on in the front room and Obote was sitting there alone. He looked like he was watching television; the flickering light reflected around the room. He had a can of beer in his hand which he was swigging as he watched. I drove on, turning round at the end of the road so that I was facing down the hill. I parked as close to the top of the hill as I could and sat and watched. I was outside a house which was for sale and looked empty. Nothing happened. I sat even longer. Still nothing happened. I guessed that Obote was now in his house for the night and I was in for a long and very boring, not to mention cold, night.

I revisited what had happened at the other house. My memory of Darnold and Obote's argument had been dimmed a bit by the events that had followed, but I tried to recall as much as I could. Thoughts of Darnold's head twisted round on his shoulders, and his staring eyes, came unbidden into my brain. I shook my head as if it might make the image fall out of my ears or something, but it didn't work. Each time the image reappeared I closed my eyes and breathed, concentrating on what they had been arguing about and trying to piece it all together. Darnold had wanted out. But out of what? He'd clearly been telling Obote to pass the message on to someone, someone who was too big for their boots. And the name he had mentioned was Townsley. And what were the children doing in a locked and bolted house? Darnold had said 'they're ill'; had he meant the children? Or had he meant the people keeping them there? He'd gestured round at the house when he had said he'd wanted to be out of "all this." Was what was going on centred on the house? Could they be using the children for prostitution? It was a horrible thought, but I knew from my research that that was a common—in fact the most common—reason that young people were trafficked into the country. Was that what was going on? Had the police been covering up a child sexual exploitation ring and Darnold had had enough? Would they be earning enough money from it to make it worth their while to kill Darnold to keep it from getting out? Probably, although more to the point, it would be very damaging. Townsley was a world-renowned and well-respected professor, researching treatments for cancer —if he were the head of something like that, then his career would be ruined if it came out. Not to mention the lengthy prison sentence that would be likely to be meted out.

But something was not right. Obote had said that Townsley had been paying Darnold; paying him to cover up, I assumed. Clearly he'd helped to cover up Dr Neasden's death, but something had pushed him too far. Something, worse than covering up a death, had made him want to get out. What could be worse than that?

By ten o'clock I had eaten the sandwiches and most of the fruit. I had also started on the crisps. I was cold and bored, but I didn't want to risk turning on the engine to warm myself up in case I attracted attention. So I continued sitting and watching. A man came out of a house further down with a small white dog. He led the dog up the hill and let it go on the wasteland behind the wall at the top. The man stood smoking a cigarette whilst the dog ran off for a last wee and a quick run around and then they returned to their home. That was the most exciting thing that had happened in the last three hours.

Whilst my attention had been diverted away by the man with the dog, the light in Obote's front room had gone off. It was gone 11pm and I guessed he was going to bed. Lucky him. An upstairs light was on—probably on the landing—and then the front bedroom light came on. Obote appeared briefly in the window, closing the curtains, and then after about fifteen minutes the light went out and the house was in darkness. I settled in for a long night, staring out into the darkness. A few drunken revellers walked past the end of the road, presumably on their way home. They looked like students, shouting and not caring that most of the people would be asleep. Their voices carried up the hill, and one of the girls let out a shriek of laughter.

There was little going on down Obote's street. Lights started going off in houses on either side. Occasionally a light would come on upstairs in one house or another. Presumably someone going to the bathroom, or possibly waking up to feed a baby. I wanted to turn the radio on to relieve the boredom but I didn't dare make any noise.

I weighed up my options, debating whether to call for help, whether to alert someone to the dead body in the house. But I knew deep down there was little choice but to deal with this on my own. I couldn't call the local police, because I had no way of knowing how many were involved. Dr Neasden had uncovered some of them, but who knew if there were others? His cryptic coding showed how fearful he had been of these people. And my experiences over the last week had confirmed that. Plus, I knew at least one policeman from Nottinghamshire was involved, so I couldn't even inform neighbouring authorities. "Trust no one," played over and over in my head as I gazed across at Obote's darkened house. I slunk down in my seat and closed my eyes, just for a moment. Just to rest them from staring into the darkness.

MONDAY

Chapter Thirty-Seven

I'm lying on the grass on a warm summer day, with my eyes closed. I've just finished a picnic with someone, although strangely I'm not clear exactly who. There's a lot of noise and I open my eyes to find a massive wasp in front of my face. I shout out and flail my arms, but it gets louder and bigger and more menacing.

I woke with a jolt, unaware of where I was. The dream dissipated, floating away from me like soft clouds as I dragged myself into the real world. Thoughts scrabbled in my head and I swivelled this way and that as I tried to make sense of my surroundings. A streetlamp overhead cast an orange glow into the car, and the blinking lights of the clock informed me that it was half-past four in the morning. A noise outside the car thumped me back into the present. I twisted around, trying to locate the source, as memories of the previous night came hurtling back. The noise came again, like a scraping. I peered around me. A shadow fell across the car, blocking out the light from above; I stared out through the back window and straight into the menacing eyes of a man.

My heart flipped up into my throat, and I drew in a sharp breath. As he bent down and squinted into the car, the sight did nothing to still the beating in my chest. This was the man who had peered at me in the shoe shop on Steep Hill, the man who had followed me after I'd fled my ransacked home. I wondered if it had been him who had done the ransacking. Still crouching forward, he took a step away and lifted a baseball bat out to his side. Everything slowed down. With a fearsome grin plastered across his face, he drew the baseball bat up in slow motion. I sat transfixed, unable to move. The bat smashed into the back window with a dull thud, the safety glass cracking into hundreds of pieces. They remained stuck together, held within the frame of the window. Another blow caused the glass to bend precariously into the car. The man stood away, as if admiring his work, and then he approached once again. I shouted at him, through a throat so tight that little more than a squeak came out and I just sat there, not knowing what to do.

He swung the bat again, hitting the rear lights and then the boot. Thank goodness for the extra insurance I'd taken out. He came round the side, leering with a blackened, toothless smile as he stared through the window of the back door. His arm formed an arc as he lifted the bat, then brought it down again on the side window. As this one was not safety glass, the window exploded into the car, sending glass flying all over the back seat and onto the floor. My body buckled as I jumped, almost hitting my head on the roof of the car. I thumped at my temple, trying to knock loose a sensible thought amidst the chaos. I had to do something. Fumbling in my rucksack, I located one of the bottles of home-made pepper spray. I grabbed one of the small knives and put it in my pocket, then stuffed the pepper spray into my right hand so that it was partly hidden up my sleeve. The man came further round the car towards the driver's door. The handle rattled as he tried to open it.

I barely had time to dodge out of the way, just managing to turn my back to the door, as the bat smashed into the window. The glass shattered into fragments, not shards; they weren't sharp but they went everywhere. They rained down on my head and the inside of my jacket, cascading down my neck and back and even into my shoes. As I sat upright again, the man leant through the door and opened it up. His horrible, toothless smile spread once again across his face. I tried to twist round to aim my pepper spray at him but he grabbed my arm and dragged me out of the car, throwing me onto the road. I gripped the pepper spray tight in my hand, not wanting it to roll away, and my knuckles scraped across the tarmac. A boot appeared by my head and the smell of stale tobacco wafted around as he bent down towards me, grabbing the back of my jacket and lifting my head and chest clear off the ground.

"Back off," he hissed in my ear, and then threw me onto the ground again.

I scrambled to sit up and as I turned, he took a swing with the baseball bat. I managed to roll out of the way so that it came down on the road and not my head.

Once again, he hissed through his barely there teeth, "If you don't want to end up like the last person who interfered, then take it from me…Back. Off." His voice was menacing, and the fact that he was so calm was frightening. I took it that he was referring to Dr

Neasden and I wondered if it had been him that had fired the fatal shot. I looked at his scruffy jogging bottoms and remembered the man who had pushed past me when I'd been on my way to the doctor's house, unaware of the carnage that would greet me. They could easily have belonged to the man who'd run past me down the hill, but I couldn't be sure.

I turned and sat up; he was swinging the bat again, ready to strike, and I was now up against the car so I had nowhere to escape to. I put the pepper spray in my left hand and reached in my pocket for the knife. As he lifted the bat, I pulled the knife back and sank it hard into his leg, just to one side of his shin bone. The bat clattered to the ground and he cried out, clutching at his leg. I took the opportunity and scrambled to a standing position, grabbing the bat as I moved. He snarled at me, his face just inches from mine. Holding his hands out in front of him, he growled and rushed forwards, as if he were going to push me back against the car. I let him come as close as I dare, and then I held up the pepper spray and pumped it into his eyes. The little pump action bottle did a sterling job. It wasn't as efficient as an aerosol, but it pumped the spray all over his face and coated his eyes. He clutched at the air in front of him, reaching for the bottle, but the spray worked almost instantly. And as he cried out, I pumped more of the spray into his mouth.

He fell to the ground, clutching at his face, drooling from the heat of the spray and clawing at his eyes. I grabbed my rucksack and the book that I had taped into the carrier bag. Lugging them up to the top of the road, I jumped over the wall and into the waste ground that stretched uphill beyond. I looked back. The man was still writhing on the floor; my pepper spray seemed to have worked well. In the dull light of the streetlamp, I could just make out the outline of the knife sticking out of his leg, but it seemed that the pain in his face was distracting him from that. I needed to hide; I was convinced the police would arrive soon. In fact, thinking about it, I was surprised that they hadn't already shown up. Perhaps no one had heard anything. The billowing wind would have carried the sound away from most of the houses, and the one I was parked outside was empty. The car alarm hadn't gone off because I'd been inside and I'd just locked my door manually, not with the remote. It didn't look as if disturbances were a usual occurrence around here. But then, I supposed if you heard some glass breaking in the middle of the night, you might just assume it was bottles or something. If I were asleep in bed, would I be bothered to get up to have a look and check it out? Maybe not.

Chapter Thirty-Eight

I glanced back at Obote's house. It was still in darkness. Had it been him who had realised I was outside? I thought I'd been really discreet, but perhaps sitting outside in a car all night was too much of a giveaway. Not for the first time, doubt and uncertainty gripped me; I had no idea how to progress. A pink glow to the east told me that it wouldn't be long before the sun rose above the city once again. I stood behind a tree and debated with myself about what to do next. Every muscle in my body was telling me to get further away but I needed to track Obote. I needed the keys to the house and he was the only link I had. The only way I could see was to wait for him to leave and then lay a trap for his return. He was a massive man who had killed someone with one swing of a shovel and I had to get the upper hand if I had any hope at all of getting the keys off him. I leaned against the tree and sighed. I really didn't want to be in the middle of all this. But what else could I do? I couldn't go back to my house until this was all sorted out or the chances were even greater that I'd go the same way as Neasden and Darnold.

I searched for a new vantage point. I could circle through this bit of ground, go back down the hill further along and watch the end of the road until I saw Obote leave. The advantage would be that I would be able to see what direction he went in. But my focus had to be, actually, when he came back. No, I would wait where I was. Here I could watch the door discreetly. I could make sure that he had gone and I could stay well hidden. The danger if I went to the bottom of the road would be that either he would see me, or someone else would see me loitering around; there was nowhere to hide down there and if the police did arrive, I'd be out in the open. Here, I could hide behind the trees and I didn't think Obote would come up and look for me. He'd make the assumption that his goon had frightened me away, or that I'd run off or something. And even if he did come up this way, the trees and the thick undergrowth would hide me. Unless he actually came determined to look in every corner, I had good cover. And I really didn't think that he would.

I sat on my rucksack behind the tree and fished out the bits of glass from inside my clothes and shoes. I watched as the light came up, gradually illuminating the street below. My knuckles throbbed where they had been ripped against the road. I wished I had thought to buy bandages and painkillers on my shopping expedition. I wrapped my scarf around my hand and tried to ignore it. At some point, the man who had smashed up the car had hobbled off down the hill. I wondered if he would call in at Obote's house, but he didn't. He didn't even give a sideways glance as he hopped past. I couldn't tell if the knife was still in his leg or not, but he was limping quite badly. He didn't look back up the hill to where I was standing. I wondered if he was connected to Obote and the mess they were involved in in any way, if he knew that Obote lived here, or whether he was just a hired thug who had been asked to batter a woman in a Vauxhall Insignia.

As the light came up, the street came gradually to life; curtains were thrown back, lights came on and then off again. More people were getting up and leaving their homes. It was Monday morning and people were going to work. Some left quite early; I assumed to either catch the train or start a shift somewhere, depending on the way they were dressed. Some carried small children and put them in cars or buggies and took them off to childcare. I felt sad for a moment that this would be something I would never experience. Then one of the toddlers started screaming and refusing to get in the car, the mother running her hand through her tousled hair, and I felt more relieved than sad. A postman came up the hill and then down again, calling in at several of the houses along the way, sometimes causing a dog to bark from within the house. Obote got no mail that day. People didn't seem to notice the broken and battered car. Maybe it was because it was parked near the top of the hill so most of them didn't actually go past it. Maybe people thought it was none of their business. Maybe it wasn't an unusual sight. Although I was pleased that no one seemed to care about it, or think it was anything to do with them, I thought it was a sad reflection of society that I could have ended up with more than bloodied knuckles and nobody would have done anything about it.

After the initial flurry of activity, the street

quietened down a little. The sounds of a school nearby filtered over, children running and shrieking in the playground; then a bell and quiet once more. I sat and watched Obote's house in the near silence, hidden behind the tree, only leaving my post for a brief few seconds to answer nature's call. I couldn't afford to move again. I needed to get the keys to the house; I needed to figure out what was going on, and for both of those things I needed Obote. I still wasn't quite sure how I thought I was going to overpower him, but I pushed that thought to one side. I had no alternative. Whilst I waited, I tried to come up with a plan. It wasn't a particularly well-formulated plan, as there were a number of unknowns to contend with, but it was the best I could do.

Chapter Thirty-Nine

It was about 11am when Obote's front door opened and he emerged. He zipped up his light-weight jacket and pulled the collar up around his neck, then locked the front door, making me even more convinced that he had been in there alone. As he approached the front gate, he rummaged in all his pockets. Clearly he'd forgotten something, and he returned to the house, leaving the front door open before re-emerging a few seconds later. Without a glance at either his car or the battered hire car, he scurried off down the hill, crossing the road halfway down and then he turned right at the end. He was heading in the direction of the house with the young people; the house with Adrian Darnold's twisted body on the kitchen floor. I waited about fifteen minutes so that I could be sure he wasn't about to return for another forgotten item, and then I came out from my hiding spot behind the tree.

I looked around. The street was pretty much deserted. Everyone seemed to have gone to work, or school, or be inside their house. I carried my things down to Obote's house and crouched down behind the garden wall. It was about four feet high at its deepest so it was a good cover. Plonking myself down on the ground, I got my things ready. I put the book that I had Sellotaped into the carrier bag on the ground next to gate. I got out the full bottle of pepper spray and put that down next to the book, along with one of the knives with a six-inch blade and one of the pairs of handcuffs I'd bought in Ann Summers. I took out the gun, which had no bullets in it, and tucked it into the top of my trousers, sticking over the waistband, a bit like Clint Eastwood might do.

Then I studied the gate; it was open and resting against the wall between Obote's and the house next door. Some sturdy hinges attached it to a post that ran up the inside of the wall. They looked in reasonable repair. Another metal post was attached to the brickwork on the other side of the gap and this housed the closure mechanism. I fished out my clear curtain wire and stretched it across the gap, hesitating a while about attaching it to the gateposts. It worried me that Obote would see it. But then, when you walked to your door along the same path every day, did you always look down? I thought about it and decided, on balance, that it would be worth it. I guessed that, if Obote saw it, I would at least have a warning that he was here, and I could try to get him with a knife to the calf like the toothless thug from last night. So I crawled over towards the gate without putting my head above the level of the wall.

I attached the wire easily around the post that supported the gate. There was a gap of about half an inch and it was easy to thread the wire through and wrap it round the post a couple of times. I tied and retied the knot and positioned it so that it was behind the post to make sure it wouldn't be visible from the road. It took me a lot longer to attach the wire to the other side of the gate. There was hardly any gap at all between the wall and the gatepost and I had to thread the wire painstakingly through. There was a fastening about six inches above the ground and I pushed the wire through the gap just above this, pushing it a little at a time until it was past the post and then pulling it hard to tighten it. When I had wrapped the wire a couple of times around the post, I pulled it as tight as I could make it and then tied it off and hid the knot, just like the other side.

I crawled away to the far side of the yard and looked back at the gate. The wire was visible, but only just, and I knew that it was there. The distance between the front gate and the front door was probably about five feet. If Obote fell flat on his face, he would actually hit the front door as he was so tall, but I didn't think he would fall completely on the ground, so I would have to move really quickly. Thankfully, I would have the element of surprise. I certainly didn't think he would be expecting me to be waiting with my makeshift armoury, especially if he was behind the attack on me and my car last night. My knuckles were swollen and raw, the skin hanging off several of them. Hopefully, I could do this without wounding them any further. I stuffed my bloodied scarf into my rucksack —I didn't want to have anything around me that Obote might be able to use to hurt me.

I sat down on the ground behind Obote's wall and surveyed my weapons—a book, some homemade pepper spray, a gun with no bullets, and a knife. I sighed, hoping it was enough. Reaching back into the rucksack, I fished out one of the other knives and tucked it into my sock just in case I needed something extra. I touched everything, making sure that my hands knew exactly where everything was. I couldn't afford to make a mistake. Obote was huge and not afraid to kill. If I gave him a chance he'd have the upper hand in no time and I didn't want to risk Townsley having the chance to sign off my death as natural causes.

The noise of footsteps drifted up from further down the road. I held my breath but then realised that the footsteps were accompanied by the sound of wheels rolling along the pavement. A buggy I assumed. The footsteps stopped before the house, and then a series of sounds—a mother talking to the child in the buggy, the cooing of an infant, a door opening and closing, then the stillness returned. It was irritating that I couldn't risk putting my head over the wall; not only because Obote might see me, but also because I didn't want anyone else to see that I was here. This was, thankfully, a quiet road, but people might get suspicious if they saw me peeping out from behind the wall.

I waited patiently for over three hours, my bottom gradually going numb with sitting on the cold ground. I was bored beyond description, sitting there staring at the front of the house; but I couldn't risk getting my iPad out to amuse myself because I couldn't afford to be distracted. I had to stay alert. My only chance of getting the better of Obote was to be ready to pounce the minute he arrived. I needed to surprise him. So I sat and counted the bricks in the wall, and the blades of grass in the yard to try to maintain my alertness.

Then, after all the waiting—footsteps. I knew immediately it was Obote. The firm, regular footsteps belonged to someone with a long stride and they were walking purposefully up the hill. I took hold of the carrier bag and waited, holding my breath and sitting perfectly still.

Chapter Forty

Time slowed down. I seemed to be sitting in a vacuum; the air rushing past me, the leaves blowing across the yard in slow motion. The footsteps progressed, heavy and slow. They were loud, and getting louder. It was all that I could hear. *Thud, thud, thud.* Like a giant from a fairy tale stepping up the hill. There was no other noise. Silence apart from the footsteps. What probably took seconds—from the time I'd heard the footsteps to the time I saw Obote's toe through the gap in the wall—seemed to take minutes. I had been holding my breath for way too long. Then, all of a sudden, things changed. Everything whooshed into sharp focus as the adrenaline my body was producing hit my brain. The world was still operating in slow motion, but every detail was crystal clear.

The toe of Obote's right shoe appeared in the gap in the wall. It was a dark brown leather toe. Expensive shoes; beyond the budget of a young people's advocate. These were the shoes of someone being paid off. The full shoe and the bottom of Obote's jeans came into view and then his shin caught on the wire and

Obote fell forward. His massive body fell heavily through the gap and onto the path. He fell onto his left knee, his leg buckling underneath him as the wire disturbed his natural momentum. His right leg folded and his arms went out in front of his chest to stop his fall. He was unaware of what was happening, tumbling to the ground.

I jumped up. Before he even had a chance to turn his head, I sprang over to him. I swung the carrier bag at the side of his head and it twisted to the left as the heavy book made contact with the right-hand side of his face. He looked to the side with a dazed expression, and I swung again, this time hitting him on the back of the head as hard as I could. He fell forward, trying to turn around, trying to see what was happening and who was behind him, clearly a little stunned from the two blows. I snatched up the pepper spray and as he moved his head towards me, I pumped the spray action of the little bottle as fast as I could into his eyes and nose and mouth. He choked and spat, shaking his head.

I picked up the handcuffs whilst he was trying to rid his facial orifices of the pepper spray. He yanked his wrist away as I tried to grab it to attach to one end of the handcuffs; even with the distraction of the pepper spray and some harsh blows to the head, he was strong. I hadn't incapacitated him as much as I had hoped. Even though he couldn't open his eyes, he scrambled for my knee and pulled it sharply from under me. I fell, hard on the concrete floor, cracking my shoulder against the wall. The pepper spray rolled out of reach across the yard as I desperately tried to keep hold of it. I fumbled to grab the bag with the book, but he was dragging me by my leg and it slipped out of reach. I clawed at the ground, desperately trying to hold on to something but there was nothing within reach. All I managed was to clutch hold of the gun in my waistband. A gun with no bullets; great.

As he pulled me closer to him by my leg, I managed to twist round. He was still struggling to open his eyes, drool pouring down his chin from the spray. I drew my other leg up and, with as much force as I could muster, I brought the heel of my sturdy boots down straight onto his knee cap. He let out a sharp cry and released my leg. Whilst he bent over and took hold of his knee, I hit him again with the butt of the gun. He gave another yelp and turned his head upwards, furiously blinking as if he were trying to diminish the pain in his eyes. I wanted to tell him to be quiet, or someone would start taking notice and call the police, but instead I raised the gun. He was clutching at his knee with his right hand and leaning on the floor with his left, he hadn't noticed the gun yet. I lifted my foot up again, and this time I stamped it down on his left hand. There was a crunching sound that made my stomach churn; I'd definitely broken something. I scrambled far enough away from him to make sure that he couldn't reach out for me again and, maintaining a crouching position behind the wall, I pointed the gun at his head. There was a trickle of blood coming from his forehead; I'd caught him just above the eye with the handle of the gun. I'd hoped to knock him out, but he was a massive man and it would clearly take more than a couple of blows to the head. As he struggled to open his eyes, he looked at me through what must have been very blurred vision.

I had to bluff. I had to hone my newly discovered talent to lie and I prayed that he didn't spring for me. I hoped my tough-girl act would wash. I continued holding the gun at his head as steadily as I could and reached for the pepper spray with my other hand. I was about four feet away from him; just too far for him to try to reach and grab the gun. I held it up, and as he caught sight of it, he flinched. A flicker of something, fear perhaps, crossed his face. His eyes were regaining some ability to focus, but he was still struggling to keep them open for more than a few seconds. I had to take my chance.

"What's going on, Obote?"

His eyebrows lifted and his mouth opened, as if it surprised him that I was calling him by his name. He shook his head but said nothing. I had to bluff as much as I could. And that meant faking a little bluster and bravado.

"What is Townsley up to?"

He shook his head once more; but I'd surprised him again by mentioning Townsley's name. He wiped his chin with the back of his good hand and then cradled his bad hand in his arm.

"What is going on with the children in the house?" I got up onto my knees and knelt on the floor. I put the pepper spray down and held the gun with both hands outstretched in front of me. "Look at me!"

He moved his head in my direction and tried to focus.

I held the gun so that it was pointing at his kneecap, the one I hadn't just broken. "Obote, tell me about the children."

"Who are you?" he rasped, barely able to speak.

"Who am I? I'm a fucking interested bystander, that's who I am. Now, tell me about the children." I surprised myself with how confident I was sounding. I was feeling anything but.

He tried to focus on the gun. "They're ill," he said,

his voice like sandpaper. I guessed the pepper spray must have burnt his throat a bit.

"Ill? How so?"

"I'm not telling you anything, you're not my boss, you're not paying me." He struggled to get the words past his throat.

"Well, if you hadn't noticed I am currently pointing a gun at you, so perhaps it might be better to worry about that later." There was a slight crack in my voice and I hoped I sounded suitably convincing. "How is Townsley involved?"

He looked up and blinked into the light, still struggling to open his eyes, which were red and swollen and weeping down his cheeks. He wiped his nose with his sleeve. His whole face was blotchy and swollen. I indicated the pepper spray. He understood.

"Townsley is treating them. It's his research," he said, and then added sarcastically, "He's going to cure the fucking world."

"Cure the world? What's he researching?"

"Cancer."

Townsley, the cancer specialist. Of course. His biography said he was leading some research. But it still didn't add up.

"Why are you keeping them in the house?"

He shook his head. He spat out into the yard and wiped his mouth again with the sleeve of his jacket.

"They're not supposed to be here, are they?" I offered.

He shook his head again, more to say no than to refuse to answer this time.

"Is someone trafficking children here? Children with cancer? And then Townsley is treating them?"

"Townsley. He arranges it all. He has contacts. They bring him the kids."

Contacts. Of course; I remembered the man in the car park.

Obote coughed and spat again.

"And he treats them?" I asked.

He nodded.

"Hasn't anybody noticed?"

"Why would they? He sees people all day long."

The well-respected Professor. Why would anyone take any notice of him treating patients?

I changed course a little. "What kind of cancer?"

"I don't know."

I pushed the gun a little closer, and he said it again, louder, "I don't know."

Jesus. Townsley was treating young people who were here illegally, as part of his research. *Bloody hell.* And if he found a treatment that worked effectively, he could make a fortune. Drugs were worth millions.

"Why are they locked up?"

He shrugged. "They need the treatment."

"But why lock them up?"

"To make sure they take the treatment and get to appointments."

Is that what Darnold was doing when he took the young girl to the house? Was he bringing her back from an appointment? I almost said something, but then I thought that now was probably not the time to let Obote know I had seen him kill Darnold, so I didn't ask that question.

"You don't want them to get away?"

He shook his head again. Through the mess of his swollen face, he looked sad. He was supposed to be an advocate for young people. I remembered the children smiling up at him in the photo. I could imagine that he had been tempted by the money he'd been offered to get involved but had then got into something beyond his depth.

I whispered almost, "But what if there's a fire?"

He glanced up at me. The light in his eyes obviously hurt and he immediately looked away again. I don't think he had thought about that before. He slumped a bit. He seemed resigned; he blinked up again at the gun.

"Where does Townsley see them?"

"Fuck off and leave me alone and stop asking questions."

That irritated me. Before he could open his swollen eyes, I lifted up one of my legs and brought my heel down onto his already broken hand. It crunched again and he winced in pain. I picked up the pepper spray and prepared to pump it into his eyes again.

"Where does he see them?" I hissed between clenched teeth. Luckily, my anger was compensating for my fear and keeping any self-doubt out of my voice.

Silence.

"Don't make me use the pepper spray again, Obote."

He whispered, "He sees them at the hospital."

"Where? Does he have a clinic? A surgery?"

He shook his head. "No, he sees them later, in the evenings. When it's quiet."

"Where?"

"In the outpatient's unit."

"Outpatients?"

"Yes, they finish in there by the end of the afternoon. He has some rooms there." He made a half-laughing sound and rolled his red and puffy eyes. "He can do what he wants," he said, with a note of bitterness ringing through his words. He spat again, perhaps to get rid of the remains of the pepper spray, perhaps in contempt of Townsley. "He could ask for the moon and they'd give it to him. He boasts about it; he thinks it shows how important he is. They think he's God. His research brings them big money. They need to keep him happy." He clearly had no respect for him at all.

I got the impression that Obote would be glad if Townsley was exposed and this whole thing could shudder to a halt. He was now guilty of murder; maybe he realised it had all gone too far.

"Every evening?"

"Most. He sees them one at a time."

That would make sense, I supposed, in terms of them not being able to run away or compare notes. If they were isolated, they were less likely to be able to find safety in numbers.

I gathered my thoughts. Townsley was seeing the children in the evenings when the hospital was quiet and the research was happening without anyone knowing. At least without anyone knowing who the subjects were. If he could lie about other stuff like the cause of Dr Neasden's death, then what was to stop him lying about who he was treating? I doubted that using illegally trafficked children as part of a research study would be viewed particularly well by the ethics committee. It would completely discredit him. I also wondered about the children's families; had they paid for their children to be sent to the UK in the hopes that they would be cured? Had they struggled to find the money? Or got into debt to do so?

"What's the treatment? The research? Is it working?"

"He says he hasn't got it quite right yet."

"So the children aren't getting better?"

"Not all, no."

I struggled to focus. I needed to keep the gun pointed firmly at Obote but I felt like sinking to the ground. He sounded weary now, as if he'd had enough too. But I really needed to do something, and quickly. I toughened up.

"Give me the keys to the house."

"No." He hung his head down so that he could keep his eyes open a bit more.

I moved closer and pointed the gun directly at his good knee cap. "Obote, give me the keys. Don't make me shoot your other kneecap."

He sighed. He seemed resigned, as if he had thought that things would be found out eventually. I put the gun closer to his knee. His eyes flicked up to meet mine. My heart flipped. I thought he was going to dare me, but he looked down and fished into his pocket. I glared at him, as if I shot people in the kneecap on a regular basis. Or at least, that was the look I was aiming for.

He handed me a bunch of keys. "My house keys are on there," he said.

"I don't think you'll need them for a while." I reached down, all the while maintaining my stare into his eyes and with the gun pointing at his knee. I picked up the handcuffs. "Give me your wrist."

Once more, he shook his head. I pointed the gun back at his head.

"Oh, Obote, don't play silly buggers, come on for crying out loud." I aimed the gun back at his knee. It seemed like a more realistic menace.

He shrugged his shoulders and held out his hand. I didn't think he really thought I was going to shoot him in the head, but he seemed to be taking my threat on his knee a little more seriously. I put the handcuffs round his wrist with one hand. I surprised myself at how steady I could keep my hand. I was still crouching and I had the gun close to him. I quickly put the other end of the handcuffs around the gate and locked them, and then I backed away, wanting to get well out of reach in case he tried to kick the gun out of my hand and disarm me. If he found out it had no bullets in it, heaven knew how he would react. He rattled the handcuff against the gate and they sounded surprisingly secure.

"Now, give me your phone."

"What?"

"I don't want you ringing anyone the minute I leave you here."

He looked down and said nothing.

"Obote, for fuck's sake just give me your sodding phone."

He carried on looking at the ground.

I hissed at him through clenched teeth. "Obote, if I have to fucking kill you I will and then I will have to rummage through your pockets for your phone. One way or another I will get it, so give it to me now."

I had handcuffed his good hand up, and his other hand wouldn't work properly. I wasn't sure if he had broken a finger or two, or some bones in the main part of his hand but he clearly couldn't use it. That was good; it would hold him up for longer.

"Tell me which pocket it is in."

With his head he indicated his jacket pocket so, being sure to keep the gun pointed firmly at his head, and keeping my crouching position, I moved round and felt in his pocket. I pulled out a Samsung smartphone, which I put in my pocket. I looked at the key ring; it had about a dozen keys on it.

"Does this have all the keys for the house?"

He nodded.

"Including the inside bolts?"

He looked surprised, raising his eyebrows high, but nodded again. I thought he was about to say something, ask me how I knew maybe, but he stayed silent.

I kept the gun held up and felt in his other pockets, patting the pockets of his jeans and rummaging through his jacket. I found a wallet in his jacket, which I threw over to my rucksack, but nothing else. No other keys. I guessed he was telling me the truth. I backed away and when I was right across the yard, too far for him to reach, I began to gather up my things and put them back in my rucksack. I stuffed his keys and wallet in my pocket next to the phone. Finally, I lowered the gun and placed it in the rucksack with everything else.

I found my phone and got it out ready and then I zipped up the rucksack, picked up the carrier bag which had the book inside, jumped over the wall and, without a backwards glance at Obote, I left. I hoped it would take him a long time to alert someone's attention and to get free. I figured he wouldn't be in a hurry to call the police, although I obviously wasn't sure if Darnold was the only bent policeman around, and Obote could have other contacts.

I had no time to lose I had to get to the house as quickly as I could, and I had to go alone. I just didn't know what else to do. Charlton was at least a couple of hours away, and what good would it do to call him? If he was fearful for my safety, which, frankly, he ought to be, then he might call the local police to try to help out. And then we were back to not knowing which of them we could trust. That might make things even more dangerous. I had to make sure the children were out of there as soon as I could. And definitely before Obote could get free and alert someone. He might just recover his resolve and want revenge. I wouldn't want to come across him when he was angry. I'd seen what he'd done to Darnold; I had only got the better of him because I'd waited for him and surprised him.

I got a move on.

Chapter Forty-One

After I had leaped over Obote's wall, I started running down the hill. I ran as fast as I could go, crossing the street and heading towards the house where the children were. As I ran, and without stopping, I dumped the carrier bag with the book inside in a bin at the side of the road. I got out my phone and paused briefly whilst I found Collette's number and punched "call" as quickly as I could. *Pick up. Pick up.*

She picked up after a few rings, clearly not recognising the number that had called her. I couldn't even remember if I was ringing her on my newest phone, or the first one I'd bought. I began running again and shouted into the phone.

"Collette, it's me. I need you to do something. It's urgent—"

She interrupted me, "Vee? What are you on about? Where are you—?"

This time I cut her off. "I don't have time to explain. You have to trust me. Honestly, Collette, this is the most important thing that I have ever asked you to do." I stopped running and stood still. "Collette, I need you, really badly. I need you to help me. No questions. I don't have time to explain, okay?"

She sounded unsure. "Okay?" I had stunned her into silence.

"Listen, Collette, I need you to get hold of Robert and Keith. I need you to meet me at a house." I gave her the address. "And, Collette, I need you all to get there as soon as you can. Tell Robert and Keith to come in separate cars. Have you got that?"

She repeated the address. "Separate cars? What if they are at work?"

"Collette, they have to come. This is really urgent. If they're at work, tell them to leave." I quietened down. I didn't want her to think I was being over-dramatic but at the same time I wanted her to get a sense of the urgency. I couldn't afford for her to not believe me. She had to come to the house, and she had to get the guys there too.

"Collette, it could be life or death, please."

"Verity? What? What did you just say?"

"Just do it. Now. I can't waste any more time. Honestly, it is really, really important. Do it. Collette, please." And I put the phone down. I didn't have time, and it certainly wasn't the place to feel guilty about being so abrupt with her. I just hoped she'd come through for me.

I started running again. I ran along the road, ignoring all the stares and I turned into the road the house was on. Thank God the whole trip was down-hill, but even so, I was seriously out of breath by the time I reached the house. *Maybe I should use my gym membership to do some actual exercise rather than just sitting in the sauna.* I ran around the back and, before I attempted to open the door, I looked through the kitchen window. There was no sign of Darnold's body. Obote must have been round and done something with him this morning. Unless someone else had been called to come during the night to get rid of him. The kitchen looked clean; whoever had come round had washed all the blood away too. There was nothing to suggest that there had been a fight here, let alone a death, the night before.

I fumbled with the locks, no longer concerned about leaving fingerprints; I just wanted to get inside. There were about a dozen keys on the key ring and I had to try each of them in four different locks. I kept forgetting which keys I'd tried and it took me ages to get the right ones for the right locks. Eventually, I had all four locks open and I cautiously opened the door. The kitchen stank of a potent mixture of cleaners. I guessed I had to be grateful that someone had been and cleaned up, otherwise I would have had the stench of death and a dead body to contend with. It would also have made things very difficult to explain when, or if, Collette and the others turned up. They might have taken a negative view of leaving a dead body lying in a kitchen and not reporting it to the police. I glanced around the kitchen—there was nothing much to see that I hadn't been able to see from the outside. There was a sink below the kitchen window, with units beneath it that had no doors. A sponge and a pair of rubber gloves lay on one of the shelves and several half-empty large-sized containers of what looked like industrial strength cleaners, but nothing else.

I moved across the kitchen to the door that led through to the hallway. I found the key for the bolts reasonably quickly and, luckily, the same key fitted them all. I turned the three bolts and opened up the door. A strong smell of faeces and urine stung my eyes, making them water and I brushed away tears with the back of my hand. It took a moment for my eye to adjust to the darkness of the hallway, so I stayed where I was for a second, glancing around me. I knew the door immediately to my left led to the dining room, and I also knew it was bolted from the other side. The kitchen and dining room doors were close together at this end of the hall, and the hall then stretched away towards the front door. To my right a door led to an under-the-stairs cupboard. The door was open, but the only thing inside was an old iron bed frame. Along the hallway there was a door on the left just before the front door. This had to be the front room. I tried the door but it was locked. Probably bolted from the other side again. I imagined someone attaching the bolts, and then what? They had to have climbed out of the bay window and shut the windows somehow from the other side.

I turned towards the stairs, took hold of the banister, and slowly began to climb. There was no carpet but the wood was painted white at the edges, as if the carpet that had been there before hadn't quite reached the edges. The stairs creaked and cracked as I climbed them and I wondered what the children were thinking. I assumed they were still here. Oh my God, I hadn't thought of that; my stomach lurched. What if they weren't here anymore? What if Obote was sending me on a wild goose chase?

"Hello!" I shouted out, but there was no reply, just silence. I carried on climbing. The stairs turned sharply at the top at a ninety-degree angle and led to a long landing which ran along the length of the house with two doors off to either side. I pushed the first door to the left, which was open. It was a bathroom, but clearly hadn't been used for ages. The smell of shit was not coming from there. Some sort of grill covered the window, similar to the one that was in the serving hatch between the kitchen and the dining room.

I looked down the landing. The other three doors were all bolted from the outside. "Hello," I shouted again, but again there was no response. I paused and listened, but I couldn't hear a thing, not a single sound. I tried the door opposite the bathroom, the first door to my right. The bolts were closed and locked so I found the keys and used the bolt key to unlock them. This was the room that was directly above the front door. Gingerly I opened the door but there was nothing in there; the room was completely empty. This was a small room, little more than a box room. Then I noticed the windows. There were bars on the inside of the windows. *Bars for heaven's sake.*

I carried on down the landing. I undid the bolts on the next door on the right and cautiously entered. Again, it was empty. I glanced around; it did look as if there had been someone here at some point, but I wasn't sure how recently. There was a soiled mattress on the floor and some filthy bed linen slung over to one side. But there was no one in here now. I was in despair. Obote must have let me come here, knowing that the children weren't here. Where could they be? He had said Townsley saw them in the evening, but perhaps he had been telling me a pack of lies to throw me off the scent. I turned to the last door. This one was next to the bathroom and would overlook the back garden. I unlocked the bolts, slid them across the door and slowly opened it. I stopped, open mouthed. *Oh. My. God.*

Chapter Forty-Two

What I saw made little sense. I scanned the room to try to comprehend what was in front of me. The stench was overwhelming. I gagged, trying not to throw up. The smell of ammonia from urine stung my eyes, and tears began to flow, unbidden, down my cheeks. The smell of faeces overpowered the smell of urine and together they formed a fowl, rancid odour that invaded every part of me. In the room, by the far wall, a double bed mattress lay on the floor. It had no sheet or cover and was hideously dirty. A couple of overflowing potties sat in the corner and next to them a bin with used toilet paper spilling out onto the floor. And there, sitting on the mattress, huddled together and blinking at me with wild, open eyes, were five young people. There were the two boys, or girls, I still couldn't quite tell, I had seen Obote pick up in the Toddington services car park yesterday afternoon, the black girl I had seen brought round by Darnold the previous evening, a young white boy who looked about twelve, and an

Asian girl, perhaps from Vietnam or Cambodia or somewhere similar. She had a tiny frame but appeared a bit older than the others, maybe sixteen or seventeen. They all stared at me with their questioning, terrified expressions and I instantly knew that they had all suffered horrors I couldn't even imagine. The scars were writ large across their faces.

This room, like the other bedrooms, had bars on the windows; these kids had no chance of escape. In the corner of the room an old television played some daytime drivel. It had a coat hanger for an aerial and the signal was really poor. There was nothing else to keep these children amused; no books, no games, no cards, nothing. There was no light bulb in the fitting and there was a makeshift shutter behind the bars of the window, meaning that the only light was coming from the flickering television. Presumably the shutter had been put there to prevent anyone from seeing any light that the television might throw. I ran across the landing and opened the opposite door to give a little more light. I ran back and glanced around the room. Scattered about the floor were a number of empty pill bottles. I picked one up; it had a name on it that I couldn't pronounce and the name of a drug which I didn't recognise. There were more bottles lining the windowsill, only these were full of pills. I looked back at the frightened children. I had to get them out of here fast.

"I've come to help," I said, directing it at no one in particular, and wiping the tears off my cheeks.

I was rewarded with blank, scared stares.

"I'm here to help you," I said it slower this time.

Still the blank stares.

"Do any of you speak English?" I asked.

The children shuffled about. One or two had understood that. I asked them again and then one of the young people that Obote had picked up sat up.

"A little," he said with a heavy Eastern European accent.

I crouched down so that my face was closer to his and asked him what his name was.

"My name Andrei."

Definitely a boy then. "I want to help. I want to take you away from here." I indicated the house with my arm.

The boy opened his eyes wide, his forehead deeply furrowed. He looked terrified. *Of course he was terrified.*

"Can you talk to the others?"

"No speak." He gestured at the two girls. One was Asian, one African. No wonder they didn't speak. He turned to the boy who had been with him in the car with Obote. "Radu, he Romanian." And then the young white boy. "Stefan. Romanian too."

"I'm going to take you away."

"No." He shook his head violently, tears welling up in his eyes, the terror returning to his face.

"What is it? Why are you so scared?"

He shrank away as if I were about to hit him. He stared at me and said nothing.

"I'm not here to hurt you," I said gently. "I want to help you. What is it that is scaring you so much?"

"Stefan had friend. Friend try." He struggled to find the right English words. "Run…he try…they lock him. In prison. Policeman lock him."

I thought of the young lad that Dr Neasden had been helping, the one who had been arrested for burglary by Sanderson. Could it have been him?

"Where was the friend from?"

He turned to Stefan and spoke to him in what I took to be Romanian and then turned back to me. "Rwanda," he said.

That was it, that was it. Was that what they had done? Could they have been punishing him for trying to run away? By staging an arrest and getting him convicted? I couldn't comprehend this. Then I remembered; Neasden had been helping him access medical treatment as part of his support. *Oh shit, this is getting worse.*

"He was ill?"

"Yes, he very ill. He die."

"He died?"

"Stefan say he die soon." He looked back at the floor. His utter helplessness overwhelmed me.

I knew he had only been here, in this house, for a night, but who knew what had happened before that. He clearly felt that he had nowhere to go, no one to turn to, nobody who could help him. He looked desperately alone. The others looked as if they had been here for some time. They leant against the wall, shoulders hunched over, arms circling their bodies, seemingly resigned to the fact that they had no control over what was happening to them; that their lives, literally, were in someone else's hands. I wondered if the dying child had access to medication now and prayed that he was hopefully in a hospital somewhere. If Neasden had been helping him access treatment, had Townsley stopped treating him because he had tried to run away? As well as being locked up, he had been denied further treatment. No wonder these kids were scared. *Bloody hell.*

"I'm not one of them. Do you understand?" I had to try to get them to trust me, but I was fighting a losing battle. Why would these children trust any adult?

He looked blank again. His staring, vacant black eyes suggested he was completely world weary. He couldn't have been more than thirteen or fourteen; as I looked at him, an aching desperation gripped at my chest.

"I'm going to help you."

"Help?" It was as if he had just recognised the word. He turned to his companion and said something in Romanian.

I gestured to the pills on the windowsill. "You're ill?"

"No," he said, pointing to himself. "Not ill."

"You're sick? The pills are for you because you are ill."

"No. Not sick." He pointed at the small Romanian boy. "He sick." Then at one of the girls. "She sick."

"But." I tried to phrase it in as easy language as I could. "I thought you came here, to England, because you are sick?"

"Not sick." He pointed at his companion. "Radu not sick"

"What are you saying? You and Radu are not sick?"

He nodded.

"But the others are?"

He nodded again.

"Stefan not sick."

"You said he was sick?"

"He sick now."

"He is sick?" My head was spinning, the confused thoughts colliding within it. I thought these children had been sent here illegally for treatment because they were ill.

"He come here. He see doctor. Now he sick."

I shook my head "What? What, what are you saying? Are you saying that Stefan was well, not sick, when he arrived in England but after he saw the doctor, then he became sick?"

Andrei looked up at me with those desperately sad eyes and just nodded.

The realisation hit me like a physical blow; like someone had punched me in the chest. I fell back onto the floor. All the blood drained out of my head and a loud rushing pulsed in my ears. The room went black. I struggled to regain my composure, breathing heavily and putting my hands down to steady myself. I crouched for a second, allowing the blood to return, then stood up and gazed at these displaced young people. Townsley wasn't trafficking children here who were ill to take part in his research. He was trafficking healthy children here and *making* them ill. He was giving these young people cancer and then experimenting with treatment. *Fuck, fuck, fuck.* No wonder he didn't want anyone finding out. I pushed the thought of Townsley out of my head. I had to get these children out of here. I had to get them out. I had to persuade them that I wasn't going to hurt them.

I reached over and touched Andrei on the arm. "I won't let the doctor make you sick."

He looked up at me, his eyes full of disbelief in what I had said. I hoped I could come through on my promise.

"Get the others to come with me," I said, standing up and gesturing that they should follow me.

They all seemed reluctant. I stood near the door and indicated that they should follow me. I looked directly at Andrei.

"Get them to come. I'm going to help you. I'm

going to get you out." I wanted to scream at them to hurry up, to get a move on before Obote broke free and came and hit me over the head with a shovel, but I couldn't. I just hoped they would trust me. Andrei eventually stood up as I implored him with my face, and he grabbed his companion Radu by the arm, dragging him to his feet. The other boy and the two girls slowly, timidly, followed suit.

A loud knocking pierced through the stillness of the rancid room, and then a shout from downstairs. A rush of relief flooded over my body. *Thank God, Collette.*

"Collette," I called out, trying to maintain my composure. "Hang on, my darling. I'll be down in a minute. Just wait in the kitchen."

"Okay." The reply drifted up the stairs with a distinct note of uncertainty.

I tried to indicate with my gestures to the children that they needed to hurry.

"Quick," I said to Andrei. "Hurry." And I demonstrated running with my arms.

I thought he might be about to smile at my mime. A flicker passed over his lips and he hurried the others along, speaking in Romanian to those who could understand him. I led them down the stairs and into the kitchen. My three friends were standing there, bemused expressions on their faces, and I indicated to them with a finger across my neck and then against my lips, that they should stay quiet. I wanted to run over and throw myself at them; I wanted to hug them and bury my face in their necks and breathe in their clean, familiar smell. Instead, I ushered the children forward.

"Guys, thank you, thank you so much. I've no time to explain. You need to take these children, now, away from here."

Now it was my friends' turn to stare at me, open-mouthed.

Robert said, "Vee, what are you doing? Where are these children from?" Then he blinked and paused and said, "And more to the point, darling, what *have* you done to your hair?"

Just like Robert, in the middle of a crisis, to focus on my new hairstyle. But I had forgotten. I had got so used to it; it hadn't occurred to me that my appearance might be a bit of a shock to my friends. Thank goodness the cut had healed on my lip and the red mark had gone from my neck. And at least they couldn't see my aching shoulder where Obote had pulled me into the wall earlier.

"Rob, darling, I can't explain right now, except that these children need our help. They need to get away from this house as quickly as they can. Someone might turn up any minute and catch us. They're hurting the children, making them ill. Please?"

He swallowed and looked into my face, beseeching him for help. Then he looked at the children, huddled together in a bewildered group. His face crumpled in disbelief and he shook his head; after all, it was completely out of character for me to be behaving like this. He must have seen the look of desperation in my face, because he looked again at the children and suddenly switched to "efficient" mode.

"What do you need us to do?"

"You need to take the children. You need to look after them, just for a short while. We can't phone social services right now."

Keith raised a sceptical eyebrow.

"I'm sorry, you'll have to trust me, we can't phone them just yet."

Collette looked at me as if I had just utterly taken leave of my senses. I ran over and hugged her.

"Collette, you are my dearest, dearest friend. Please, you have to trust me."

"Why not social services?" She moved away.

I wanted to snap at her, but now was not the time. Taking in a deep breath to slow myself down, I tried again. "Not yet. We can call them soon, but not yet. You have to trust me. I will explain, but I need to make sure that these children are safe and I need to make sure that the person who is hurting them is brought to justice."

Silence.

"Please, please. There is a really good reason we can't call social services or the police just yet. We will. I promise, but you have to believe me for now."

Collette was wavering. She knew what had happened to Dr Neasden. She looked across the room at me.

"The notebook," she whispered.

"These kids have been trafficked here, they are here illegally." I was begging now. "Some of them are very sick. We have to get them out of here. We'll deal with the rest of it later. Please."

I was met with another silence. I appealed to Collette's maternal side. "Collette, I know you think I'm mad, but these children are in real danger." I pointed at the huddled group. "Imagine if they were yours, you'd want someone to help, wouldn't you? If your kids found themselves at real risk, you'd want a random stranger to help out."

"Vee, are you sure we are not doing anything illegal?" Robert asked, and I wanted to weep. I wasn't at all sure that this wasn't illegal but I didn't have the time to debate the law with him. I took another deep breath, reminding myself that this was all very new to my friends; they hadn't been on the journey that I had over the last few days.

I looked him in the eyes and repeated my mantra. "They are here illegally already, Rob. They've been trafficked, and they are sick. They need our help."

I could tell that my closest friends all thought I was bonkers, but eventually, after a little more imploring on my part, they seemed to accept what I was saying and agreed to take the children. They also agreed to hang fire with calling social services for now.

I fought the urge to feel relief, knowing we were not out of danger yet and we had to get a move on. I took Radu by the shoulders and crouched down so I could look him straight in the eyes.

"You are going to be safe now," I said to him. He looked back and nodded slowly. He turned to the others and without saying anything he indicated with his shoulders that they should follow his lead. I gestured to them all with my hands that they should go with my friends.

The children made no effort to resist, to argue, or to ask where they were going. I sensed that they were used to being taken from one place to another by people they had never met. I felt a sense of unease; that perhaps I was exploiting their vulnerability. But at least I knew that this time they were being taken somewhere nice, where they would be treated well and that it would be for their benefit. I just needed to get them away from the house.

As we got out the front to the cars, the children naturally divided. The three Romanian boys followed Robert and Keith, and the girls latched onto Collette.

I was scanning around for any sign that someone was coming down the street to prevent us from leaving; I couldn't risk being interrupted now. I bundled the children into the cars, made sure everyone had their seat belts on, and bid them a hasty farewell. Time was pressing and I had a professor to get to.

Chapter Forty-Three

The sun was almost down by the time the children went off in the cars. After spending most of the day whiling away the time waiting for Obote to come back, all of a sudden the time had rushed past. I needed to get to the hospital and find the room that Townsley used for seeing the children. I needed to be in there before he turned up. The element of surprise seemed to have worked well with Obote; there was no way I could have overpowered him if I hadn't lain in wait, and I wanted to use that again with Townsley. I hoped that Obote hadn't worked his way free and hadn't been able to tell anyone that I was on to them. I didn't want Townsley to be expecting a visit from me.

I didn't want to walk past Obote's road, preferring to remain in the dark as to whether he was free or not. I figured that the only way he could have got free would be if he had alerted a neighbour and I wasn't sure he would want to do that. I supposed he wouldn't want to remain handcuffed to the gate for too long, but he couldn't ring anyone as I had his phone. He wouldn't be able to use the hand I had stamped on, and one of his knee caps was pretty well smashed up. As I walked along, I wondered what Charlton would make of all this. Then I thought I'd probably committed several crimes in the last few hours, including grievous bodily harm, but I pushed that thought to the back of my mind; I'd have to cross that bridge when I came to it. The important thing now was to get to Townsley as soon as possible and prevent any more children's lives being ruined in the name of his research.

The hospital wasn't too far away from the house and I walked up a small road that led up the hill and came out near the back of the site. It took me about ten minutes to get there. I walked in through the staff car park and paused a while near the curb. I quickly got out my iPad and Googled the hospital website, where I found a map of the site. This told me where the outpatient clinics were, over to the right from where I was standing. I thought or a while about what to do. I watched a couple of people come into and out of the car park and hovered around, trying not to look too suspicious. Each time someone came in, I watched them to see what they were doing. Most had an ID badge around their neck and they walked towards various different entrances, some disappearing off round a corner out of sight.

After watching about a dozen or so people come into the car park and walk off to work, I spotted someone I thought could help. She wasn't wearing her badge; she was carrying it on top of a bag that was spilling over with paperwork. I ran up to her, doing my best to look a bit flustered.

"Excuse me! Excuse me!"

She stopped and turned towards me.

"I'm really sorry, I seem to have got a bit lost. Can you tell me where the main entrance is please?"

She seemed happy to help and turned round, pointing in the direction I should take. I leant in close to her as if following the line of her finger with my vision and gently, slowly, and without looking, I picked up her badge and slipped it into my pocket. I thanked her and ran off in the direction in which she had been pointing. I didn't think she would realise I had taken her badge, she would probably assume that she had left it at home. There would be some procedure for getting a new one, I was sure. It would be a bit of an inconvenience, but never mind. I had bigger problems to think about.

Once I was out of her sight I stopped. I turned round and headed over to the other side of the hospital, where the entrance to outpatients was. Having been here last year, I knew my way; I'd had a referral for a painful swelling in my knee. It was, apparently, a problem with the ligament which actually had gone away of its own accord in the end. But I had been here for a consultation.

The pass I had stolen identified me as Gillian Legge and I hoped no one would take too close a look at the picture; it showed a round-faced woman with shoulder-length curly hair. There was little resemblance to me, even if you had thought I'd cut and dyed my hair and been on a diet since having the photo taken. As I put the badge around my neck I made sure the photo was against my body, then I strode through the corridors, hoping that no one would have cause to ask to look at it. I thought the key was to walk along with a confident air, as if I was in a hurry to get somewhere, so that was what I tried to convey.

Several bustling nurses pushed patients along in wheelchairs, scurrying past me. Others almost ran in the opposite direction. No one gave me a second glance. A few patients wearing night clothes and dressing gowns sat on chairs outside the wards, their blank expressions screaming boredom. Hopefully, it would be visiting time soon. Just past a café area, all shuttered up for the night, I found the outpatient unit. I had to access it with my card and I paused and took a deep breath before entering. *Come on Verity, you've found a new talent for acting as well as lying. You can do this.* I pushed the door open and went in.

One person stood alone in the waiting room; the last of the day's clients I imagined, or a relative waiting for someone else to emerge from a clinic. The deserted reception desk looked as if nobody had sat behind it for some time. Several of the lights further down the corridor had gone out and, as I walked along, they flickered back into life. Signs for the clinics pointed a little further along, and I slowed a little when I reached the consulting rooms. Some had a sign on the door with the name of the consultant who was seeing patients that day, some had a slot for a name but the name had been removed. I looked through any open doors; there was nobody about. Two nurses whispered in a corner, glancing over at me as I passed, then they turned away again to continue their conversation. It amazed me how I could get by unnoticed because I had a name badge around my neck, especially as I was dressed as if I was about to go on a hike. I'd been lost in hospitals before and had only got a couple of yards before someone had asked me what I was doing.

Then I saw the name. Professor Kenneth Townsley; consulting room five. Obote was right; Townsley had a consulting suite in the outpatient department. I wondered how much money his research brought to the hospital; probably a lot. Obote had said they thought he was God. I'd known consultants before who acted as if they owned the place and no one ever questioned them because they were so powerful. They ruled the hospital. Townsley was probably even more powerful; he was a professor, a well-renowned professor who was bringing lucrative research to the hospital.

Nobody was around so I opened the door and slipped inside. I flicked on the light, revealing a typical hospital consulting room. An examining table almost filled one side. Beside the desk, some cupboards on wheels almost spilled over with various sorts of medical equipment. A connecting door led through to another room and I peeped in there. This had a desk and a chair, some lockable cabinets, some shelves that were filled with books and another chair off to one side.

Gazing into the room beyond, I realised that I hadn't a clue what to do. I really needed to get myself a bit more prepared for these occasions. It had seemed so important to get here before Townsley, that I hadn't given a thought to what I was actually going to do, or say to him when he arrived. I took my rucksack off my back, then fished out a knife and a pair of handcuffs, hanging the handcuffs from the waistband of my trousers. Then I put the rucksack on my back again; I didn't want to trip over it in the dark and I certainly didn't want to leave it anywhere if I had to go in a hurry; it had everything in it, most importantly all my notes and figuring outs. Nerves were threatening to overwhelm me; I needed to calm myself down. Sitting down on the bed, I reached over and turned off the light, holding the knife in my hand and taking in some deep, slow breaths. Then I just sat and thought about what I needed to do.

Chapter Forty-Four

I wasn't allowed the luxury of being able to think for very long, because about ten minutes later the opening snick of the door in the next room alerted me to someone's arrival. Just when I could have done with some waiting time, he had turned up before I had expected him. I assumed it was Townsley. I didn't know what he looked like; I hadn't been able to find a decent photo, so I would have to guess. I held my breath and sat there in the dark, listening to the movements next door. A scraping of a chair—he was sitting down at his desk. A drawer opening—looking at a file? Maybe he was studying the file of a person he was expecting to see tonight. Unless he had other children in another house somewhere, he thankfully wouldn't be seeing anyone this evening. And unless Obote had worked his way free, and felt inclined to hobble up here with his gammy leg, Townsley would still be expecting them.

I clenched my jaw and gripped the edge of the examining table, breathing in and out to try to quell my speeding heart. The chair in the next room scraped again. He was standing up. Footsteps, and then the door handle rattling. The door opened; the sudden illumination of the light causing me to blink as my eyes adjusted. A tall, thin man, who I took to be Townsley, strode into the room, taking a small stagger backwards when he saw me sitting on the bed. He ran a hand through his grey hair, the air of self-importance momentarily wavering.

"Good evening, Professor Townsley. I've a few questions I would like to ask you." The words came out with a confidence I wasn't feeling.

He opened and closed his mouth a few times before taking another step back. Then, pausing before he moved towards me, he spread his shoulders wide and lifted his chin. Obote had obviously not been able to warn him. Or maybe hadn't felt the inclination to.

"What the hell do you think you're doing in here? How did you get in?"

I held the knife up in front of me so that he could see it and he took a step back.

"I'd like to ask you about the children you've been using for your 'research.'" I made the internationally accepted sign for inverted commas with both hands.

"Get out of here. I'm not talking to you or anyone else. Get out of here, go on." He pointed to the door as if to reinforce his point.

I sat tight and said nothing.

"Get out of my room. You have no idea what you are talking about. Believe me, you should just go now." He wasn't shouting; he was calm and measured. That made him all the scarier. He just looked at me directly in the eyes and spoke in a slow, cold tone. I could see how he frightened people into doing what he wanted. But I had no intention of going anywhere.

"I know what you are doing, Townsley."

He made as if he were about to move closer, but stuttered when I held up the knife again. I had the upper hand; he didn't really know what to say and I wasn't about to leave voluntarily. I was inwardly congratulating myself on getting the better of him. I was about to tell him that I had taken the children somewhere safe, but the sound of a commotion outside in the corridor disturbed my thoughts.

A woman was shouting from in the corridor. "Stop! You can't go in there."

And a man's voice replying, "I will go anywhere the fuck I like."

The woman again, "I'm calling security."

And with that a man burst through Townsley's door, followed by a flustered middle-aged woman in a nurse's uniform.

"I'm so sorry, Professor," she stammered. "I tried to stop him. I'll get security."

"No!" Townsley shouted, whilst still maintaining an air of calmness. "No, no need for security. You go home. I can handle this."

The nurse frowned. She glanced from Townsley to the intruder and back again. She didn't even appear to notice me sitting on the bed with a knife in my hand. The curtain at the end of the bed partly obscured me, but she wouldn't have been looking for anyone else anyway.

"It's okay," Townsley reassured her. He put a hand on her shoulder and ushered her to the door.

She shook her head doubtfully and glanced over her shoulder but Townsley reiterated, "It's okay. You go home. I'll be done here soon." He shot a glance at the intruder.

The nurse disappeared through the door and Townsley closed it behind her.

He turned to the man, ignoring me for the time being, and hissed at him, "Sanderson, what the fuck do you think you are doing here?" He then turned and gestured at me. "What is going on tonight?"

Sanderson. The last of the acronyms. I'd found them all now. Sanderson pulled at the sleeves of his suit and shot a glance across at me. Then he stared directly at Townsley. He ran his hand over his shaved head and took a couple of paces in one direction, then a couple back in the other. His gaze shifted to the floor, then putting his hands into his pockets, he looked up. He kept his voice low. "Darnold is dead. That's what the fuck I am doing here. You've gone too far this time."

"He deserved it, the little prick," Townsley snarled at Sanderson and paced further into the room, but Sanderson was just getting warmed up.

"I'm going to report you. I'm going to ruin you. Murdering a police officer. That's too much. I'm going to have your veneer of respectability in tatters before I'm finished."

"Don't be stupid, Sanderson. No one is going to believe you. He was a bent police officer anyway, I'll discredit him as fast as you can blink." Townsley continued pacing around the room, puffing himself up with importance. He had moved away from Sanderson and closer to me but he carried on pacing backwards and forwards.

"Bent because of you! You're the one who corrupted him."

"Like you. Ha! You're all the same." Townsley curled his lip and spat the words out the corner of his mouth. "So easy to buy off. Who on earth will believe you over me?"

"You're not infallible, Townsley. I have evidence

that even you can't get changed or fabricated. Your reputation will come tumbling down round your ears when people realise what you are really up to."

And then, catching me completely unaware, Townsley turned towards me. I didn't have time to react. Before I could think about stabbing him, he grabbed my knife and poked it towards me. He yanked me off the bed by my arm and turned me round, holding me by my neck and putting the knife to my throat.

"You think Darnold's murder was too much? What about this bitch? I can slit her throat easily."

"You can't keep covering up one death after another."

"Ah, well, that's where you're wrong. The benefit of working in a hospital is that I get to sign the death certificates. I can do what the hell I want. They need me here. What do you think she will die of? A disease? Pneumonia perhaps? Trauma? From a car crash maybe?"

Chapter Forty-Five

I couldn't move. The knife pressed hard against my neck; the blade digging into my skin. He gripped my neck in the crook of his arm, and I grabbed at it with my hands, trying to pull it away. I could barely touch the ground with my toes, and my weight was adding pressure onto my neck. It had only just recovered from being strangled in my hotel room a few days earlier.

Sanderson looked shocked, but he was still quite cocky. He still obviously thought that knowing about Darnold's death was enough to bring Townsley down. He spread his arms. "Townsley. You've got to realise. It's gone too far."

"No, no...It hasn't. We're back on track now. Or we will be when we've got rid of this interfering cow. Everything was going okay, Sanderson. It was all going smoothly. It still would be now if you hadn't let that stupid, snooping Neasden poke his nose in where nobody wanted him. Everything was going fine until then." He was getting emotional, and he gripped my throat even tighter.

I thought about kicking him with my walking boots, but I didn't want to risk him stabbing me in the neck. I was helpless.

"You'd cut that lad off." Sanderson was getting louder now. "He was dying and you'd cut him off. Getting him locked up is one thing but he had to get treatment. You just left him to die."

"He was going to die anyway. Why bother?"

"You were supposed to be treating him."

"He tried to run away." Townsley took a few steps back, dragging me with him. "I," he said, gesticulating towards himself with the knife as if to emphasise his own importance. "I was making him better and he tried to run away, the little fuck. He didn't deserve my help."

Sanderson seemed taken aback at Townsley's arrogance. He paused, took in an audible breath, and frowned. His voice took on a higher tone. "What about the others? Will you cut them off too?"

"They should be grateful. I'm making them better. They're getting the best care available." He shouted, "They should be falling at my feet."

I couldn't stand it. I tried to shout out, "They're not ill!" but it came out more like, "hmm hmm hmm."

But Townsley knew what I was trying to say. He squeezed my neck tighter in an effort to stop me speaking and pushed the knife against my neck a little more. I let out a sharp squeal through my nose; my mouth was pretty much covered by Townsley's arm. Sanderson could tell that Townsley was trying to silence me and he moved a little closer.

"What did she say?" He looked at me and then at Townsley, his frown deepening. The fear of what he had got himself into etched across his face. "What did you say?"

I forced my mouth above Townsley's arm and shouted out. "They're not ill." But before I could say anything else, Townsley jabbed the knife back into my neck. An intense pain took over all other thought, and would have knocked me off my feet, had Townsley not been holding me up. The pain increased as the point of the knife dug into my skin, and a trickle of blood ran down my neck. It was all I could do not to start panicking but it seemed as if I was getting Sanderson on side. He came towards us, a look of incomprehension playing across his face.

"What do you mean?" he asked. He scrunched his eyebrows together in a knot and looked at me. "What does she mean, not ill?" He looked back at Townsley. Then he shouted at the top of his voice, his face contorting, "What does she mean?"

Townsley tried to back away, still gripping me by the neck. Sanderson lurched towards him and pulled at the arm he had around my neck. Townsley tightened his grip but Sanderson managed to pull his arm away from my mouth enough so that I could shout out.

"They're not ill when they come here. They're healthy kids. He makes them ill so that he can use them in his research."

But Townsley was strong and he pulled his arm back over my mouth again and dragged me away from Sanderson.

Sanderson paced around the room, one hand on his hip, the other rubbing back and forth across his head. He walked to the far wall, swung round, then pointed a finger at Townsley.

"Townsley! You lied to me. You lied to everyone. Is this why Darnold wanted out? You told us the kids were ill. You told us their parents had paid for them to come here to get treatment. You made us think it was all for the good."

"A white lie," Townsley said. His calm and calculated demeanour contrasting with Sanderson's fury. He pulled me back a few paces towards his desk. I scrabbled for purchase with my feet, trying to maintain contact with the floor.

"You wouldn't have helped otherwise. It was for the greater good. Think of the lives we'll save. Think of the money we'll make." He took the knife away from my neck.

I didn't understand what was happening or why he had done that. He moved his arm, although I couldn't see why, and the knife ended up beneath the examining table. He must have thrown it away. What was he doing? He still had his other arm tightly round my neck and I couldn't turn round to see what was going on.

"Well it's gone too far," Sanderson shouted back at him, stabbing his finger towards Townsley. "You have to stop. You have to be stopped."

"No! I'm too close."

"You can't keep on just killing people."

"I can!"

Sanderson didn't seem to have noticed, but Townsley had reached down to his desk. As he bent down and twisted me round, I had a clear view of what he was up to; he was putting his hand out towards the desk. Sanderson didn't appear to be paying attention. He continued stomping across the room, backwards and forwards.

"You arrogant bastard—" he started to say, but he was cut off in mid-sentence, stunned into silence when he realised that Townsley had opened a drawer in his desk and pulled out a gun.

Still gripping me round the neck, Townsley held up a black handgun with a long thin barrel with his free hand. It was very different to the one I had in my rucksack. It had something attached to the end but I wasn't sure what it was; it looked like an extension of the barrel.

Sanderson reached for the door handle whilst still staring at Townsley. His jaw flapped open and although I couldn't see Townsley's face, the horror on Sanderson's told me all I needed. Sanderson opened his mouth to speak and he lifted his hand a tiny way upwards, as if to make a gesture. He managed to do neither. A thumping 'pop' from behind me rippled the air, and Sanderson's head exploded onto the wall behind him. He smashed against the wall with the force of the shot and then slumped down onto the floor, a trail of blood following as he slid to the ground. As Townsley had pulled the trigger, his grip on my neck had loosened, and I pulled his arm away from me and ran to the far side of the room. The noise the gun had made had not been loud and I realised then that the extension on the barrel must have been a silencer. It had worked. Although it was far from silent, if there had still been anyone around they wouldn't have heard anything that would have alarmed them.

I couldn't take my eyes off Sanderson. His mouth remained wide open; the horror of what was about to happen to him still etched on his face. A tiny trickle of blood ran from a neat hole in the front of his forehead, falling across his left eye and down towards his ear. The back of his head had completely disappeared. There were bits of it all over the wall; little bits of skull stuck to the wall behind him. There was blood, loads of blood in a massive swoosh, as if someone had thrown a bucket of red paint onto the wall. And there were bits of other stuff. I wasn't even going to start thinking about what they were.

Chapter Forty-Six

I gasped, listening to echoes of myself breathing heavily, as if the breaths were coming from someone else. The smells that whipped around the room were almost overwhelming. The stench of excrement where Sanderson's body had emptied itself, together with the smell of blood and brain. Into this mix swirled the tart smell of a recently discharged gun and I heaved as I tried not to throw up. I tore my eyes away from the remains of Sanderson and looked at Townsley, my mouth open in astonishment. He was still holding the gun in front of him. He turned to me.

"You should have left that meddling Doctor Neasden in his poky little house and got out."

He knows who I am. Of course, the man in the night with the baseball bat. Townsley had been on to me.

I tried not to let that thought show in my voice. "And let you carry on getting away with what you're doing?"

"I'm curing people! I'm doing good! It's my mission to save lives!" he shouted, spit pouring from his mouth in an arc, landing on the desk and the floor.

I shouted back, the rage burning inside me, shaking my finger at him, "No, it's your mission to be a hero. You want everyone to see you as a saviour, as some kind of god."

"I am," he roared. "I'm going to cure the world."

I leant forward and pointed, gesticulating with my whole arm. "You can't cure people by killing other people. Those children haven't asked to be part of your grand plan."

"They're doing good too. They're doing good for the world."

I quietened my voice. "They're children. You bring them over here, telling them I don't know what stories to get them here and then you use them for your own ends."

"No. Not my own ends. For the greater good. You've got to look at this from the perspective of all those people I will save."

"But doctors don't kill."

He glanced over at Sanderson, still propped against the wall, still with that look of horror on his face.

He looked back at me. "In the future, I will go down as a hero. No one will care how I did it. The ends will justify the means." He puffed out his chest and threw his arms out wide.

"Making children ill? Making them die?"

"But it's only a few." He had calmed down now. "And their families don't care. They're prepared to send them over here. No one will miss them." He sat on the desk and spoke quietly, "We have to continue studying how the cancers grow and how they hide in our bodies so that we can find an effective treatment." He paused, glancing over at Sanderson again, and I thought I saw a look of recognition, of shock, pass over his face. Then it was gone. "Treatments only help once the cancer has grown but if we can understand how they grow, make that less unpredictable to us, we can attack the cancer at the earliest stage. Maybe even before that if we can understand *why* they develop."

He looked up at me. "Do you know how many people a year die across the world because of cancer? What these children are doing, they are doing for the good of the world."

"You're a doctor and you don't care about them. The boy in prison, you just discarded him." I was horrified by what he was doing but I had to keep a check on my emotions.

An edginess returned to his voice; the words snapping out of his mouth like more gunfire. "He was dying anyway."

"Because of you!" I couldn't believe the arrogance of this man. If he hadn't had a gun in his hand I would have stomped up and smacked him in the face.

"My research will save thousands of lives!"

"But you can't do it like this. You can't make some people ill, let them die, to save others. You just can't do it like that."

Townsley looked at the gun in his hand. He lifted it up and aimed it directly at me. I couldn't think straight, I couldn't even breathe. I leant against the wall, gripping it behind me with both hands to stop myself from falling and just stared at the gun. *This is it.* This is it. Maybe those were John's last thoughts too as the lorry hurtled towards him. This is it. My mouth had become so dry the words would barely pass through it. But I had to try something.

"What about the oath?" I tried to keep my voice as level as I could.

"Oath?"

"The oath you take as a doctor."

"The Hippocratic oath?"

"Yes. Doesn't it say something in there about saving lives, not taking them?"

He sighed and looked at me as if I was being particularly stupid. This wasn't going well. He spoke slowly and calmly, "The end will justify the means. We will be saving lives."

"You're ruined, Townsley." I indicated towards Sanderson. "Killing me won't help. You're ruined anyway."

"I think killing you will help me greatly," he said. He lifted the gun up and aimed it at my forehead. "All you meddlers will be out of the way then, and I can carry on with my research in peace."

"And who will you get to cover up for you the next time?" I swallowed, forcing the terror back down my throat. I couldn't give in to it now.

"I don't need anyone else. I'll take care of everything. Everyone else just gets in the shit anyway. I'm better off operating on my own."

I kept my eyes riveted on the gun. Fear clawed at my chest and I gulped in some air. "I moved the kids out of the house," I said, unable to stop my voice from wavering.

Townsley looked genuinely surprised at this, his mouth twitching before he forced it into an unnatural smile. He exhaled sharply and took a step backwards, lowering the gun. He opened his mouth as if to speak but said nothing.

"They're safe. You won't find them. And the Human Trafficking Unit is on to you too."

He looked over at Sanderson. That flutter of something passed over his face once again. Perhaps a recognition of what he had become; something as far removed from a doctor as you could get. He looked back at me, and this time his eyes were filled with sadness and horror.

"I've got an iPhone in my pocket, Townsley, I've had a call in to DI Sam Charlton from the Unit. It's been on since before you arrived. All this has been going through to him. He's probably recorded it. Townsley, killing me will make no difference at all. Either way, you're finished."

"You're lying."

"You're through."

Townsley looked up at me again, the fire back in his eyes. "No, I'm going to carry on. I'm going to finish my work. The world needs me."

"The world doesn't need you to be killing people who have no one to turn to. Or,"—I indicated Sanderson—"people who have been covering up for you but got fed up with your megalomaniac tendencies. I don't think the world wants to be saved by someone like you."

He looked at Sanderson again, then at the gun, then at me.

"You're a doctor, Townsley, you're supposed to save people not kill them. No end justifies that method. That was the argument the Nazis used; it didn't wash with the world then, and it won't wash now."

"I want to go down in history," he said quietly. "I want the world to remember me."

He lifted the gun up, and for a moment I thought he was going to aim it at his own head. I held my breath. I had seen enough death over the last few days and braced myself for another. But then a phone beeped in his pocket, and he took it out and looked at it. A smile spread slowly across his face.

He pointed the gun back at me.

"We'll see who's finished. Come with me." He nodded towards the door into the next room.

What was he doing? Where was he taking me? I checked my rucksack was firmly on my back and made towards the door to the adjoining room. Although the thought made me feel queasy, there was no way I could get out of the door without trampling all over Sanderson's blood. I looked at his body, still slumped against the wall; his face a vision of horror, the rest of his head splattered across the room. The blood had pooled around him and spread out, covering the area near the door. Shiny hospital floors were not designed to stop the flow. I pitied the poor person who would stumble across this scene in the morning.

Townsley followed closely behind me as I left the room, pushing the muzzle of the gun into my side so that I knew not to try anything. I wasn't about to try anything; I had seen what this man was capable of and now was certainly not the time to make a move. *Pick your moment, Verity.*

Chapter Forty-Seven

We walked through to the adjacent room in silence but as I approached the door to the corridor, he grabbed my arm and stopped me.

"Don't try anything stupid. Just walk. I'm going to cover the gun with my coat. If we see anyone, just keep walking. You know I am not afraid to use it." Reaching up, he grabbed a coat that had been hanging on the back of the door and put it over the gun. He positioned himself so that it looked as if we were walking closely, perhaps father and daughter visiting a relative, and hid the gun between us. The muzzle stuck into my side.

I didn't take this as an idle threat so I walked as calmly as I could through the now deserted outpatient department and through the corridors of the hospital until Townsley pushed me towards a side entrance. We passed a few people but they didn't give us a sideways glance, so there was no way I could even try to attract their attention with my expression. Townsley shoved me through the door, closed it behind him, and pushed me down the path towards one of the staff car parks. He kept his coat over the gun and continued to stick close behind me so there was no chance of getting away. I looked round to see if there were any bushes or buildings I could run to and hide behind, but I knew that I would only get a couple of yards and he would have pulled the trigger. The gun had a silencer and there was no one around; he could easily kill me and then drive away without anyone noticing. If I was going to make a move, I had to do it at the right time.

The car park was almost deserted; there were a few cars dotted around but I guessed that it was generally used by people who worked during the day. In one of the bays at the front, marked "consultants parking only", there was a dark grey jaguar. I noticed the missing apostrophe and thought what a stupid thing that was to notice in a moment like this. Townsley blipped the car open. He led me to the passenger side and told me to get in and then slide over to the driver's side. Doing it that way meant he could keep the gun aimed at me the whole time.

Once I was in the driver's seat, he got in beside me. I hoped he wasn't expecting me to drive; my legs were making jelly look fairly solid. The rucksack dug painfully into my back as I sat in the driver's seat but I ignored it. I wasn't letting go of it under any circumstances. It had my remaining armoury inside it and I was clinging to it like a security blanket in the hope that I might, just, get a chance to break free at some point.

He passed me the keys. "Here, drive to the house."

"House? Which house?"

"The one where you reckon you've stolen my patients from."

I put the key in the ignition and tried to concentrate on getting the car going. It was a huge car. I had never driven anything like it and I didn't want to scratch it; I didn't want to do anything to antagonise the man pointing a gun at my chest. Trying to forget that there was a gun pointing at me, I focused on pulling away smoothly.

"You've probably condemned them to death, you know?"

I was silent. I couldn't hold a conversation *and* drive with a gun pointing at me.

"They need their medication and treatment. I hope you don't mind having that on your conscience."

I wasn't going to get into an argument in the car, so I let that pass and ignored the irony of his statement. Hopefully, if I ended up shot and dumped in the boot, my friends would make sure those children were looked after.

I drove carefully out of the car park and along the roads to the house. The dark streets and pavements were almost deserted. The few drivers who passed wouldn't have noticed anything distinctive about the Jaguar passing the other way. How would anyone know that I was driving along with a gun against my ribs? So I concentrated hard on getting there as smoothly as I could. When I turned into the road, my heart sank; cars lined the side of the street and there was nowhere easy to park. I slowed to a crawl, searching for a space.

I found a space right at the end of the street, near the corner. The car was partly on the double yellow lines, but I thought I would let Townsley worry about the parking ticket. He held the gun at me whilst he got out of the car and then made me slide over and get out the passenger side. He pointed in the direction of the house and without saying anything poked the gun in my side and pushed me forwards. Why was he bringing me here? I thought of all the locks and the bars on the window. Things were not looking good.

My legs shook, barely holding me up as I led the way to the back of the house. A light shone out from the kitchen window. Someone was in there. Townsley pushed me up the steps and into the kitchen and there, standing in the middle of the room, was Champion Obote.

Chapter Forty-Eight

Champion Obote cradled his broken hand, now heavily bandaged, a thunderous look on his face. As I walked into the kitchen, he curled back his lips, baring his teeth, and looked me directly in the eye. He held up his hand, but said nothing. He didn't need to; the look said all that was necessary. Payback time.

"Look what I found," exclaimed Townsley.

Obote limped heavily as he moved forward a little and I shuffled a little closer to him. I glanced around me, trying to get a sense of where Townsley was. Feigning even more terror than was actually whipping through me, I whimpered and tried to look as if I were about to cry. When Obote was reasonably close, but far enough away that he couldn't easily grab me, I stopped. The barrel of Townsley's gun pointed in a direct line through me and towards Obote. I hoped that Townsley wouldn't want to risk killing Obote by mistake, although I could be sure of nothing under the circumstances. I kept up the whimpering, hoping that this would make them both relax their guard. Obote was smiling a dreadful, sickening smile as I moved towards him, and a wave of nausea passed through me. He clearly hadn't relished being overpowered by a woman. I positioned myself as well as I could, gave another little whimper and then dipped down really quickly, grabbing the knife from my sock and standing up in one smooth movement. As I stood up, I caught Townsley by surprise and punched at his hand from below, sending the gun flying up in the air and across the kitchen.

I had caught them unawares. I stabbed the knife at Townsley, getting him deep on the thigh. He screamed out in pain. Obote was behind me, but the sound of shuffling feet alerted me that he was about to make a move. I yanked the knife out of Townsley's leg, keeping hold of it, and spun round, slashing Obote across the arm. I wrenched the handcuffs off my belt and rushed towards Townsley, pushing him to the floor. But Obote was too quick, even with a smashed kneecap; he was tall and it only took him two paces to stride across the room. He struck me from behind and pushed me to the ground. The knife fell out of my hand. He snatched at my shoulder and turned me round, slapping me hard across the face with his good hand. He pulled the handcuffs from my hands and dragged me by my wrist towards the sink. I managed to reach the knife, which had fallen near the sink, picking it up and stabbing wildly behind me but I merely grazed his leg. He pulled me under the sink, where he attached my wrist to the water pipe. I was trapped. I pulled on the handcuffs but there was no way they were going to come loose. *Fuck, fuck, fuck.* What the hell was I going to do now?

Townsley hobbled across the room for the gun.

Obote grabbed him and pulled him away, kicking the gun out of his reach.

"I'm going to kill that fucking bitch," Townsley spat. But he was so much smaller and shorter than Obote that he couldn't fight him off.

"Leave her," Obote snapped at him. "There's been too much killing already. We'll fit her up for something. Sanderson can have her put away for years. Give her twenty years in a high-security prison and she'll soon wish you'd shot her." He glared in my direction, and I imagined myself in a prison somewhere, charged and convicted of some crime I hadn't committed.

Townsley set his mouth in a determined line, drawing in his lips and breathing heavily through his nose. He tried to make another run for the gun. Obote grabbed him and threw him on the floor. Townsley skidded like a bowling ball across the floor and landed in the pile of leftover cleaning products. I thought for a moment that he had been knocked unconscious but he suddenly leapt up. He had a plastic container in his hand.

"Sanderson's dead," he shouted at Obote and then he threw the contents of the container into Obote's face and over his clothes.

Obote screamed and fell to his knees, and Townsley dropped the container onto the floor near his feet. Obote was scratching at his face; the pain in his eyes must have been agonising, they had to have still been tender from the pepper spray earlier. He writhed on the floor, trying to peer up at Townsley and summon the energy to charge at him another time.

Townsley stood up. He calmly took a cigarette out of his pocket and lit it. He looked down at Obote crawling on the floor, clutching his face. Obote stared up, his jaw dropping, as Townsley lit the cigarette and took a couple of drags on it, standing there as if he didn't have a care in the world. Obote's eyes opened wide, despite the pain he must have been in. He knew what was coming, and so did I. He scrambled across the floor in an attempt to get through the kitchen door and into the hall. I clutched desperately at my back, trying to reach into the rucksack for the last set of handcuffs, so that I could use their key to undo myself. Townsley glanced towards Obote and then to me; suddenly the calm demeanour left him and a manic grin spread across his face. Slowly and deliberately, he threw the cigarette at Obote as he struggled for the door. The vapours of the cleaning product caught fire and flames engulfed Obote. He thrashed about and threw himself into the hallway, madly trying to beat his body against the walls, screaming for help. But the vapours also led back to the container that Townsley had dropped at his feet. The floor in front and to the side of him lit up in a sheet of flame, trapping him in the corner of the room.

The flames quickly spread as the liquid left in the container caught fire, and flames began to lick at Townsley's legs. He was beating himself frenetically with his arms, but I ignored his agonised calls while I tried to get the opening of the rucksack within reach. It wasn't easy with one arm attached to a pipe and I had to contort myself right round so that I could reach the zip. I held the material in my teeth whilst I battled to get the zip open, and then I twisted my body as far as I could and fumbled blindly into the depths of the rucksack with my loose arm. I struggled to pull the handcuffs free from the bag as my lungs began to fill with noxious fumes. Thick, dark, acrid smoke billowed into the room. Townsley was trapped in the far corner, behind a wall of flame and smoke; his legs were well ablaze. He was still frantically wafting his arms at his legs in a futile attempt to stop the flames from climbing further upwards, although he appeared to be fanning the fire in the process. Agonised screams poured from his open, contorted mouth. The pile of discarded and half-filled cleaning containers whooshed up into a raging fire, licking at the curtains and sending the temperature of the room to a searing, unbearable heat.

I grappled with the spare handcuffs, releasing the keys and fighting to unlock the pair around my wrist. Twice the keys clattered to the floor before I managed to unlock them. I yanked my hand free and covered my mouth as best as I could with my arm, desperately trying to stop the fumes from getting into my lungs. Grabbing onto the sink for leverage, I pulled myself up and turned the tap on, hoping to soak Townsley in water but nothing came out. The water had been cut off. Of course, that would be why the children were using a potty and not the toilet. Townsley was trapped, unable to move through sheer terror, the flames climbing higher up his legs; his screams now high-pitched and inhuman. Obote crashed about in the hallway, trying to do something. He had stopped screaming now, which somehow seemed much more sinister.

I choked and spluttered; the fumes going to my head. Everything was becoming fuzzy. I got back down on the floor and crawled to the back door, hitting the knife with my knee as I crawled along. I picked it up, stuffing it back into my sock, where it had been for most of the day. The door handle was slippery and hard to grip onto. Eventually I managed to get a firm hold and yanked at the door, all the time trying not to breathe in the thick air. There was a rush and a strong breeze as I pulled the door open, as if the air from the garden was being sucked from the outside and into the house. The sudden increase in oxygen fuelled the fire, raising the temperature levels, and the leftover chemicals exploded into a ball of intense heat. The flames leapt instantly to the ceiling, brighter and hotter than before. I didn't glance back at Townsley. There was no hope, and I had no desire to see what had become of him. Apart from the crackling of the fire, the house was now silent. I wrenched the door fully open and staggered outside, gulping the air into my lungs, coughing and choking as my body readjusted to the clean air.

I was about to reach for my phone to call the emergency services but as I did so, the sound of approaching sirens pierced through the air. Someone had obviously called them already. The fire must have taken a stronger hold of the front of the house than I had realised. I stumbled to the back of the garden and climbed through a hole in the fence, throwing myself onto the lawn of whoever's garden this was. The cold night air stung as it hit the back of my throat and I leant on my knees, taking a minute to regain my composure. I didn't want to be seen anywhere near this place, so I quickly gathered myself together and headed through the back gardens of the neighbouring houses until I found a passageway through to the adjacent road.

I walked through there as calmly as I could and headed into the night.

Chapter Forty-Nine

I slowed down to a stroll. I didn't want to do anything that would draw attention to me. People milled about on the pavements and spilled into the road; coming out to see what emergency the sirens were signalling, or attracted by the flames to watch the horror unfolding before them the way we humans like to do. A story to tell at dinner tomorrow. I plodded through the streets, aiming to go more or less straight downhill towards the river. When I reached the river, I was about half a mile from the city centre, opposite a small business park made from a group of disused warehouses. A high-arched bridge crossed the river at this point; it was likely built that way to let taller boats sail underneath it. Moonlight glistened on the water below as I walked onto the deserted bridge, stopping when I reached the apex of the arch. Nobody ventured out there at that time of night; even dog walkers avoided that stretch of water. I pulled the gun from out of my bag and wiped it all over with one of my tops. Then, double checking that there no one watching, I dropped it into the middle of the river, listening as it sploshed down beneath me. I zipped up my rucksack, put it over my shoulder and hurried on across the bridge.

As I walked along, I fished out my phone and called Charlton.

"Verity, how are things?" he asked calmly.

On hearing his voice, a rush of emotions over-whelmed me and I collapsed in a heap on the far side of the bridge, near the car park of the business park.

"Tense," I mumbled, trying hard to maintain control. "A little tense." I slumped down onto the tarmac and leant against the wall of the nearest build-ing. Charlton was gentle, asking just a few questions. There would be time for that later. I described briefly what had happened, giving a less than graphic description of what had happened to Sanderson, so as to spare myself from reliving that scenario. Then I attempted to tell him what had happened when we'd got to the house. I had to stop mid-sentence.

"I'm sorry," I said, gulping in heavy breaths between the words and just about managing to fight back the tears. "I can see him beating the flames, flap-ping uselessly. And the screams." I stopped again, trying to erase the howls that were on repeat in my head.

Charlton made all the right sympathetic noises down the phone; but really, what could you say to help in that situation?

"What do you think I should do?" I asked Charl-ton. "Should I call the police now?"

"No." He was emphatic.

"But…"

"No buts. Go and check into a hotel. I'll come and find you. I've been meeting an old colleague in Stevenage, so I'm already near the A1. I'll be there in a couple of hours."

I ignored the first part of this advice. "But, what…?"

"No buts. Listen, does anyone know you were at the house?"

"No."

"Is there anything of yours at the house?"

"There'll be my fingerprints from earlier, when I went for the children."

"It sounds like there won't be much left of it, anyway."

A vision of Townsley flapping and twizzling and screaming came back into my head, and I stifled a sob.

"There's nothing specific that will point to you being there just now?"

"No. I don't know why I thought I might need it, but I took my knife with me."

"Instinct," he laughed.

I laughed too. It was a bit of light hysteria, I thought.

He insisted on driving up to Lincoln that evening. I couldn't persuade him not to. Having said that, I found myself looking forward to seeing him. We agreed that he would drive straight up. I would go and check into the Royal Hotel and get cleaned up and he would let me know when he had arrived and checked in himself. I put the phone down and stayed alone on the car park tarmac for some time. Was it finally over? Was that it? I had got the children to safety and Townsley, by his own stupid actions, had ensured that he would never harm another young person. A wave of relief washed over me, quickly followed by a wave of nausea; the memories of the last couple of hours would stay with me for a long time to come. And then it hit me; I was liberated, free from the tension of the last week. I stood up and headed into town, suddenly light-hearted and giddy from the reprieve.

The chimes of the cathedral from up the hill drifted down, telling me it was now eleven o'clock. I strode all the way into the city centre along the south side of the river and then I crossed the main road via the footbridge and headed towards the train station, where I knew I would be able to climb into a taxi and go straight to the hotel.

Chapter Fifty

I was almost at the taxi rank when a shout interrupted my thoughts.

"Hey!"

And again, "Hey!"

I turned round, beyond surprised to see Stephen Ibbetson running after me. I stopped and let him catch me up.

"Ibbetson," I said, my voice coming out slightly higher than I'd intended. "What are you doing here?"

"Same as you, I guess." He smiled. "I've been figuring this all out a few paces behind you, it seems. I got to the house and it was ablaze. It looked like quite a fire."

I was so relieved to see a familiar face in front of me; my shoulders drooped as the last remnants of tension drained out of me.

I let out a great sigh. "I thought I was going to die in there."

"Was there anybody still in there?"

"Townsley and Obote. Do you know who they are?"

"The organ grinder and one of his monkeys, yes. Thank God you're all right, though. I've been really worried about you. I couldn't drop it, after your phone call. I felt really bad about what had happened and I had to try to find out what was going on." He put a sympathetic hand on my arm.

I looked at him and smiled a weak smile.

"Are you okay?"

"I'm fine, thanks," I lied, not really feeling fine but desperate to get into a hot bath.

"What else has been going on? It looks as if you've had a tough time."

"Have you been up to the hospital?" I asked cautiously.

"No, should I?"

"I wouldn't. When did you get here?"

"A couple of hours ago. I finally realised exactly what was happening, and I headed straight for the house."

"Well, welcome to the madness."

"What about Charlton?"

"He's on his way up, actually. He's been a great help. Thanks." I smiled at him. "We're meeting up at the Royal Hotel when he gets here." The relief of seeing a face I recognised overwhelmed me and I staggered forwards a step. Ibbetson took my arm and steadied me.

"Let me give you a lift," he offered. He indicated a car park a street away and we walked over to his car together.

I took off my rucksack and threw it in the back of the car, relieved that the makeshift armoury had reached the end of its usefulness, then I jumped into the passenger seat.

"I am so looking forward to a long, hot bath," I

said, stretching out my arms and noticing my body start to relax from the strains of the last few days.

Ibbetson pulled out of the car park and started heading down the High Street. He seemed to know where he was going so I didn't offer directions. I guessed he must have been up here before as part of his work with Dr Neasden.

"How did you know where to find me?" I asked.

"I saw you leave the house."

"But I left out of the back of the house, through the garden."

"Yeah." He glanced over and smiled. "That's where I saw you."

That seemed a bit strange. "You were following me?"

"I followed you from there for a minute or two. I saw you heading along the river, and I thought you might need a moment to yourself. So I drove up here and headed back towards you."

"And how did you figure out who was involved and what it was all about?"

"Same way as you I guess, information and a bit of digging. I've got contacts."

"Have you been keeping in touch with Charlton?"

"Charlton," he mused. "Yes, Charlton has been keeping me informed."

I sighed and relaxed into the seat.

"You did well, figuring this all out." He sounded impressed.

"Yeah, well Townsley won't be hurting any more children, although the outcome for him was a little bleak."

"And the police you were so untrusting of?"

"Did Charlton not tell you?"

"No. I haven't spoken to him for a while."

"At least two of them. They're both dead too." An image of the mess in Townsley's room at the hospital flashed into my mind, and I wondered if anyone had found it yet. The thought made me sick.

We sat in silence for a minute, staring out at the dark.

Ibbetson glanced over at me. "Townsley must have been paying someone a lot of money to bring him those children."

I closed my eyes. "Well, that's unfortunate for them. But good for the children and any potential future children."

"Have you any idea who that was?"

"No, and I will leave that for someone else to work out. All I want now is a long soak in a hot, bubbly bath."

"Where are the children now?"

I opened my eyes and looked at him. He smiled his rugged smile.

I smiled back. "They're safe, with some friends."

"Which friends?" He sounded inquisitive.

"Some old friends, that I can trust. You won't know them."

"In Lincoln?"

"In Lincoln, yes, why?"

"I'm just curious as to how you got to the heart of what was going on so quickly."

"They're safe, Ibbetson."

"Thank God," he said. "I'm just concerned, that's all."

"You've really got into all this, haven't you?" He seemed to have genuinely figured it all out.

"I'm interested."

I said nothing, just looked out of the window.

"And what did you do with the notebook?"

The hairs on my neck prickled, and I shivered involuntarily. "You knew about the notebook?" My stomach sank into the pits of my pelvis.

"Of course."

I sat upright, peering into the darkness beyond the window. "Ibbetson, this isn't the way to the Royal Hotel. You've turned the wrong way."

"I haven't," he said.

"You have." I turned towards him.

"You should have left that notebook well alone."

"Ibbetson, what are you doing?"

He pulled the car to a stop at the side of the road. I grabbed at the door handle, but the car was locked. Panic rose inside me.

I looked over at him. The smile was still there, but it was no longer rugged, it was a smile of hatred. His face contorted. I rattled the door handle in a vain attempt to get out of the car. He drew back his fist.

And then nothing. Just blackness.

Chapter Fifty-One

As I came to, a searing pain pierced the front of my forehead, as if someone was driving an ice pick into my head. I didn't want to open my eyes. I hadn't a clue how long I had been out cold or where I was. I moved my head and then immediately wished I hadn't.

Sharp pains shot up my arms and legs as I tried to move, but it was useless. There was nowhere to move them. My hands seemed to be tied behind my back and my legs squashed unnaturally underneath me. When I opened my eyes, it did no good; the space I occupied was in complete darkness. There was movement, though, and a rumbling noise. I was in something that was moving. A car. I was in the boot of a car. *Oh fuck.*

I tried to remember what had been happening. Ibbetson. *The prick.* What the fuck was he doing? How was he involved in all this? One minute I had been as close to a bath as I'd been in a long time and the next I was tied up in the boot of a car as far from a bath as I'd ever been. I pieced together the sequence of events. Ibbetson had been there, near the station, when I'd gone to get a taxi. I had been surprised, but it had seemed feasible that he had figured things out too, and had come up to Lincoln where his old work colleague had lived. But then he had asked about the notebook, hadn't he? And the children. Where was he taking me?

Once again, a wave of nausea came over me. I had no idea where he was taking me, or why. And who would know where I was? I suddenly remembered the phone in my back pocket. With my hands tied behind my back it would be difficult to reach, but maybe if I manipulated them a little I could pull it out. I shifted around in the boot, as much as the limited space would allow, and tried to free my arms from the weight of my body. Pushing my hands towards my back pocket, I fumbled around for the phone. I tried to press the buttons that I knew by memory would unlock it, but the phone slipped from my grasp. *Shit.* Blindly, I scrambled around on the floor of the boot with my tied-together hands and, after what seemed like ages, located the phone. I couldn't be sure if it was locked or unlocked, but I held it tight and started pressing the buttons again. In the darkness of the boot a light shone out from behind me indicating, I assumed, that I had unlocked the phone. Groping with my fingers, I pressed what I thought might be the call button and hoped for the best. And then Charlton's familiar, deep voice pierced through the rumbling of the engine. I shouted at the top of my voice. "Help!" I just kept repeating over and over, "Charlton, help! Help!" hoping he could hear me. I wasn't sure what I thought he could do, but I had to try something.

"Verity! Shut up! Shut up and listen." Charlton's voice crackled through the emptiness, shouting to make himself heard over my anguished pleas. I quietened down.

"Okay." It was little more than a whisper.

His disembodied voice came back at me. "Where are you? What's happened?"

"I don't know," I shouted back, breathless from the lack of air. "I'm in the boot of a car. I think it's Ibbetson's car."

"Verity, whatever happens keep your phone on. Okay? Keep this call open."

"I'm scared."

"Keep the phone on. Okay?"

And then I remembered the knife in my sock. I lay the phone on the floor of the car boot, touching my thigh so I could feel exactly where it was, hoping that I didn't accidentally turn it off. Pushing my ankles as close to my hands as I could, I tried to retrieve the knife. I inched it out of my sock and clasped onto it, as if my life depended on it. Maybe it did. I tried sawing with the knife against the rope tying my hands together. It was hard to get much purchase, and I couldn't move it very far or very fast, but I could feel the strands of rope begin to give a little. My hands didn't feel so tightly bound. My wrists jerked apart a little as one of the pieces of rope broke and I sawed with a renewed vigour at the others.

Charlton's voice echoed into the boot. "Verity, are you okay?"

I was just about to answer when the car stopped. The jerking movement of the brake made the knife fall out of my hand and I cursed under my breath. I felt around but my hands were still tied and I couldn't locate it. The sound of the car door being opened and then slammed shut brought the panic back into my chest as I realised I didn't have time to hunt for it. Instead, I grabbed the phone from next to my leg and shoved it up the back of my top, stuffing it under the elastic of my sports bra. I thought it was less likely to get turned off there than back in my pocket. Fresh air flooded the boot as the door flew open, and I gulped in several breaths. Ibbetson grabbed my arm, dragging me roughly from the car. My legs wouldn't move fast enough; they'd been curled up beneath me and wouldn't straighten, so I fell head first over the edge of the boot. Ibbetson yelled at me to get up, kicking me hard in the back, then pulling once again at my arm and yanking me to my feet.

I seemed to be in some kind of garage. Shelves lined the walls, piled high with tools, batteries, wrenches, and tins. Jacks, ladders, and other items hung from hooks scattered around the sides. As Ibbetson held my arms, the car backed out coming to a halt just outside the door. A thickset man jumped out and locked the car, then ran back inside. He pulled the garage door down, then stood to one side, lurking in the shadows where I couldn't really see him.

Ibbetson shoved me away from him and, unable to break my fall, I crashed onto the floor. My knees thumped into the ground, sending a jarring pain up through my body. Ibbetson kicked me again and shouted for me to stand up. Without a free hand it was a struggle, and he tutted, grabbing my arm and dragging me to my feet. He walked round and leaned into me.

"Where are those children?" He screamed into my face, baring his teeth, his friendly smile firmly replaced with a grimace.

"Why do you want to know? Ibbetson? What are you doing?"

He laughed. "What am I doing? I'm trying to recover my property is all."

"The children?"

"Yes, the fucking children," he screamed at me. "Have you any idea how much those kids are worth to me?"

"But some of them are ill." I was dumbfounded. I couldn't believe Ibbetson was involved in this.

"Ha! They'll bloody stay that way now that you've killed off their doctor."

"They're safe now. Out of harm's way."

He screamed at the top of his voice, "They're mine. I want them back."

"You've known all along?" I could barely speak, I was so stunned.

"Yes, I've known. Of course I've known. How do you think Townsley got the kids in the first place?"

"You? You were getting him the children? But the paper…"

He laughed again. "The stupid, meddling, interfering, *Doctor* Neasden. If he had kept his nose out, everything would have turned out alright. And *you*. You're as bad. Why didn't you just give up? Charlton was supposed to get you back here. You just couldn't keep from snooping, could you?"

Charlton. I gulped. He was on the phone. I didn't know how much of this he could hear and I worried that keeping the phone line open might not have been a good idea. *Shit. Not Charlton too.* With my hands hidden out of the way, I twisted and pulled at the rope, trying to free them. The knife had done some work and they weren't as tightly bound but I still couldn't free them.

"Charlton?" I asked.

He threw his arms wide. "The great Samuel

Charlton," he laughed. "I should never have introduced you to him, he's too clean for his own good. He was supposed to just call the police up here, get you out the way before you knew anything. But you just wouldn't give up and he actually wanted to help you. Idiot."

Ibbetson calmed down. He took a step back. The thickset man stepped forward out of the shadows and I instantly recognised him as Kevin Lambert, the flabby man from my hotel room. He grinned at me and rubbed his hands together.

Ibbetson nodded towards me. "Lambert, get her to tell me where *my* children are."

Lambert moved towards me, and I backed away, trying to keep him in my vision, but I stumbled over a paint pot and slammed into the floor. I struggled to stand up. Lambert waited for me.He grinned again. "Got to be an equal fight," he said and threw a punch which hit me on the shoulder, causing me to spin round and hit my head on the corner of one of the shelves. A bright light had exploded over my eye and the pain seared through my forehead. I turned to Lambert.

He indicated with his hands; *come on, fight.*

"I have no arms free," I shouted. "How can that be equal?"

He laughed. "Well, almost equal." And he threw another punch.

This time I saw it coming and I span out of the way, his fist piercing the air close to my ear. He took a step forward to steady himself and I kicked out my foot to try to trip him over. I caught his ankle, but he only stumbled a little. As he steadied himself against the wall, he reached up and grabbed a wrench from one of the shelves. Then he turned towards me again, tapping the wrench against the palm of his other hand. I ran across the garage, but Ibbetson grabbed hold of me and pushed me back towards Lambert.

"Tell me where my children are," he screamed as he pushed me away, and Lambert swung with the wrench.

I managed to move my head out of the way quickly enough, but the wrench hit me on the shoulder and I shouted out in pain and fell to my knees once again.

I stumbled back onto my feet and moved away from Lambert, closer to the wall, stretching my arms behind me and scrabbling against the wall with my hands. I grabbed something that felt like a jack and held it behind me as I moved closer to Lambert. He was still had the wrench and he swung it round above his head. As he tried to bring it down, I ran out of the line of fire. Spinning as fast as I could, I brought the jack round and slammed it into his back. Because I was holding it behind me, I couldn't hit with as much strength as I wanted. Still, the force of it, coupled with the momentum from him swinging the wrench, made him lurch forwards. I ran up to him and kicked him as hard as I could on the back of his legs, so that he fell face first onto the garage floor.

"Lambert, you girl," shouted Ibbetson from the sidelines, and then he ran over and pushed me away so that Lambert could get up.

As he pushed me, I dropped the jack and I would have stumbled over but he yanked my arms back and dragged me to the other side of the garage. As Ibbetson held my arms behind me, I tried to pull away and the extra tension was enough to finally snap the last piece of rope. I felt my hands come free and even though the rope was still wrapped around each wrist, I finally had my arms back. I pulled my leg forward and smashed it behind me as hard as I could into Ibbetson, thankful that I had bought the new walking boots. The shout he let out indicated that I had hit him, although I didn't know where. He gripped my arms even tighter and I kicked backwards once again, harder than the first time. I connected my heel with his shin and this time he let me go, so I span round as quickly as I could and kicked him hard in the balls.

Lambert came up behind me and swung another time with the wrench, glancing a blow at my elbow, causing a temporary loss of sensation in my arm. I scrambled about along the wall of the garage with my other hand, and took hold of the nearest thing, which turned out to be a wooden mallet. Lambert was coming at me again with the wrench; Ibbetson was writhing on the floor still, clutching his balls, so I circled around Lambert, tempting him to lash out. As he lifted up the wrench one more time, I swung high with the mallet, knocking the wrench out of his hand and probably breaking a couple of his fingers in the process. He shouted out as the wrench clattered across the garage floor and rushed forward but I swung the mallet again, moving slightly to the right as I did so. This time I hit him squarely on the back of the head. He sank instantly to the floor, out cold for the second time that week.

I snatched at the door, still clutching the mallet, desperate to get out of that place. I couldn't figure out how the door opened, and Ibbetson was coming after me. I knelt down on the floor to try to lift the door but Ibbetson grabbed at my feet and pulled me. I found a handle in the middle of the door and twisted it round, heaving the door up an inch, but he was dragging me away. I got hold of the mallet and tried to swing it round. I barely caught him at all. As he dodged back, I turned and lifted the door another inch. Ibbetson gripped my ankles tighter. I clutched at the floor, clawing myself back towards the door, kicking out with my boots to stop him from being able to hold on to my feet. I managed to push the door up another inch or two and I took a strong hold on it, this time leaving the mallet and pulling with both hands. I pulled myself slowly under the open door, scrabbling to get away, aware that he had picked up the mallet and was preparing to bring it down on me. I rolled as quickly as I could, feeling the mallet coming down on my foot, feeling the intense pain but glad that my boots must have deflected the worst of it, scrabbling under the door, feeling the phone at my back shatter and break, groping, clutching at the door, rolling out the other side of it, escaping, grasping.

And then I felt a pair of hands helping me, pulling me away from the door, lifting me up and out into the night.

I was lifted up and into the arms of Detective Inspector Sam Charlton. I looked around and saw that there were about half a dozen police cars lined up outside the garage. I didn't ask how long they'd been there; I didn't care. Finally, it seemed that I might be safe.

As Charlton pulled me away, several police officers rushed into the garage. Someone was checking Lambert and calling for an ambulance; someone was grabbing Ibbetson and handcuffing his hands behind his back. The flurry of activity around me faded into the background. Charlton took me further away, taking me by the hand and suddenly noticing the rope still tied around my wrists. He fished into the pocket of his jacket and pulled out a pen knife, then took first my right hand and then my left and gently cut the rope away. Deep red marks wrapped themselves around my wrists; they would be sore later on.

Charlton let my arms drop by my sides, rested his hands on my shoulders and looked me in the eye. "You okay?"

I nodded. And then I rested my head on his chest, and he held me to him.

TUESDAY

Chapter Fifty-Two

It was the early hours of the morning before we finally made it to the hotel. I had given a brief statement to the police, and exhaustion was raking at my body. I knew I would have to talk to them more formally, but they seemed happy for me to do that at a later date. For now, they were happy to know the bare bones of what had happened. They had wanted to know where the children were, and I was anxious that the powers that be would make sure that they were alright. They assured me that they would make arrangements with social services to ensure they were safe and well cared for. Charlton wanted to take me to be checked over at the hospital, but I managed to persuade him that I really didn't want to go back there right at that minute. I agreed to go in the morning if anything appeared more than just bruising. Lambert was taken to hospital under a police guard, and Ibbetson had been carted off to the police station, hopefully to be locked away for a very long time. After what had seemed like an eternity, I had retrieved my rucksack from Ibbetson's car and been glad to get away.

"Can I help?" The receptionist said when we arrived at the hotel, her voice rising as high as her eyebrows as she eyed me from head to foot.

I asked for a top-of-the-range room, and although she bit the corner of her lip as she tapped on the computer, she kept quiet about my, admittedly rather dishevelled, appearance. I was so shattered I didn't care anyway.

"Ground floor, on the left," she said, pointing down a long corridor.

Charlton walked me to the door and we agreed to meet up and chat over breakfast. There was nothing to say that wouldn't wait until then. When we got to my room, I turned to him to say goodnight. He looked down at me and took my elbow in his hand. For a fleeting moment, as I glanced up at his face, I saw something in his eyes that I really wasn't ready for, and I lowered my gaze quickly. As I looked back up, I caught his eye again, but whatever it was that I had read in his face had gone. I gave him a peck on the cheek and rushed into my room.

Sighing with relief, I flopped onto the bed, marvelling that I wasn't shaking or crying; I was just thankful that I would be able to go home safely. Hopefully, very soon. I'd have to let the guys and Collette know that I was safe but that could wait for another half an hour; they were probably all in bed, anyway. What I really needed right there and then was to get clean.

Paying for a top-of-the-range room had been one of the best decisions I'd made. I stretched out in the enormous bath, used up all the luxury toiletries, and filled the bath with bubbles. Periodically, I dunked my head under the bubbles, blowing out through the water. Tension fell from my muscles, and I lay there, with my eyes closed, until the water had gone cold.

Once out of the bath, I twisted round to examine myself in the mirror, studying my assortment of scratches and bruises. My foot hurt the most where Ibbetson had hit it with the mallet, but it didn't appear to be anything more than bruising. Blue splotches mottled my arms and legs and arm. Townsley had left a cut on the right side of my throat where he had held the knife against it. I had some difficulty bending my elbow where the wrench had caught it. Still, it was all superficial and would heal within the next few days. The images of Obote and Townsley in flames, and of Sanderson with the permanent look of horror etched on his dead face, would take longer to leave me. I wrapped myself in the oversized bath robe, put on the slippers, and made myself a cup of tea.

Once I was in my pyjamas, I fished out my spare phone. I wrote out a message and sent it first to Collette and then to Robert. I knew it was late, but I needed to let them know I was okay.

All ok. I'm safe! Hope the kids are doing ok? Police may be in touch about them. Everything will be sorted tomorrow, latest. I will be back at home soon! Will talk in the morning. Thanks for all your help. Lots love V xx

Then I climbed into the king-size bed, curled up under the duvet and fell into an instant and deep sleep.

Chapter Fifty-Three

C harlton was already tucking into a full English when I arrived for breakfast in the morning. I ordered coffee and porridge and we chatted until all the other diners had left and the waiting staff had set up all the tables for lunch and abandoned us.

I spoke more than he did, telling him all that had happened over the last two days; how I had followed Obote up the motorway and found the house where the children were being kept, how I had seen Darnold being killed through the kitchen window, and how I'd lain in wait for Obote and overpowered him with my homemade weapons. I wasn't sure if Charlton was more impressed with my ingenuity or cross that I had put myself in such danger, but he let me carry on. Then I filled him in on the events at the hospital and how I was concerned about the grisly mess that must have been discovered this morning by cleaner or a nurse.

"Ah, that wouldn't have happened," Charlton said. "I rang the local police on my way up." He clearly saw my anxious look. "Don't worry," he interjected. "The scene needed to be secured quickly. There was no way I was going to let someone stumble across that. I've made sure the powers that be know about this, it will be all above board. No more cover-ups."

Charlton had also spoken to the emergency services and discovered that it had taken several fire engines quite some time to put out the fire. Townsley had been found dead in the kitchen and Obote had been taken to hospital. He was alive, barely, but was covered in third-degree burns. His prognosis was not good. If he survived, which was looking unlikely, he would be in severe pain for the rest of his life and would need months of intensive treatment.

We sat in silence for a minute, thinking.

Charlton looked up. "What about Ibbetson, then? I didn't think he was capable of that."

"Absolutely. I thought he did all sorts of work to *help* children."

"He did," Charlton pondered, "but I guess it must be easy for someone in that position to fall prey to the lure of 'easy' money. He passed those children around at several thousand pounds a time."

I said nothing, just sighed.

"And he was in such a good position to cover up what he was doing. He was a weak man and they can be the most dangerous."

I was deep in thought. "I'll need to sort things out with my friends." I wasn't sure where to begin with that one and, lost in my memories, I pursed my lips and looked off to one side. I hoped those poor children got the medical attention they needed. I sighed, shifting my thoughts onto other matters. "And what about me?"

"What about you?" Charlton smiled and raised an

eyebrow.

"Well, I think I may have committed a few crimes over the last few days and have probably been an accessory or witness to several others."

"I can't see Lambert or Ibbetson putting in a complaint to the police. Obote isn't going to survive and even if he did, it would be easy to connect him to the murder of Darnold without there being a need for a witness. Ibbetson is in so deep with the trafficking offences he'll be put away for some time."

"And Lambert?"

"He is a hired small-time criminal and thug, well-known as a serial offender; in and out of prison like you and I go on holiday. I think he was brought in for the job."

"The job of beating me up." I smiled. I had still failed to tell Charlton about Lambert's gun.

"Once he's recovered from the blow to his head, I think they will have a small string of offences they'd like to do him for."

I said nothing.

"There is one thing you might be needed for, though."

"Oh?" I stared up at him.

"Well, they will probably be re-opening and investigating the case of Dr Neasden's murder. Apparently, at some point, Nash had complained to his superiors about Darnold getting involved, but had been turned away. I think the corruption went further than him, but how much others knew will obviously need to be investigated. And there will be a proper inquest into Neasden's death, I imagine. It'll be referred to the coroner, anyway."

I nodded.

"Hey," he said. "You'll come out well in all this."

Chapter Fifty-Four

After leaving the hotel, Charlton and I drove up to my house. I was a different person to the one who'd walked in a week before to find it ransacked, and I was cautious as I opened the door. But the place was spotless. Books and ornaments filled the shelves, interspersed with photos in new frames; frames that went together but didn't match, just the way I liked it. A vase of fresh flowers sat on the table and another empty vase on the bookshelf. When I looked a second time, I realised that this one was John's heirloom vase and it had been carefully, professionally, glued back together. I knew it would be worthless now, but I didn't care about that.

Whoever Robert had hired to clean up had done a fantastic job, but I suspected his hand in this as well. Not everything was in the right place but that would be a small task to sort out and, actually, I thought it might be the right time to jumble things around a bit.

I left Charlton in the kitchen whilst I had a shower and got changed. I looked in the rucksack; everything was still there—the almost used up pepper spray, the knife, the handcuffs; it was all there. I wasn't really sure what to do with it all now, so I threw it into the corner of the room whilst I showered. Sam and I walked the familiar route down the hill to the city centre. I gave a running commentary as we went.

"That's the road where Dr Neasden lived, look." I wondered if his house had been cleared up too. "And that's where he dropped his notebook," I said as we reached the bottom of the hill.

I took him into the coffee shop where I had met Collette that morning. I went and sat down whilst he ordered and paid for coffee and cake, and I watched him at the counter. He was a good man and I was grateful for the help he had offered, especially in getting the police to the hospital and keeping my name out of it all. Well, out of most of it. I didn't know what he had said to them, and I wasn't about to ask. He never offered an explanation, and I thought it was best to leave it unsaid. As he turned away from the counter and walked towards me I thought that, out of all this mayhem, there had come something good. I'd met Sam Charlton, and I knew that he wouldn't be leaving my life with the closing of this rather tempestuous chapter.

"Goodbye, Verity," he said as we left the café. "Promise to keep in touch?"

"I will," I said. And we arranged to catch up later in the week.

Charlton went off to find his car, and I headed towards the High Street. I bumped into lots of people I knew, although many didn't recognise me with my short hair. One elderly neighbour stopped me to comment on it.

"I just fancied a change," I said.

She patted my arm, tilted her head, and said that

she understood. She didn't really understand, but I smiled and nodded all the same. I walked down the steps from the High Street to the river and dodged down behind the stairs. I worked the brick loose where I had hidden the notebook. It was still there, wrapped in several sandwich bags, and I retrieved it and replaced the brick. When I got home, I stood in my living room and assessed John's repaired vase. I took the notebook out of my pocket, flipping through its pages and remembering how, what seemed like a lifetime ago, I had sat in the kitchen puzzling over what it had all meant.

I held the notebook in my hand and then said aloud to the empty room, "Dr Neasden, I hope you can rest in peace now, knowing that your notebook led me where it needed to. And, John, my darling, I hope you are up there somewhere, showing him the ropes in the hereafter." And with that I put the notebook into the vase, the symbols of the closing of my old life and the beginning of my new one together in one place.

Epilogue

Two weeks later, I was sitting at the dining table with my closest friends. There was loud chatter as several conversations were going on at the same time, and laughter drifting across the room. I had spent the day preparing dinner and I had really enjoyed it. It was the first dinner party I had hosted since John had died, and I looked around the room. It wasn't a big gathering, just those closest to me. Collette and her husband Marcus were there, having drafted in Marcus' mum as a babysitter, as well as Robert and Keith. I was eternally grateful for having such good friends; I couldn't have got where I was without them.

They had taken the young people off and looked after them without question. Marcus had arrived home that night to find Collette entertaining two young girls who could speak no English. They had been sitting on the sofa with Charlotte and Sophie and playing a video game. They could all understand this and there was no need to be able to communicate with actual words. Collette didn't really understand much of what had been going on for me, or the children. But she must have done a reasonable job of convincing Marcus not to call either the police or social services on the spot, because he had resisted picking up the phone.

It turned out that finding foster homes for the children wasn't as easy as I'd thought. I had just assumed there were people out there, waiting, but the social workers who'd become involved had found it difficult to find places for them to go. They'd hastily done checks on Robert, Keith, Collette, and Marcus, who had all agreed to hold on to them for a few days. After a couple of days, the girls had gone off to a foster family in Market Rasen; they'd seemed happy to go together. The boys had left Robert and Keith's separately over the following few days and I thought the guys had actually been quite sad to see them go. They had bought them games and books and new bedding, which they'd insisted they took with them. The children who had needed medical treatment, I'd been assured, would get good care and would be allowed to stay in the country until their treatment was completed. All the children would be assured foster placements and a school place until they were adults and then their future would be decided through the normal legal channels. At least they would get the decent education they had been promised. I hoped that they felt able to stay where they were and weren't frightened into leaving like so many of the children I'd read about in the research.

And so, there I sat, amazed at the goodness of my friends and how they had given their time and energy willingly to help me out. It was lovely to be here, watching them laughing and chatting and having a good time. I thought that I had changed almost beyond recognition in the last few weeks, but I slipped easily into this company and had no problems sharing their jokes and small talk. I thought that, for the first time since John's death, I actually felt happy—really happy. A momentary waft of guilt threaded its way through my body but I glanced over to a photo of John, one of my favourites, where he was dressed in his dinner jacket and bow tie; he was holding up a glass to the camera and saying cheers. He was smiling broadly at me, at my position hidden behind the camera. He wouldn't want me to feel guilty for being happy. He would want me to feel happy. I held up my glass to the picture and said, "Cheers!"

Everyone turned round and shouted, "Cheers!" in return, and I laughed.

"Here's to not going back to work." I clinked glasses with everyone around the table.

"Not going back to work?" Collette asked, and raised her eyebrow.

"I've made a decision," I said emphatically. "I am not going to go back to the college, but I think I will be working."

"What are you going to do?"

"Oh, I don't know for sure, but I think after all this, jobs will somehow find me."

From the Author

Thank you so much for reading No Deadly Medicine, I hope that you enjoyed it. As an independent author, without the marketing budget of a big publishing house, I rely heavily on reviews of my book and word of mouth to ensure that people know about it. Reviews, especially good ones, help elevate my books when people search on Amazon, so each one helps. If you liked it, it would make me really happy if you could find the time to write a review, and tell all your friends. I do read all the reviews. If you are interested in finding out more about Verity, me or my writing, you can follow me on Amazon. I am also active on Twitter and try to respond to all tweets and messages.

@ladyermintrude

Happy reading!
Trudey

References

References:

The Children's Society (2013): *Still at Risk: A review of support for trafficked children.*
https://www.refugeecouncil.org.uk/wp-content/uploads/2019/03/Still_at_Risk-Report-final.pdf

The United Nations (2009): *Global Report on Trafficking in Persons https://www.unodc.org/documents/Global_Report_on_TIP.pdf*

Andrew Boff (2013): *Shadow City: Exposing human trafficking in everyday London*
https://www.west-info.eu/human-trafficking-modern-slavery-children/shadow-city-exposing-human-trafficking/

HM Government (2013): *Second report of the Inter-Departmental Ministerial Group on Human Trafficking.*
https://assets.publishing.service.gov.uk/government/uploads/system/uploads/attachment_data/file/251487/9794-TSO-HMG_Human_Trafficking.pdf

Your free book is waiting

Claim your free book!

EVEN MONEY A Verity Spencer short story

After uncovering a web of corruption in No Deadly Medicine, Verity has to decide what she wants to do with her life now. Still mourning her husband, she's started to fill her time by chasing errant husbands and wives for money. Susanna Means approaches Verity believing that her partner, too, is being unfaithful...but as Verity looks into his life, she realises he may be holding a much darker secret...

Visit the website to download:
https://trudeymartin.co.uk

Acknowledgments

Firstly, my heartfelt thanks to Sarah Smeaton for her editing and for helping the story flow. Thanks also to all my friends who read initial drafts and gave constructive comments. And to the various professionals who read the manuscript and gave such helpful technical advice. And, lastly, to my longsuffering husband, who endured several weekends of inattention as I finalised the book ready for publication.

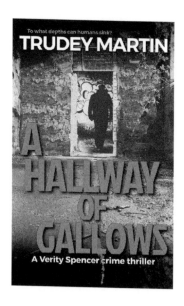

A Hallway of Gallows

Gloria is missing...

The police have drawn a blank...

Gloria's distraught foster carer turns to Verity Spencer for help. As Verity gets closer to finding out why Gloria is missing she uncovers a horrifying web of manipulation and abuse. Can Verity get to the truth before more lives are shattered...or worse...

Ever wondered to what depths humans will sink?

Verity is about to get closer to the answer than anybody would ever want to be.

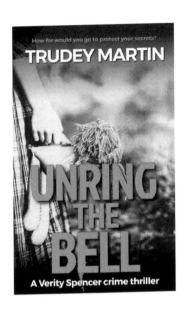

How far would you go to protect your secrets?

TRUDEY MARTIN

UNRING THE BELL

A Verity Spencer crime thriller

Unring the Bell

A murdered child...

A prime suspect about to be released...

How far would you go to protect your secrets?

Ten years ago a child was brutally murdered, but nobody was ever charged. Verity Spencer is asked to look into the case of eleven year old Margaret-Elizabeth who was taken from her bed and strangled while her parents were out at their book club. There was only ever one suspect; currently serving a sentence for inciting racial hatred, he is about to be released.

But somebody is prepared to go to any lengths to stop the truth about Margaret-Elizabeth's murder from coming to light.

As Verity delves into the happenings on the night of the murder, it seems a ruthless killing spree is about to commence. Can Verity stop the killer before any more lives are lost?

Printed in Great Britain
by Amazon